Praise for Colette Gale:

"Erotically wicked! Spellbinding! A unique retelling of *The Phantom of the Opera*." — Bertrice Small on *Unmasqued*

"Colette Gale leads us through a labyrinth of dark, extravagant eroticism, to the romance at the story's heart. Grandly conceived, wildly inventive in the smallest details—I for one will never hear harp music in quite the same way again." — Molly Weatherfield, author of *Carrie's Story*.

"Lush and sensual." — Erotica Romance Writers

"Inventive and steamy and clever all at once." — M. J. Rose, author of *The Resurrectionist*

Books by Colette Gale:

The Erotic Adventures of Jane in the Jungle
(published as separate ebook volumes)

Entwined: Jane in the Jungle
Entangled: An Unexpected Menage
Enthralled: The Sex Goddess
Enticed: An Erotic Sacrifice
Enamored: The Submissive Mistress
Enslaved: Prisoner of the Amazon Queen

Unmasqued: An Erotic Novel of The Phantom of the Opera

Master: An Erotic Novel of The Count of Monte Cristo

Bound by Honor: An Erotic Novel of Maid Marian

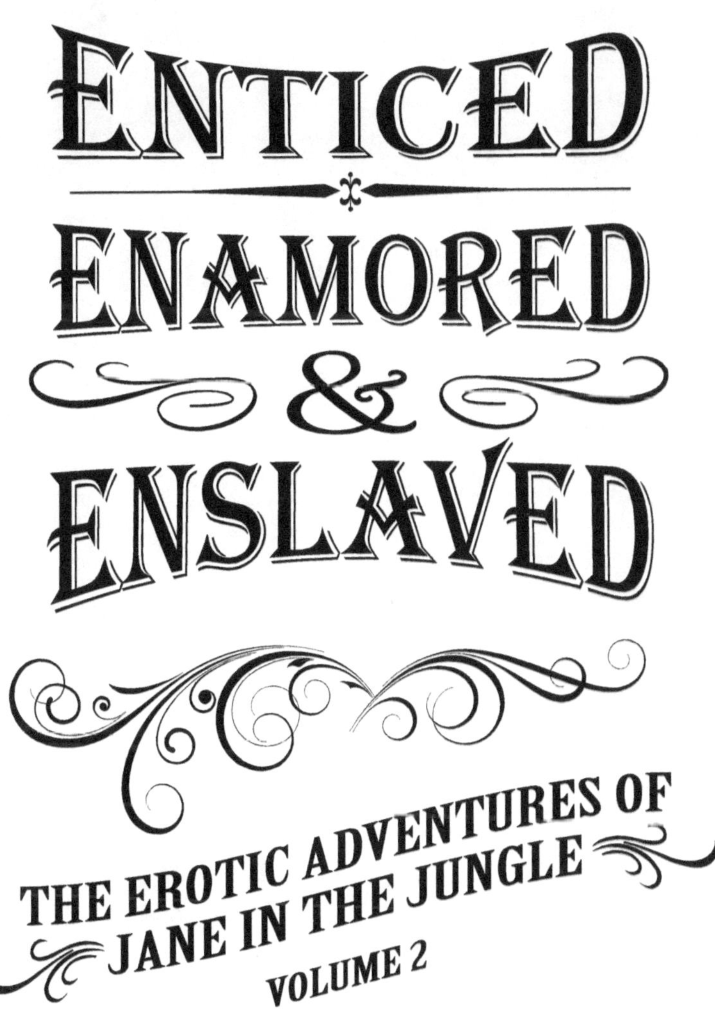

ENTICED, ENAMORED & ENSLAVED

THE EROTIC ADVENTURES OF JANE IN THE JUNGLE

VOLUME 2

Colette Gale

AVID PRESS

ENTICED

Colette Gale

Dear Reader:

Welcome to the fourth volume of Miss Jane Clemons's adventures in the jungles of Africa.

If you have already read the first three volumes, you need not continue with this introductory epistle, but move directly to the first chapter. For those who have not enjoyed Entwined, Entangled *or* Enthralled, *please feel free to read on below.*

During the late 19th century, the British indulged in much exploration of Africa, searching not only for gold and gemstones, but also for knowledge of this fascinating Dark Continent.

Professor Everett Clemons, the famous lepidopterist, and his daughter Jane were two of the most famous British citizens to embark on these travels, and although Jane published a book of her drawings and notations about the butterflies her father studied during these trips, there remained little information about her own thoughts and adventures—until now.

For, not long ago, I was fortunate enough to come upon an old trunk filled with Professor Clemons's journals and butterfly specimens, and there, within, I also found the treasure of Miss Jane Clemons's personal (and highly intimate) journals. They detail her experiences in the jungle—being captured by natives, being abandoned by her fiancé Jonathan—as well as her passionate relationship with the wild man of the jungle known as Zaren.

Incidentally, after careful analysis and research, I have come to believe the jungle man Zaren—whom Jane eventually brought back to London for a time and who was quite well-received by Society— was the inspiration for Edgar Rice Burroughs's well-known Tarzan character (a thesis, unfortunately, that is sharply denied by descendants of Mr. Burroughs).

I leave the reader to his or her own conclusions regarding this theory.

Because there were so many volumes of Jane's journals, I have chosen to publish a series of short segments over time in order to make them publicly available as quickly and efficiently as possible.
I do hope you'll indulge my decision to follow the popular form of literature from this era and publish Jane's journals as a serialized collection. Not only does this enable me to be more efficient in releasing sections of her work (for it is quite an arduous task to pore over the very intimate and detailed descriptions of her experiences), but it also allows you the reader to experience the story in segments rather than in one overwhelming gulp.

I must also warn you: I have kept with the tradition of the times, ending each serialized episode on a cliffhanger.

The previous volume ended with Zaren helping Jane to escape from a small village of natives who believed she was a Fertility and Sex Goddess. The man known only as Cold Eyes was the leader of the tribe, and he agreed to take Jane (for her so-called powers) in exchange for giving her worthless fiancé Jonathan the map to a diamond mine. We don't expect to see or hear from Jonathan again, for the map led to a mad lioness's den and we heard the feline roar as she attacked the encroacher.

As Jane and Zaren swing from tree to tree in their escape from Cold Eyes and his companions, something happens to Zaren and they begin to tumble down through the trees…

I hope you find Jane's adventures enlightening, exciting, and titillating as we follow her further adventures as a young woman in the Madagascar jungle.

Colette Gale
December 2013

JANE FELT ZAREN JOLT with a low grunt. She looked down to see an arrow protruding from the side of his torso. Before she could react, he jerked again sharply and then they were falling through the air.

She stifled a scream, clinging to him while grasping wildly for a vine, a branch--anything that might slow their descent. Her fingers closed over one of the thick ropes, but she could not manage the weight of their fall. The vine slid through her grip, burning and rough, and then they were tumbling once more.

Zaren grunted and gasped, then moved suddenly as he snagged a vine at the last minute. Their descent slowed as his muscles bulged against her…then something gave away and they were in free-fall again. But the ground was closer now, and all at once they thudded into it in a tangle of limbs and loose leaves, his arms curled protectively around her. Jane landed on top of him, and felt him go still.

"Zaren," she gasped. Though the breath was knocked out of her, Jane scrambled off him in a swirl of flower bedecked hair. "Zaren," she cried again, when he didn't move. The sound of voices and thrashing through the jungle was much too close.

The arrow had snapped in half during their fall—probably causing his second jolt as it torn up through his skin—and blood oozed from its jagged wound. He was panting, and she noticed a second arrow in his leg as he shifted and his eyes fluttered open. He'd protected her from the worst of the fall, twisting at the last minute to take the brunt of the impact after slowing their tumble as much as he could.

"Jane," he said, reaching for her even as one hand went to touch the broken arrow still in his side. His blue eyes were fierce despite the tremor in his fingers. He pulled to his feet more slowly than she would have liked, and the crashing sounds and voices were too close. He tensed, like a cobra ready to strike. "You run. Go!"

"No," she said, tugging at his solid arm, trying to pull him into the jungle with her. But even stunned and injured, he was as immovable as a boulder. "Not without you."

"No. I will fight them." His eyes blazed with the fury of a wild animal and for a moment even Jane was afraid of him. "I will stop them."

"You're hurt. They're coming! Zaren, please!" Why wouldn't he listen? She saw his heaving breaths, the blood leaking stubbornly from the two injuries, the gingerish way he moved. He wouldn't last two minutes if they attacked him.

"Not hurt!" As if to prove this, he yanked the arrow from his leg. Blood spurted from the wound, and before Jane could stop him, he pulled the other one from his side—this time with a roar of pain and outrage. "You go!"

But it was too late. Their pursuers burst into view, spears and arrows at the ready, and all at once they were surrounded.

Cold Eyes stumbled into the clearing behind them, brandishing the biggest spear of all. He was panting, and his eyes were bright with fury. He snapped something to his tribal companions, and two of them lunged forward with their sharp blades.

Jane dodged in front of Zaren, spreading her arms wide, knowing they wouldn't dare hurt their "goddess." Zaren growled in her ear, and tried to yank her away, but she ducked out of reach and stomped on his foot as hard as she could.

"No," she hissed back up at him. "*No.*" Perhaps there was something in her eyes, for he didn't attempt to move her again—though he clamped a solid arm around her waist from behind as if to be prepared to do so if necessary.

"Let us go," Jane said boldly to Cold Eyes. "You've had your pleasure, taken it all from me, and there is nothing left—"

"We aren't finished with you, Goddess. There is still much more to come." His eyes glittered darkly and he stepped closer to her as his men eased back.

Zaren's arm tightened around her waist. He growled low and threatening, sounding so much like a feral cat that some of the villagers glanced uneasily up into the trees.

Cold Eyes looked at him closely for the first time, and his eyes flared in surprise. A little, ugly smile twitched his lips. "You. The Wild Man who was raised by wolves. I have heard of you."

Zaren's only reply was a sneer, with a different deep, guttural sound. The threat and his antipathy couldn't be more evident.

"So he doesn't speak? Nevertheless, I cannot let you go, Goddess. You won't make it far. This man is weak and bleeding. His injuries will attract the animals and you won't last the night. He might not last at all."

"He knows how to protect himself," Jane replied. But she felt Zaren sway against her, and the blood that had been flowing from his side now seeped all over her torso, wet and warm. More blood had pooled on the ground, spattering her leg and foot. Was he even leaning on her now, ever so slightly?

Her heart thudded harder and uncertainty weakened her resolve. He was badly injured. He needed treatment and care. And if his blood would attract predators...

Cold Eyes seemed to recognize her concern. "Your savior interrupted our ceremony. We must finish it, or they will be sorely disappointed." He gestured to his spear-toting companions. "I do not wish to face their wrath should I allow their goddess to go free."

At that moment, Jane realized Cold Eyes had only tentative control over his people. One false move and they would rebel—likely violently. No wonder he had grasped at the opportunity to present to them a fertility goddess. It was his only hope of retaining leadership over the unhappy, desperate villagers.

He and she both knew that her presence would make no difference in the procreation aspects of these people. But Cold Eyes didn't care. He, like every other man, wanted power and control. He was greedy. Just like Jonathan had been.

Jane narrowed her eyes thoughtfully. "I will go willingly with you and will…submit…to whatever you require of me, short of bodily injury. *If*," she added, holding up her hand to forestall his triumphant speech, "you allow me to administer to him, and to tend to his wounds. Provide me anything I require to make him well, and you may do what you will to me. If you do not—or if he dies," she said, stepping closer to him while holding his gaze, goddesslike, with her own, "I will show your people that you have brought my wrath upon them…and an angered goddess must have a sacrifice in order to appease her fury. I shall make certain to make my choice of sacrifice known. If you agree to my terms, you must bow to me. Now."

Cold Eyes recoiled as if he'd been struck, and black fury burned in his gaze. But he kept his lips in that flat, cool smile and bowed deeply to Jane.

All at once, there was a shift in the place and bows and spears descended along with their owners as the rest of the men made their obeisance to Jane.

Yet Cold Eyes was on his feet almost instantly, giving sharp orders to his men.

Zaren started as they moved toward him, his arm tightening around Jane's waist. He bared his teeth like a ferocious beast and she felt the unyielding shift of his muscles against her.

"We will go with them," she said, turning to look up at him. "I will see to your injuries."

"No." The sound was little more than a growl.

She pulled away—that in itself a testament to the disturbing fact that he was becoming weaker. "Zaren, we must go with them. You cannot bleed all over the jungle." She smiled, forcing her expression into something light and unconcerned.

But he was very experienced with reading the slightest body language of in the wildlife he'd faced, and it was clear from his expression he didn't fully believe her. His mouth was taut with pain and she felt the renewed surge of blood from his side. His eyes had dulled, and that worried her the most. He could just as easily die from a fever as from his injuries.

"Please," she said, aware that the villagers were watching with naked interest. She must remain goddesslike, and yet she must somehow convince Zaren this was the right thing to do. "Come with me. I will care for you. And then we will leave," she added softly.

She pulled away, heart thudding as she waited to see if he would follow. He made another of those warning noises, scoring their captors with an equally feral gaze, and nodded once.

But behind the dullness, the darkness in his gaze told Jane he had little patience for her so-called bargain with Cold Eyes. Zaren would not be caged and protected for long.

She only hoped that would, indeed, be the case.

FLANKED BY THREE OTHER MEN, Jane followed Cold
Eyes toward a compact hut near the center of the village.
It appeared to be new, and hastily erected.

She'd been bathed and massaged with oils as before, and
then draped in ropes of flowering vines and feathers. None of
which did anything to cover her nudity. Her hair had been
braided and twisted into a pile on her head with only a few
tendrils curling over her neck and shoulders. The weight of her
coiffure felt odd, especially since she no longer had her hair's
curtaining effect to help clothe her.

At the entrance to the hut, Cold Eyes turned to her. A small
smile curved his thin lips. "Your ceremonial chamber awaits,
Goddess." He spread his hand to encompass the space as he
gestured her inside.

The small building had been constructed to resemble a
primitive, albeit comfortable, boudoir. The floor was strewn
with pallets, pillows, and furs, and a huge altar-like bed sat
in the center. The four posts at each corner were connected
by bamboo rods that created a sort of canopy decorated
with flowers, vines, and fabric. A fire crackled in one corner,
safely confined by a large stone container, and the scent of
woodsmoke mingled with a sweet, cloying essence that had
become very familiar to Jane. And giving the chamber an even

more exotic flavor, the walls were covered with more furs and thick tapestries woven of some unidentifiable material.

The space was hardly larger than a parlor would be back home, where one would receive and entertain guests and callers. But in this case, Jane had a suspicion she knew precisely what sort of "guests" would be entertained herein.

At one end of the chamber was a large pedestal or dais. Next to it burned two tall, slender pedestals which held shallow bowls with live coals that gave off a soft red-golden glow. A table near one side of the room boasted a variety of containers that appeared to offer food and drink.

There were no windows. There was one door.

And in the corner there were ropes, sticks, and something that appeared to be a crude whip.

Jane's insides swirled nervously. She drew in a deep breath and released it slowly. *They want only my pleasure and my blessing.*

She would endure it.

She could endure anything, knowing that Zaren was safe…at least as safe as she could make him. A dart of fear shot through her. Not for her own fate was she terrified, but for him—the man she loved, who even now lay feverish and injured in the hut belonging to the village healer, who was a wizened old woman with sharp black eyes. He'd been so since they returned with Cold Eyes and the others late last night.

"Your subjects were disappointed by the interruption of last night's ceremony," Cold Eyes said, urging her into the chamber. "But I assured them you would bestow even more grace and favor upon them because of the delay. Still, their impatience grows."

Jane refused to ask the obvious questions: what was she to do, what was required of her to provide "grace and favor" to her "subjects."

"And thus, there is no time to waste. Your throne, Goddess." He made a gesture to the massive bed, and before Jane could protest, two of the guards directed her onto the large platform. But instead of forcing her to recline, as she might have expected, they directed her to stand on the edge of the mattress at one end, facing the bed.

Then they lashed her wrists high onto the bedposts so she stood, spread-armed, looking down onto the large pallet strewn with furs, pillows, and flowers. One of the men stirred up the fire, and another sprinkled leaves into the shallow bowls on the two tall pedestals. Almost immediately, the sweet, exotic scent she'd come to associate with these ceremonies grew stronger.

"Behold," said Cold Eyes as the door opened. "Your subjects, Goddess."

A man and woman—Jane had a moment to spare for gratitude that there was only the two of them—entered as Cold Eyes and his men left the hut. She recognized the couple as one of the pairs who'd made an offering to her during the first part of the ceremony last night.

They came in, dressed in beautiful, ceremonial clothing complete with feathers, flowers, and animal skins, moving immediately to the table of food and drink. Jane watched with some apprehension as the woman filled a crude bamboo goblet with a dark liquid and the man placed an unfamiliar red fruit on a small plate.

The couple approached the bed with their victuals and climbed onto it, settling upright on their knees in front of her. Apparently, the fact that their "goddess" was tied up and nearly hanging in front of them caused no consternation whatsoever.

With earnest faces, the man and woman looked up at Jane and spoke in a chant as they swayed gently, proffering her the food and drink—which, of course, she was physically unable to accept. Then, both collapsed in obeisant bows, still holding the offerings, and remained prostrate for a long moment.

Jane was just about to speak when the man rose and brought his selection to her. She opened her mouth and he slipped the fleshy red fruit between her lips, then licked the juices off his fingers with an enthusiastic, red tongue.

The fruit was sweet and had an effervescent, almost fermented element. But she hardly had time to taste it before the woman rose and tilted the cup to her mouth. Much of the pungent liquid spilled down the front of Jane, but she caught some of it in her mouth and drank. This too was unfamiliar, but not unpleasing. Slightly bitter, it warmed her from the very moment she swallowed, and she felt the flush roll from her belly throughout each of her limbs.

As soon as she'd finished her offering to Jane, the woman tossed away the empty goblet. This seemed to be a signal, for the man—presumably her husband—pulled her toward him. The two kissed passionately on the bed below Jane, tongues twining and delving, mouths devouring. As she looked down, the couple began to pull off each other's clothing to reveal sleek, dark-skinned bodies.

Soon, they were both naked and entwined on the massive pallet in front of Jane, seemingly unaware or uncaring of their goddess's presence. She could do nothing but watch, suspended by her arms, as the two feasted upon each other with crazy mouths and stroking hands. Jane tried to close her eyes, but the scents and sounds surrounding her were intense and distracting, and she couldn't seem to block them from her mind.

The man flipped his partner expertly onto her back. She sprawled on the bed with a soft, pleased *whuff* and a large jolt beneath Jane's feet. Her coarse, dark hair brushed her goddess's toes as the man arched over her. She had small, tight, cocoa-colored breasts with taut red nipples that glistened in the dim light, thrusting up teasingly at Jane—who'd never seen aroused female breasts other than her own. She found it startlingly erotic and could not pull her eyes away from them.

Like Jane, the man seemed unable to get enough of the woman's tits, for he fondled and teased as she gasped and shuddered beneath his busy hands. When his dark head dipped to them, Jane could hear the erotic sounds of sucking and licking, the enthusiastic lapping of his tongue, the low, aroused moans and sighs. The woman cried out softly, her face turned up with an ecstatic expression, her full, wet lips parted. Clearly, she loved her man, and was fully enjoying his attentions.

Jane realized she, too, was having a hard time breathing, and that the more impassioned the couple became, the less able she was to look from the tableau before her. The enveloping, sweet smoke in the air combined with whatever they'd given her to eat and drink made her both hazy, and yet sharply awake and aware. Even when she managed to close her eyes ever so briefly, she saw and heard them, she smelled the musky scent of man and woman and arousal as it filled her nostrils.

The twining, writhing, dark-skinned bodies—smooth, shifting muscles, tight breasts, a thick, full cock, and even the flash of a moist pink quim—had her full attention, and the images combined with the sounds of moans and suction and lips and tongue caused Jane's body to tighten, shiver, and dampen. A dart of arousal shot up from her needy little pip, then settled into a low, insistent pulse.

Jane shifted as her own quim swelled and grew warm as the couple below her became louder and more passionate with their sighs and groans and cries. When the man eased back, kneeling on his haunches, Jane's mouth dried at the sight of his ready cock. Not as large as Devilish Grin's, and not as beautiful as Zaren's—but turgid and ready. She imagined she could see the gentle vibration of its need as the man closed his fingers around it, preparing to slide into the wet, red heat of his woman.

Jane clamped her knees together, needing the pressure on her tiny pearl as it began to throb gently. But even that did nothing but tease her as the man shifted his hips and shoved inside his partner.

Both cried out, and Jane bit her own lip to keep from doing the same. Heat rushed over her, and she felt clammy and lightheaded. The bed on which her toes rested rocked and shifted violently as the man slammed and thrust against his woman. The sounds of flesh slapping flesh, of the soft suction of her wet quim accepting the dark red length of his erection, the scent of musk and pleasure, sweat and incense had Jane panting on her own, writhing against her own restraints.

She crossed her legs, pressing them hard together, feeling the slippery moisture and the hard little nub tucked in there, shifting her hips desperately—but she was unable to find the relief she needed. As the writhing, undulating couple pumped and jolted and she saw the dark red length of cock slide in and out of the woman's pussy, Jane found herself moving in the same motion, her hips shifting, her legs glued together as she tried to find pressure, and rhythm, and heat…

At last the woman cried out, arching up beneath her man. Jane saw her fingernails drag down her partner's back, leaving deep red weals all the way to his muscular buttocks. The man's head reared back as he gusted out deep moan only moments later, then he fell back over his woman, breathing heavily.

Jane closed her eyes, her body tight and throbbing and full. Her pip was ready to explode, her inner thighs wet from her useless juices, her quim swollen and sensitive, her nipples pinpoint taut. She realized she was panting nearly as harshly as the couple before her, and tried to pull herself under control.

But the days and hours of intense pleasure she'd experienced since arriving in the jungle—from Zaren and Jonathan and even the people here in this village—had taught her body *need*, and arousal, and had caused her to become so sensitive to scent, touch, and sound that she couldn't fight it back.

And so Jane stood there, sagging by her arms, her knees squeezed tightly together, her body hot and damp and pulsing insistently, her nipples tight and jutting against the vines and leather wrappings around her. and her quim throbbing wetly between her thighs, and she waited.

Now that the couple was done, what would happen?

It seemed a long while before either of the prone figures moved—a long while in which Jane hung in a state of uncertain arousal—but at last, they stirred.

Slowly, the man ran his hand along his woman's body, and she shivered and smiled as a lover often does. Then she smoothed her hand over his belly and as Jane watched, the woman closed her hand over his relaxed cock. He smiled, arching into her grip, and his eyes rolled back with pleasure as the woman began to stroke him.

As his partner began to coax his cock back to life, the man slid his fingers between her legs. Jane's mouth went dry as the woman's knees spread apart and she could see the moist red of her nether lips below the thatch of dark hair. She smothered a desperate moan as the man slid his hand over his woman's quim, slipping and sliding through the musk-scented juices with soft, sleek suctioning sounds.

The woman shivered and sighed, her hand moving faster up and down his erection. Now Jane could hear the sounds of friction, of a hand over the velvety skin of a cock, and the soft, wet splats of fingers sliding into the depths of the woman's hot pussy. The man gave a soft, erotic chuckle and bent to lick a saucy nipple, lapping and sucking vigorously.

Jane moaned, curling her fingers around the cords that bound her gently to the bedposts, drawing in a deep breath and trying to block away the growing strength of her pearl and its desperate throbbing. *Please,* she mouthed the word…not knowing what she really wanted, just wanting *something.*

Her nipples were so tight they hurt, and the unfulfilled arousal between her legs was sharp and tingling, and still the couple played and licked and sucked and stroked. The woman shifted on the bed and knelt to take her man's cock in her mouth. Jane's eyes latched onto the sight of her juicy, red lips sliding up and down the thick length and she trembled, somehow wanting to taste it herself.

Not once did they look up at her. Not once did they appear to even notice her presence, let alone her need and desperation. They were completely, utterly engrossed in the body of the other, and Jane was nothing but an unwilling spectator. An untouchable goddess.

When the man thrust himself inside his partner once more, Jane gusted out her breath in a moan that matched the woman's, and she could not tear her eyes away from them as they mated, coupling wildly in front of her, flesh slapping, bed rocking, muscles bunching and sliding. The long, red cock moved in and out, faster and faster, and Jane's hips twitched in vain, desperately matching each thrust with no hope of relief. The bedposts creaked with her rhythm and that of the couple below her, and when they reached their peak, Jane cried out too.

But her moan was one of pain and need, while the other sounds in the chamber were that of pleasure and satisfaction.

Once again, the pair collapsed on the bed in front of her, and Jane had the terrifying thought that she might be witness to them coupling *all night*. Over and over, as her arms grew numb and her body overheated, and her arousal was left unfulfilled and in pain.

Please, she whispered. This time louder, this time, loudly enough for them to hear.

But she was answered only by the soft, grinding snore from the man, and a delicate, contented sigh from his partner.

They were asleep.

And Jane was left hanging there, swollen, dripping, aching. Frustrated.

JANE MUST HAVE DOZED OFF, or slipped into some other sort of stupor, for she slowly became aware of her surroundings once again.

Her arms ached, and she realized they were immovable—she was still suspended from the bedposts. The hut was filled with a soft yellow glow emanating from the fire pit and renewed torches, and she wasn't able to tell whether it was light or dark outside. The scents of musk and coitus and the titillating incense still colored the air.

She realized the altar-bed below her was empty; at some point the couple had left. Likely only recently, for surely she wouldn't have slept that heavily. Jane felt a wave of relief that they'd gone instead of subjecting her once again to their lovemaking.

For, clearly what they'd done before her was nothing less than making love. After the last days and weeks of experiencing a variety of physical pleasure and torment—both willingly and unwillingly—Jane recognized the depth of emotion between the man and woman.

The same sort of emotion and deep passion flared between her and Zaren whenever they were together—and had, from the very first time he'd touched her, when she was caught up and entangled in a web of vines.

A man like Devilish Grin could draw pleasure and coax—well, unleash might have been a better term—intense relief and erotic pleasure from Jane, but it had no more depth or emotion than taking a piss. Jane had come to understand the difference, and she realized now what had been lacking between her and Jonathan.

Zaren…his very touch was layered with love and affection and respect. He would never allow another man to touch her, or to trade her for any sort of treasure. How could she have ever thought she loved Jonathan? How could she not have *seen* through his superficial care and deceit? When he had shared her body with Kellan Darkdale, his partner in crime, she should have realized he didn't truly love her.

Jane swallowed hard. She didn't wish violence on anyone and she didn't celebrate his demise at the teeth and claws of the lion, but she was damned glad Jonathan would never bother her again.

But Zaren. *Oh, God, please let him live.*

By agreeing to come back here, she'd made the best bargain she could, she'd done the only thing that gave him a chance of being healed. She believed if—no, *when*—he recovered, they'd find a way to escape this village. But she had no way of knowing what was happening with him, or whether he still thrashed and rolled from the fever that had begun to take him. The village healer had seemed willing to help, and Jane had put her trust in the old woman.

But she wanted to see him. She needed to assure herself Zaren still breathed. *I am a goddess. I should be able to command these people!*

She pulled at her bonds in frustration no longer related to sexual need, but desperation for the man she loved. The bedpost creaked but the bonds held firmly.

She was just about to call out, to make an imperious command, when the hut door opened. Moonlight glowed on the ground outside, and in walked Cold Eyes, followed by two young women.

One carried a sort of basket, and the other a large vessel that clearly contained some sort of liquid.

"How have you fared, Goddess?"

"My arms are numb. Surely there's no need for me to be restrained," she said sharply.

The two young women—ones she didn't recognize, and who seemed hardly into their teens—jolted a little at her tone. *Good. Let them fear me.*

"Very well then. We can adjust that." Cold Eyes came to stand behind her, and Jane felt the warmth of his body pressing into her bare backside. He reached up and fumbled with the cords that held her left arm, releasing it from its raised position. But instead of leaving it free, he merely moved it down so it extended directly out from her shoulder.

The blood rushed back into her arm and Jane gritted her teeth against the sharp prickles. She was in such discomfort she hardly noticed when the two girls approached. As Cold Eyes lowered her other hand and affixed it to its post, the attendants began to unwind the flowers, vines, and leather wrappings that had acted as clothing—such as it was. Then they used warm, scented water and sea sponges to wash her nude body.

They dabbed at her tender breasts, sliding the rough sponges over her sensitive skin, down over her belly, and along her thighs. One of them used a cloth to bathe Jane between the legs, forcing her to relax her clenched knees. The friction and stroking of her nether parts with a hot, scented rag caused Jane to sigh with relief…and then to tense and throb with expectation and awareness once again. The ablutions seemed to have the effect of reawakening her body, which had temporarily gone quiet and dormant—exhausted from frustration and tension.

By the time the girls were done, Jane was quivering and wet. Her skin was damp from the warm water that now ran in tickling rivulets down her arms and legs, and her little pip was full and throbbing once more.

In an attempt to put the demands of her pulsing sex from her mind, Jane said, "I wish to see Zaren."

Cold Eyes, who had watched silently during the bathing, shrugged. "You have more to do this night, Goddess. Your grace and favor was clearly upon Timi and Greela, for they came out of your chamber with great happiness. Now you must bestow the same upon the others who desire it. And here they are—Dahla and Guri."

He turned as a man and woman came in through the hut door. The young bathing attendants squeaked in surprise, as if they'd been caught falling down on their tasks. But Jane hardly noticed, for the woman who came in the door immediately caught her attention.

Awareness darted through her as Jane recognized the newcomer. She—Dahla—was the leader of those who'd bathed her the first time, the woman who had shoved her face between Jane's legs and sucked and drank from her so vigorously, demonstrating for the others.

At the memory, her lungs constricted, and her body felt hot and trembly, shivery from top to bottom. All at once, Jane was back to that same taut, frustrated state of arousal she'd been in while watching the woman and man coupling in front of her.

And when Dahla turned to look at Jane, focusing eyes hot and dark on her, she nearly jolted from the weight of them. Already beginning to pant, Jane was only vaguely aware when Cold Eyes and the bathing girls left. Instead, she struggled to control this unusual, intense reaction to the mere presence of this woman.

The man—Guri—had gone to the table of food and drink, and he beckoned for his wife or partner to join him. Jane watched as they made their selections. Though it had only happened once before, she knew this would be a ceremonial rite, and that they would come and offer their gifts to her.

Guri lifted a cup to her lips. This libation was different than the one she'd tasted before—bitter and strong, and with a long after taste. Nevertheless, Jane was thirsty and swallowed several large gulps without any trickling from her mouth.

Then Dahla, the woman, approached. She was holding a small plate with a dark red square on it, hardly larger than Zaren's thumb. Her eyes were hot and filled with meaning as she lifted the soft reddish cake, breaking a piece off and offering it to Jane, who parted her lips obediently. Her breath was harsh and unsteady as she waited to see what would happen to her this time.

Dahla slid the bit of sticky sweet into Jane's mouth, allowing her fingers to linger over her lips then brush them in a sensual caress. Holding her gaze, still hot, still heavy, she licked her own lips suggestively as she broke off another piece of the sweetmeat for Jane.

This time, however, she brought it to her own mouth first, tasting it with exaggerated, pursed lips and the slow, swipe of her tongue. Then she lifted the bite to Jane, who wanted to turn her head away, to reject the offering…but the woman was too fast and determined. Before she knew it, the sticky fig-like cake was smashed on and into her lips and she could taste its moist sweetness. She choked a little on a crumb, and swallowed the bit that had gone into her mouth…but much of it was smeared on her lips and chin.

Dahla stepped back, her eyes still avid, and offered the last bit of cake to Guri. They spoke briefly and he nodded, his attention flickering to Jane, then back to his partner, who smiled and drew off the simple tunic-like dress she wore. She had large breasts and an unruly bush of dark hair growing between her legs, and wide, full hips.

She turned to Jane, who instinctively drew back as far as her ties would allow, arms straining with the effort. But Dahla came after her, taking Jane's face in two strong hands, bringing her naked body so close her warm breasts pushed against Jane's, and began to kiss and lick away the remnants of food from around her goddess's mouth. She was strong and determined, and not at all gentle; for her fingers dug firmly into Jane's jaw and chin as she devoured her mouth with surprising roughness.

Jane had never been kissed by a woman before, and she found the experience unexpectedly sensual, wholly unfamiliar, and more arousing than she would have expected. Dahla's tongue was strong and her lips were soft, and she ate at Jane's mouth, sliding her tongue between her lips and invading her passionately.

Jane couldn't breathe, and she couldn't move, and she found herself groaning and gasping, trying in vain to twist away from the hot, busy lips and strong, swiping tongue. Her insides were hot and moist, and by now her breasts had become crushed harder against the two hard-tipped mounds of Dahla's breasts, their bellies bumping and sliding against each other in an unfamiliar sensation, the brush of wiry hair tickling her skin.

At last the other woman pulled away, her breathing rough and fast, her eyes dull with passion. But instead of turning to her partner, Dahla smoothed her dark hands along Jane's neck and shoulders, down to cover her breasts. The expression in her face changed to one of open-mouthed pleasure as she fondled and hefted each pert-nippled handful, her thumb tracing lightly over one of them. Her other palm pressed flat into the other one as she kneaded and stroked the pale globe.

Jane closed her eyes, trying to ignore the incessant, arousing sensation, and to fight back the surge of lust that shot through her at the teasing. Then Dahla grasped her by the hips and pulled her closer, bending her head to cover Jane's left nipple with full, wet lips.

Jane arched and jolted at the sudden rough onslaught, but Dahla's strong fingers dug painfully into her hips and held her in place as she sucked and sucked, the pull hard and long and never-ending—as if she meant to draw every bit of tit into the depths of her mouth. Acute pleasure entwined with pain shot down through Jane's belly with each long tug, and she cried out, her moan filled with both desperation and need as she shuddered and trembled beneath the other woman's hands.

Still the woman went on, licking and sucking, her mouth wide and hot, closing around Jane's entire areola as she drew it in deep, sliding her tongue around and over the tight, sensitive tip. Jane bit her lip, squeezing her eyes closed as the pain-tinged pleasure rose and tightened within her, prickling and hot, arrowing down and down, over and over, faster and faster… until the sharp sting of pain lost out to bold lust and exploded into a long, undulating orgasm, rolling through her body with brutal force.

Jane sagged, half gasping and sobbing as Dahla released her, stepping back with a cat-like satisfied smile on her face. She looked down at Jane's abused nipple—red and long and taut, glistening and fairly throbbing from the torment—and then she bent toward the other breast.

"No," Jane moaned, twisting violently away, the ropes chafing her wrists, her feet digging into the mattress as she struggled to put distance between her and that greedy, demanding mouth.

But Dahla was determined, and this time when she closed her mouth around the neglected taut pink nipple, she flickered her tongue lightly over it, then faster and faster and faster until it drew up tighter and longer and became wet and red. Painful waves of sensation once again jolted fiercely through Jane's body, trammeling down to her overused pip, where it pulsed and swelled violently. Her hips were undulating wildly as she tried to free herself from the restraints, to pull away from this incessant *taking* and tasting from her…but of course she couldn't, and so Jane was reduced to little more than uncontrollable jolts and sharp waves of pleasure-pain, over and over and over.

She was sobbing, wet and damp and trembly everywhere, her quim full and hot, dripping with her juices when Dahla at last pulled away with a loud smacking suction. Her eyes burned with lust, and as Jane tried to steady her breathing, the other woman knelt in front of her.

Oh, God, no… Jane groaned in desperation, squeezing her eyes closed as Dahla dug her fingers into the soft skin of her thighs and pushed them wider apart. Her quim swelled even more, full and hot, and when the woman's tongue flicked out to touch her tiny, turgid nib, Jane screamed.

The shock of an orgasm blasted over her like a lust-filled dagger, stabbing her even as the unwanted pleasure rushed through her body. She lost the strength in her arms and knees and sagged, held only in place by Dahla's demanding fingers.

And then all at once, the woman was gone, torn roughly away from Jane. She dragged her eyes open to see Guri, his own eyes heavy with lust and his mouth tight with desire, in front of her. She didn't even have the strength to pull back, out of his reach…but to her surprise he didn't grab for her.

Instead, he said something sharp and hard as he flung Dahla facedown on the bed in front of his goddess. Dahla gave a sort of laughing gasp and looked up at Jane, kneeling in front of her. Eyes bright and lips parted, she ran a tongue over her mouth as Guri tore away his loin cloth to reveal a thrusting erection. Then he pushed Dahla onto her hands and knees in front of Jane…so that her mouth was directly level with Jane's quim.

With rough movements, Guri knocked his mate's legs apart and manhandled his cock into place, sliding it deep into Dahla's pussy with a sudden thrust. She raised her face and grunted with pleasure, looking up at Jane as he shoved into her again. Still breathing heavily, sore and sensitive and yet unable to keep her body from responding to the sounds and images before her, Jane closed her eyes and curled her fingers into fists.

Almost over.

The bed jolted beneath Jane's feet with every one of Guri's thrusts, and she shifted and bounced, hardly able to keep her balance, swaying backward then forward as far as her bound arms would allow. As the rhythm became faster and harder, Jane was no longer able to keep her eyes closed.

She looked down as Dahla moaned and lifted her face. Jane could see the hot, intense lust in the other woman's expression and she wasn't sure if it was because of her mate or the goddess she worshipped. Guri reared behind her, his own face taut with passion, and she could see just a hint of dark cock pumping in and out from behind Dahla's arse.

Jane looked away, trying to block out the sighs of pleasure and the sounds of suction and slap of slick, wet flesh. Then, fingers curled around her hips once more, and Jane felt Dahla bury her face in her quim.

She tensed and twisted, but couldn't pull away. Dahla's tongue flickered mercilessly at her dripping, swollen nether lips, sliding in and around the folds, thrusting deep into the tight depths. Jane squirmed and trembled, arching away as Dahla ate at her tender quim and sucked on her little pearl—all while Guri was fucking her from behind. Jane couldn't believe her body had the strength to respond yet again, but it did: tightening, growing hot and trembly and tense with arousal once more.

Every time Guri thrust, Dahla's face jolted harder into Jane's warm pussy, and the rhythm began to build faster and faster.

Her tongue moved just as quickly, just as rhythmically, lapping and thrusting in its own erotic dance deep and strong against Jane's hot sensitive flesh. She strained at her ropes, her arms sore from being jolted with every movement, and the pumping became even faster and harder: *bang, bang, bang…*

Dahla was gasping and moaning against her nether lips, her fingers tight and strong at Jane's hips, her face buried deep into hot, musky flesh, sliding in the juices and lapping it up as if she needed it to breathe.

Jane bit back a moan as her pleasure grew stronger, gathering up in that familiar way, spiraling into a blossom of sharp, spiked heat. Then all at once Guri slammed one last time, jamming Dahla powerfully into Jane as he cried out his release, and she exploded into a dark, raging orgasm that wrung her out like a damp rag.

But Dahla wasn't finished, and she drew Jane's pulsing little pearl deep into her mouth, sucking hard as if to coax out the last bit of pleasure. Jane cried out hoarsely, half sobbing at the sharp pain-pleasure…and then Dahla gave a moan of release as she fell, shuddering, against her thighs.

There was silence for a moment; the only sounds that of rasping, rough breathing. Jane swayed, half falling off the mattress, held in place only by her trembling arms and the balls of her feet on the edge. Her body was wet and dripping, burning and shuddering, and her pussy was so swollen and hot it felt twice as large as usual. The dull, heavy throb tolled through her torso and limbs like a low, rolling bell.

Her mouth was dry, her hair plastered to her body, her wrists chafed and her shoulders aching, and she prayed the night was over. That there would be no more couples.

But then Dahla pulled back onto her haunches and looked up at Jane, her eyes filled with that same heat.

"No," Jane whispered. "*No.*" She tried in vain to free herself, to kick and buck the woman away, but her fingers were too strong, her grip too determined....

And when Dahla rose, climbing up her goddess's hot, sticky body with her hands and lips and tongue, Jane fainted... succumbing to the welcome oblivion of unconsciousness.

KAREN WAS DREAMING.

He was hot, burning, as if he were engulfed in flames. Something seared down his side…fire…and he reached to brush it away, but it wouldn't stop blazing into him.

His world was dark, shadowy, filled with strong, heavy scents and closeness…so close. He almost couldn't breathe…

Jane.

He could see her long fire-hair, and he reached out…but the curls fluttered away, filtering through the tips of his fingers. Her sleek, creamy body, her lush pink lips…they danced just out of reach. He cried out for her, reached again…but his body was too heavy and awkward and he couldn't catch her…he couldn't touch her.

Jane. Come back.

He was hot and damp, and he struggled to throw off the murkiness, to shove away whatever it was that enveloped him, weighted him down…kept him from Jane…and suddenly there were hands on him. Cool. Firm. Comforting.

Something trickled between his dry, hot lips…cold and welcome.

The soft murmur of a voice. Voices.

Hands pressed gently at him, soothed and smoothed, massaged and stroked, and he felt himself losing the fight, easing back onto…something. Soft. Like a nest…

Or a bed.

Bed.

The unfamiliar word settled strong and stark in his foggy mind, and he suddenly had an image of something that was a…*bed*. High off the ground. With four tall poles at each corner. In a…*place*. A *room*. With walls not made from trees and…

He frowned in his memory, pain shooting through him at the temples as he tried to remember… The searing pain in his side and leg returned. Heat. Agony.

Zaren shifted restlessly, reaching out for something. He saw the bed again, and Jane lay on it. Her glorious hair was strewn around her, spread over white mounds of…clouds? Soft and rumpled and inviting. She smiled and beckoned and he reached for her…

But the dark, slushy pain seized him again and his mind melted into shadows and heat. He rolled and slept and moaned, fighting to get back to her.

And then Jane was gone, and another woman, dark- haired and heart-faced was there…beautiful and soft, smiling at him…

Mother.

The thought was dragged from somewhere deep inside him, and Zaren stilled his mind even as his physical body burned and fussed and fought.

Mother. He clung to the word, the image, and the woman bent forward as if summoned. Something glinted at her throat, something round and shiny, and he could see it…he recognized it… He reached out, his hand lifting…and then it fell heavily onto his belly when nothing was there but air.

The soothing hands were on him again, the cool touch, the trickle of icy water, the scents and taste of freshness and bitter. Something poured down his throat, smooth and cold.

Zaren drank greedily, reaching for the wrist of the hand holding whatever vessel had been brought to his mouth and keeping it in place as he gulped his fill. He saw shadows, heard voices through the dimness, and his mind was foggy and soft.

But... *Jane.*

Where is Jane?

He could see only shadows, and the faint glow of orange-yellow flames in the corner of a dim place with dancing, shifting walls. The burning in his side had eased, but he was restless and the hands...many hands...soothed him. Brushed him. Massaged, stroked, rubbed... He sighed, stretched. His abused body melted beneath the touch.

They were everywhere. Hands. Small. Delicate. Busy.

He arched and tried to move away when they settled *there*...at his *thing*...the thing that shifted between his legs and now began to grow stiff and long and thick.

Jane.

He reached for her, called out for her. Someone pushed him back down when he would have risen, and those hands... they were everywhere. He thought he heard murmurs, voices, and from a distance perhaps a soft giggle followed by a low sigh that ruffled against his skin and made him feel *hot* again...but in a way that was very far from pain.

And those hands...they brushed over his stiffening length and Zaren tried to bat them away, but they were determined— and more hands massaged and stroked his face, his shoulders, his arms, his legs. But then fingers, suddenly closing around him tight and firm, caught him by surprise.

A shock of pleasure rushed over him, and Zaren's eyes bolted open, his heart racing. The place was murky and dark,

the glow of fire in the corner revealed the shape of a woman…
no, two women…next to him. Both dark-haired, with small,
insistent hands that were touching him *everywhere*. They lifted
his sac and fondled it, brushed over the sensitive hair growing
on his thighs, his bush.

Where is Jane?

He tried to speak, tried to lift himself up, but he was too
weak…and that one pair of hands was still tight and warm
around him, enclosing the part of him that swelled and filled.
When they moved again, sliding up and down along his
lengthening rod, he gasped and felt a hard, powerful throb
of response against those tight fingers. A sizzle of heat rushed
through him, and he fell back with a moan. Stroke…stroke…
slide…

Jane.

He wanted *Jane*, not this woman…these women…there
were three of them now, somehow. The one had hold of his rod,
sliding up and down his length with long, slow movements.
Something glistened and dripped from the tip, and Zaren felt
his arousal growing. She brushed a thumb over the slick, sticky
droplet and smoothed it over the engorged head of his cock
as her hands continued to move faster and faster. He couldn't
hold back a moan, and felt his body growing damp with sweat,
weak with need.

The other two women were on either side of his torso, their
hands massaging his shoulders and face, their bodies brushing
against him with warm lips, tickling nails, and soft skin. Heat
and pleasure filled him, beating back the nagging pain at his
side, and he lay there, weak and yet thrumming with pleasure,
unable to push away his attendants. Soft, moist mouths settled
on his jaw, his shoulders, his arms…even over the nipples of his
muscular male teats, and made him shiver and tremble.

One of them took his hand and pressed it to her… smoothing it over the hard tip of her own teat, and Zaren yanked away with what little strength he had.

I want Jane.

But the women were insistent and he was too weak and confused—was this a dream?—and when the stroking on his rod became faster and tighter, he could no longer fight the hot, surging pleasure. It rolled through him like a massive wave, and his breathing rasped and became more labored. He rolled his head from side to side, reached out into the air, trying to break free of whatever murkiness claimed him.

It should be Jane who touched him like this, Jane whose hands stroked and teased…but his body cared about nothing but the rhythm, the sliding up and down, faster and faster… *faster…*

All at once a storm washed over him. He reared up a little, grunting as seed spurted from his pulsing rod and a white blaze of pleasure burst from him.

Zaren collapsed back onto his pallet, dimly aware of soft, excited voices and murmurs…of the hands that still stroked and massaged and scratched him. His body thrummed and vibrated, sated and yet strangely empty and dull.

"Jane," he managed to say. At least, he thought he whispered her name. But no one seemed to notice.

Instead, the hands remained there, adjusting him, rubbing his skin, brushing back his long, coiled hair from where it clung to his face, massaging his fingers and smoothing over his chest as if he'd accomplished some great thing. He wavered, somewhere between sleep and consciousness, the dull aching burn at his side a reminder of…something.

Then his eyes bolted back open, and his body became sharply aware…for they were rubbing his relaxed cock again, this time with something greasy and slick. It smelled pleasant, and *felt* even more pleasant on his sensitive skin…

Zaren realized he was growing hard again. A gentle prickling sensation from the cream seemed to awaken his rod, to make it lift and twitch—so soon? He shifted, moving his hips to shift away, but strong, practical hands pushed him back down onto his bed even while others massaged and stroked his cock back to life.

His chest rose and fell rapidly as lust built, his blood surging back to fill his rod…this time more urgently, with a dull, throbbing heat.

And when he was hard again, jutting up, filling the slick hands that curled around him, he closed his eyes and waited for the long, smooth, steady strokes to bring him to the peak again.

But something changed—the woman shifted, her hands moving away. He relaxed, more than ready to slide back into repose despite the throb between his legs—for he wanted no one to touch him besides Jane.

When the woman's mouth closed over him, Zaren surged, pushing weakly at the invading sensation with a low growl. But his head thudded painfully, and the searing injury in his side screamed with shock. Hands forced him back down as that hot mouth slid down over him, deep into her throat.

He groaned, deep and low like an angry cat, and blood and seed bolted through him to that hard place. He couldn't ignore it, couldn't beat back the hot pleasure from long, warm, sleek movements over him. Up and down, up and down…his world became centered there, heavy and hard and engorged. He felt himself fill and swell, and her mouth become tighter around him, hotter and damper, and he heard the soft moans and sighs surrounding him as she rose and fell.

Faster and faster…Zaren's eyes rolled back in his head and he gasped and moaned, suddenly moving his hips to drive deeper and deeper, hard and frenzied and so hot and full…

He cried out like an animal in death, felt himself explode into the warm mouth around him, then fell back, trembling and shuddering and spent.

And then she was there: warm, soft, familiar.

Jane.

V

WHEN JANE BECAME AWARE of her surroundings once more, she found she'd been released from her bonds and was curled up on the altar-bed.

She was blessedly alone and could only guess how long she'd been so. A bit of light filtered through the crack around the door, and the small fires in the braziers had sunk into nothing more than coals. Was it morning, then?

Her body ached—her arms, her legs, her shoulders—and especially her breasts and abused nipples. The little pip hooded inside her quim felt full and swollen, pressed between her legs as she slept. As she drew herself up onto her hands, hair tumbling over her face and shoulders, Jane heard a tortured cry—something like an animal in pain.

"Zaren!" She didn't know how she knew it was him, but she was certain. Stumbling off the bed, she staggered to the door.

Unheeding of her nakedness—what had she to hide?—Jane flung open the door of the hut and found herself confronted by two large, dark-skinned men. Guards.

They blocked the way with strong arms and long spears, and seemed to have no intention of allowing her to leave. Jane didn't know what she would have done if Cold Eyes hadn't walked up at that moment.

"I demand to see Zaren," she told him, standing straight and tall—very aware of the hot gazes from the spear-wielding men. "Take me to him now."

Cold Eyes swept her with a disinterested look and appeared ready to ignore her demand, but she would have none of it.

"Take me to him or I will bring down my wrath on your people," she pressed. "If I am angry, they will know whom to blame. And I can be *very* angry. And very unaccommodating." She cut a dark, warning look at the guards, who'd stepped back in the wake of her furious words…but still ogled her jaunty breasts tipped with nipples that were still bright red from Dahla's determined mouth.

Jane had no power here but the villagers' belief in her as a goddess, but she would use that advantage as long as she could. If Cold Eyes wasn't so disliked and untrusted by his people, she would never have this leverage.

"Of course, goddess," said Cold Eyes when he felt the measured weight of the two guards' attention pass from her to him and back.

Even Jane recognized their uncertainty. They couldn't understand their words—which was a benefit to her. They just knew she was angry, and that Cold Eyes had acquiesced to her.

"You may see the man. He's feverish and has yet to awaken, though he has been well-tended to." Then Cold Eyes's thin lips curved into a flat smile. "And you might wish to rest before tonight. I suspect you shall be even busier than last evening."

Jane swallowed hard and her pip gave a sudden little pulse, as if to remind her how willing her body was to accept this role. "Where is he?" she demanded by way of response.

"There, of course." He gestured languidly with a large hand, pointing to the healer's hut.

Jane wasted no further time. She didn't even grab anything with which to cover herself—what was the point?—and darted over to the hut. After that one animalistic cry, she'd heard no other sounds of pain or anguish.

She flung the door of the hut open—she was a goddess, after all—sending a myriad of young female attendants scattering with startled squeaks. The elderly healing woman was nowhere in sight, but there was Zaren, sprawled on the same pallet on which she'd left him…yesterday? Late yesterday afternoon.

He didn't move or otherwise acknowledge the sound of her entrance, and Jane rushed over to him.

He was hot to the touch, and her pulse spiked with fear. His skin had a fine sheen of perspiration glossing it, and his breathing was raspy and rough. Covered only by a scrap of cloth draped over his hips, the rest of his glorious, powerful body was naked. Jane felt a sharp pang of lust and some stronger, deep emotion as she knelt on the pallet beside him. He was so strong…surely he would fight through this.

"Zaren," she whispered, stroking his arm and smoothing the springy coils of hair from his face. Tears gathered at her eyes and a pang of fear shot through her. He had to recover. He must live.

At her touch, he seemed to become more aware. He mumbled something that sounded like her name—rough and coarse, but definitely something like "*Jaaaane*"…and he reached out blindly.

Her heart leapt with hope and she grasped his powerful hand. His fingers curled around hers as if she were a lifeline. He muttered something again, pulling her down next to him… next to his too-hot, too-damp body. His grip was surprisingly strong and Jane allowed herself to be imprisoned: brought up tight to his torso, enveloped by him.

She closed her eyes, exhausted, afraid—but *home*.

And when his breathing at last settled into something more smooth and steady, she slept.

Jane came awake suddenly to find Cold Eyes standing over her and Zaren.

The healer's hut was dark, lit only by a few meager coals in the corner. But even in the dim light, she saw the glint in the other man's eyes as they swept over her…and Zaren.

His gaze lingered heavily on the long, lean thigh Zaren had curled around Jane's leg, his muscular hip and tight buttocks… then lifted to meet her eyes.

"Come, goddess. Your subjects await."

Jane wondered what would happen if she refused…if she fought him back and clung to Zaren. But as she brushed against her lover's skin and felt the burning temperature of his fever, she abandoned that thought.

She'd do nothing to risk his health and safety. He must be left to heal, to fight through the fever and to regain his strength. He must…for she couldn't consider what would happen to her if he did not.

And so Jane pulled away from Zaren. It was difficult, for though deep in the semi-consciousness of fever, he held tight. It was as if he somehow knew it was she.

Nevertheless, Jane stood and turned resolutely from the man she loved. As she did so, she noticed the aged healer, sitting in her chair in the corner. Without another glance at Cold Eyes, Jane went to the elderly woman.

"You must make him well. Care for him. For if he doesn't recover, you'll feel my wrath—you and the entire village." She spoke sharply and firmly, and although the healer surely couldn't comprehend her words, she certainly must understand the meaning.

"Come, goddess. I grow impatient," Cold Eyes said. "There are preparations to be done."

Aren't there always? Jane thought, suppressing a shiver. What activities would they subject her to this evening?

The first one, she found—and couldn't complain about—was a warm bath. Her aching muscles wept with pleasure (a wholly different type of pleasure than before) when she sank into the large tub of steaming, floral scented water. She soaked for a while, and was just beginning to feel relaxed and optimistic when her attendants drew her up and out of the bath.

She was draped in a single tanned hide that wrapped around her waist like a very short loincloth, leaving her breasts bare and her quim hardly covered. And then she was taken once more to the hut with the altar-bed.

Inside Jane found the same arrangement as last evening, with a table filled with food and drink, pungent fires burning with the heady incense that made her feel slow and murky almost immediately. And yet her heart began to pound in expectation, and her skin tingled with anticipation.

When the two guards—the same ones who'd blocked her from leaving earlier this morning—directed Jane to her position between the bedposts, standing on the head of the bed, she wanted to resist.

"Save your strength, goddess," Cold Eyes warned, as if reading her mind. "Surely you'll need it tonight, for Ulma and Deren are *very* eager to curry your favor. And your pleasure."

Jane swallowed hard, her belly fluttering at the thought, and a sharp spear of lust and apprehension shot straight to her pip. It pulsed in a naughty reminder that her body, at least, would be willing and able to bestow "favor" on the worshipful couple.

Her wrists were tied loosely to the tops of the two bedposts, and her ankles spread and tied to the bases of the same. Standing there, she felt less like a goddess and more like a sacrifice herself, but Jane summoned her strength.

No one was about to hurt her. They wanted only her pleasure.

And she would accept that. For Zaren's sake.

The third couple was young and oddly similar to each other in appearance. Both were tall, and Ulma, the woman, had high, hardly noticeable breasts and boyish hips. Her partner, Deren, was slender and lanky. His attention strayed to Jane and remained on her even as they stood at the table of offerings, making their selections.

Jane looked over as the hut door closed, leaving her alone with Ulma and Deren, and when she turned back, they were approaching the altar-bed.

As before, she was plied with food and drink. But no sooner had Deren tipped the cup to her mouth—spilling half of it down the front of her—than he tossed it away and said something sharply to Ulma.

Then he moved off the bed and positioned himself behind Jane just as Ulma took her place in front. Deren was obviously standing on something, for when he pressed into Jane from the back, she felt the jut of his hard cock against the crack of her arse. She jolted at the unexpected prodding sensation and gave a little shiver as his hands came around from behind to cup her breasts.

Pinching her nipples and fondling her from behind, Deren kissed and licked along her shoulder and neck, sending arousing prickles over her skin. He pushed his cock along the seam of her arse, sliding it up and down, and Jane felt herself grow full and wet.

She curled her fingers into fists and tried to keep from moaning as her arousal grew, but by now Ulma had knelt in front of her. She spread Jane's thighs, roughly forcing them apart in a generous vee. Using her thumbs, she pulled Jane's quim lips so they were wide and open, allowing her little pearl to thud expectantly. Jane felt as if her pussy was about to explode, it was full and pulsing, free to swell and grow as Ulma bent forward.

Jane gave a soft shriek as the woman's tongue slipped inside her, sliding beneath the little sheath that hooded her pip. Her body shuddered with sensation and pleasure, and the tongue moved again, darting deep inside her wet opening. A streak of heat shot up, stabbing her in the belly, then thudded back down to her engorged lips. She pulsed and pounded and *needed.*

"*Oh...please,*" she whispered, straining against her bond as Ulma licked her again. A bolt of sharp pleasure made her gasp and shudder again, and Jane shook from the effort of holding herself up by her bound arms as the intense, sharp rise of lust burned between her legs.

Deren was moving faster now behind her, pressing his cock into her cleft, sighing and groaning against Jane's ear. His fingers were rough as they massaged her breasts, and she swayed and shifted with every movement, sandwiched between a busy, sucking, licking mouth and the hard prod of cock.

She couldn't move away from the sensations and the couple surrounding her pummeled her from either side, forcing her to pant and beg for release. Suddenly, just before she reached her peak, Deren growled something sharp and hard and released her.

The next thing Jane knew, he was on the bed, driving his cock into Ulma even as he looked up at her, watching with hot, dark eyes. Jane stood there, shaking and swollen, throbbing everywhere. The expression in his face told her he'd rather be fucking her than his mate.

Perspiration trickled down her spine and she tried in vain to press her knees together to put pressure on her pip, to give herself some relief from the unsated, pulsing arousal. Instead, she could only feel how wet she was, how her juices slid down the inside of her thigh, and how big and ready her little pearl had become.

Please...

Deren reached his orgasm with a loud shout and Ulma gasped and fell onto her face with his last hard thrust. The hut was silent, filled only by rasping, panting breaths and Jane's own soft sobs of frustration.

She closed her eyes, willing the sensations to ease, fighting with her body to relax and cease its insistent pounding. It was a long while before anyone moved, but at last, Deren shifted and rolled from his partner. Ulma gave a long, languorous sigh and, looking up at Jane with a feline smile, stretched and arched. Her small breasts shifted, her nipples large and red and surprisingly enticing with their tiny, delicate erections.

Jane looked away as the couple left the altar-bed and went to replenish themselves from the table of food and drink. This meant they weren't yet leaving, and therefore weren't finished with her. She shivered and swallowed hard, then turned her thoughts to Zaren.

She prayed his fever would break soon, and that they'd be able to leave. How they'd do that, she wasn't completely certain—but Jane was resourceful. She'd find a way. And with Zaren's amazing strength and abilities…

Jane pushed away a thump of uncertainty. Even if—no, *when*…it must be *when*…he did come out of the fever, she didn't know how soon he'd be recovered enough to help make their escape. If they had to go on foot, they would, but it would—

Someone touched her from behind and Jane froze, trembling. Rough hands, dark and insistent, were fumbling with the ties at her wrists. They were freeing her?

Jane quelled the surge of hope as Ulma climbed onto the altar-bed in front of her. She lay on her back, legs spread, arm shifted up behind her head. Her wet, pink pussy glistened, open and exposed, arranged directly in front of Jane.

Deren finished untying her wrists, and Jane—perched on the edge of the bed—would have lost her balance if he hadn't curled an arm around her belly from behind. His fingers twitched up to cup her breast even as his half-mast cock bumped against the bottom of her arse. He pinched and rolled her nipple, biting none-too-gently at the tendon on the side of her neck.

Jane felt an unwelcome surge of lust as he played with her nipple, teasing it back into its hard, sensitive point, and ground his hips into her from behind. The familiar heat of arousal trammeled through her, making her knees tremble and her mouth go dry. Her little pearl was already throbbing and ready, and now it swelled and stretched as if ready to burst.

On the bed in front of them, Ulma stroked herself. Spreading her nether lips wide, she used the full width of her four fingers to stroke and smooth over the slickness of her quim. Jane couldn't look away and her breath caught as her own pip filled and throbbed even more, tight and sharp with frustration.

Deren's cock was hard once again, and it prodded her arse cleft, dripping with its own sticky juices. His breath was harsh and hot in her ear as he reached around to touch her ready quim. When he felt her wetness, Deren groaned in her ear and began to slide his fingers around. Jane shuddered, trembling and quivering as he played with her—stroking and slipping while he pressed his cock into her from behind. She came almost immediately, surging an orgasm wet and hard against his hand, and sagged in his arms.

With a sharp sound of frustration, he released her with a little shove. Unable to keep her balance, Jane pitched forward, the ropes around her ankles twisting and giving enough so she fell onto her hands…right on top of Ulma.

Before Jane had the chance to recover, the woman had her hands on her breasts and was massaging them and fondling them. Propped on her hands, still tied by her spread ankles, Jane had nowhere to go as she was subjected to these caresses.

Deren was still there, and he grabbed her hips, positioning himself thigh to thigh behind her. Jane gasped when she felt his cock probing her…not in her dripping, ready quim, but in her arse—in the place Kellan Darkdale had taken her. She tried to pull away, but Ulma had one breast in her mouth, and was playing with the other one—using her fingers to tease the tip into a hard point—and Jane was held in position as Deren pulled her arse cheeks wide and pushed himself slowly inside her.

She gasped and arched at the unfamiliar, strangely arousing sensation of being filled there. He made another of those sharp sounds, then moved in even further. Jane bit her lip, her body shivering with the sensation, her eyes squeezed closed, her breath coming in short, hard gasps.

He filled her, then reached around to touch her pip. At that unexpected brush of sensation, Jane exploded into another blinding orgasm. She couldn't control a cry as pleasure washed over her, ripping through her like a blade, and that was all Deren needed.

He began to pump and thrust with slow, insistent strokes, filling her tight entrance and awakening new pleasure, unusual and intense. Jane quivered and surged, her muscles tightening around him as he pumped and thrust, faster and faster, and a dark, edgy desire rose inside her once more. She was panting and dripping, and Ulma had pulled away and was looking up at her with hot, wide eyes, her own breath puffing roughly. She shifted, lifting her hips to slide one leg between Jane's spread thighs.

As Deren shoved into her from behind, Ulma began to slide her full, wet pussy up along Jane's leg, pressing against her and moving slowly and sharply in her own rhythmic thrusts. Ulma's hot, slick juices seemed to burn into Jane's skin, and she closed her eyes, assaulted by sensations that grew hotter and more intense. The smell of musk and perspiration, mixed with the sweet incense, filled her nostrils and spread through her body.

Suddenly, Deren yanked himself free and shoved Jane flat onto her belly. She fell with an *oof* onto Ulma, narrowly missing the other woman's chin. Before she had the chance to recover, Deren moved sharply and jerked Ulma's legs between Jane's. The other woman jolted, then as Deren moved again, she cried out in surprise and pleasure—and Jane realized he'd slammed himself inside his partner.

He began to move furiously, with Jane sandwiched between them—her knees spread wide and Deren pumping violently just below her own ready quim. His hands braced Jane's hips as he thrust in and out, shoving her down into Ulma with each movement. She could feel him moving against her, felt the length of his cock brushing along her quim as he withdrew and then shoved back inside Ulma.

Her little pip was pressed into the top of Ulma's mound, banging and jolting into her warm, damp skin with every movement. The other woman writhed and arched against and beneath Jane, grinding her own hips against hers, and Deren thrust and thrust, his fingers biting into Jane's hips as she tried in vain to hold herself up, to take some control over her body.

But Ulma grabbed Jane's shoulders and pulled her down suddenly, covering her mouth with her own, thrusting her tongue between Jane's surprised lips, and devouring her. Just then, Deren shoved hard and deep inside his partner, and Ulma cried out against Jane, her teeth biting into her puffy lips as she arched up sharply.

The other woman fell back, shuddering and trembling beneath Jane, and Deren collapsed on top of her, hot and heavy and damp. Jane could feel the last bit of pulsing from his sated cock as he heaved long, deep breaths against her from behind. Her own body was hot and wet and full once more, and her little pip cried out for satisfaction, pressed against Ulma's belly.

Her breasts were flattened against the other woman's, and as Jane lay there, Ulma smoothed her hand down along one side of her torso, her fingers light and teasing.

Jane couldn't control a soft, pleading sound as those questing fingers went lower and slipped around between them to touch her full and ready pussy. She jolted and quivered when Ulma found her, and it only took two quick, sleek slides for her to explode into a long, undulating, orgasm.

She bit her lip as the hot pleasure exploded over her, shuttling through her limbs and centering there between her legs. Still sandwiched between them, still weighted down by Deren's exhausted torso and held by one strong hand, Jane quivered and shook…and then collapsed fully onto Ulma's warm chest.

Her ankles were still bound, her legs still spread, her body exhausted and replete, trapped between them.

It seemed a long time before anyone moved and when Deren began to touch her again, Jane almost began to cry. He pulled her upright, closing his hands over her breasts from behind, forcing her to kneel upright in front of him.

As Ulma watched from below them, Deren found Jane's full, exhausted quim and began to tease her once more, his hand sliding down over her belly. She quivered and trembled, unable to fight off the sensations, and soon he had her shuddering and pulsing around his fingers as they slipped and slid.

"Please," Jane begged as he nudged her into yet another violent orgasm. "*Please.*" Her voice came out in a desperate moan and tears spilled from her eyes.

Ulma said something and to Jane's surprise, Deren released her. Heedless of her bound ankles, he tipped her aside and onto the altar-bed, then grabbed his partner once more.

Zaren… was her last thought as Jane fell into a deep, dark sleep.

ZAREN OPENED HIS EYES SLOWLY.

He was aware of a dull, aching throb just above his hip bone and another one that screamed a little more shrilly in the meaty part of his right calf. Everywhere else he felt sore and stretched out. His head beat with a soft pain where it had connected with a tree branch as he fell.

Fell.

Jane!

He would have vaulted from the bedding on which he lay except that he just as suddenly became aware of her scent. And before he could even assimilate that familiar, heady essence, he saw the blazing red-gold of her fire-hair strewn across the pallet next to him.

Zaren relaxed only slightly. Jane was there, but he didn't know where they were. Fragments of memory shifted from images of hands closing over him, stroking him…to a heavy weight covering him, and heat…much heat…into the image of spear-brandishing men and their lascivious eyes that pawed over Jane—*his* Jane. His eyes widened and he remembered.

"Jane," he said, pulling himself into a sitting position as he recognized they were in a small, windowless hut. She lay next to him, sleeping. Her white skin, luminescent like the moon, glowed in the low light, and spirals of fiery curls covered her arm and shoulder, spilling into a pile where her hands crossed, infantlike, in front of her breasts. He scented her, his familiar, beautiful, delicious Jane…and something else. Something musky and titillating and unfamiliar.

At the sound of her name, Jane's eyes shot open and she lurched upright. He saw she was wearing little more than a simple cloth wrapped around her torso. When she saw Zaren, that shocked, frightened look evaporated.

"Zaren. Oh, thank God," she murmured, reaching to stroke his cheek. "I thought…I was afraid the fever would take you."

Fever. The word was vaguely familiar, and it had bad connotations, but whatever it was Zaren was certain of one thing: nothing had taken him. And nothing would take him from her. Ever again.

She was already touching him at his bare hip, where it still hurt and where he now saw the thick paste covering his wound. He remembered now how an arrow had seared into his skin and then, when he crashed into a tree trunk during the fall, the weapon had been torn up through his flesh then broken in half.

Because Jane had moved, her hair fell away and Zaren was, as always, caught by the breathtaking beauty of her. His lungs felt constricted and his hand shook as he reached to touch that waterfall of fiery curls.

Her lips parted as she looked up at him, their eyes catching in the dim light of…wherever they were.

Zaren stopped himself from leaning forward to taste her. There would be time for that later. Now… "Where are we?"

He remembered Jane thrusting herself in front of him, blocking the threatening spears. A renewed wave of rage shuttled through him—that *she* would think *he* needed protection. The rage turned into a dull throb of fury and anxiety. Jane had spoken readily to the leader of their captors… Zaren remembered very little after that—little more than traipsing through the thick brush, surrounded by the villagers…and there were those murky images of hands stroking him, massaging him…a mouth going down, long and slow and tight, over his hard rod… He felt himself shift and lift at the vague memory.

"We're in the village. They believe I'm a goddess," Jane was saying. "They won't hurt us."

Because his vision at night was as well-honed as a tiger's, Zaren saw something in her emerald eyes that might have been otherwise lost in the dimness. A trace of fear and worry, yet determination. Fierceness. And something else that niggled at him uncomfortably. Something he didn't understand.

But…*goddess*? That word he didn't know. He tried to form more questions, but although he'd been practicing and listening to Effie and Everett (or was it My Gad and Darling?) speaking, he still found it difficult to easily express himself.

"You go with me," he tried, reminding her of her words. The ache that had suddenly stretched inside him, in his heart, eased when he remembered the joy in her face when she spoke those words. *Always. Forever.* She had meant it.

So why were they back here, in the same village where she had been lying on a platform—

Zaren had to stop the thought, force away the image of her splayed over a dais, writhing and undulating with pleasure. He tightened his fingers, curling them into his palms and felt the ragged edges of his nails cutting flesh. Why had she brought them back *here*?

"But you were hurt." She touched the dried paste at his side. "You were bleeding, and weak, and the animals would have attacked. We wouldn't have been safe in the jungle. And then you got a fever—"

But he'd interrupted her with a low, outraged growl. "You think I cannot take care of me? And you? In—in *jungle*?" He fumbled for the word. His heart thudded harshly and that rage was back. "You bring us here to *protect* me?"

Her eyes had gone wide and shocked. Then her lips—the full lush ones his attention continued to wander back to—firmed and flattened. "You were very badly injured, and you could have died from the fever. This isn't an insult to your manhood, Zaren. It was practicality. I wasn't about to let anything happen to you—and I certainly didn't want to be trying to lug a deadweight man who was bleeding to death around the jungle. It was the only way to save you."

Her voice had become prim and tight, and Zaren didn't understand most of her words, but he comprehended enough. "You risk yourself to protect me?" he replied bitterly. "I would not let anything bad happen to you. This jungle is my *home*. I know it all."

Right before him, she softened and eased. "I was afraid you would die. You have been very sick for two days…and three nights." Her voice caught a little.

He relaxed some. *Fever.* He remembered that word, remembered the weakness that had overtaken him…and then a rush of shadowy memories.

"But now that you're awake," Jane was saying, pressing her hand gently against the side of his face, "we can leave."

"We go now." He made to move, but she pulled him back down.

Her eyes were wide and she leaned closer to him. Her voice was low and her warm breath brushed his cheek. "We must be careful. There are guards outside."

"Guards?"

"They are watching. They don't want us to leave."

"They cannot keep me here." Fury shot through him, and his muscles bunched. No one would keep him. And no one would touch her. "You come with me."

"Yes, oh yes, Zaren," she said, kissing him on the side of the mouth.

He turned to take her lips fully with his. She tasted beautiful…warm and soft and sweet, and something inside him filled as if to burst. When she pulled away, her amazing green eyes glittered with something hot and deep that made his belly move like butterfly wings. She drew in a deep breath and put her fingers over his mouth. "We must wait, Zaren. It must be the right time—when they won't stop us. Trust me. I—"

The door to hut opened and the man with the very cold, empty eyes stood there. "Goddess. It is time. You must come with me. The fourth couple awaits their turn."

Zaren didn't like the way the man looked at Jane—or at himself, and he tightened his fingers around her wrist. "No."

"Zaren," Jane hissed, trying to loosen his grip. "Please."

Please. A shard of heat rushed through him, for he remembered the first time she'd looked at him like that: her beautiful eyes wide and green as the sea, filled with fear and hope.

Please. He'd touched her soft skin, and she'd moaned and writhed, turned warm and damp and sweet-dusky smelling… and he knew even then he must mate with her. And once he did, he knew there would never be another mate for him.

"No," he said. "You stay with Zaren. With me." He looked fiercely at the man and pulled to his feet, wholly unconcerned with his nakedness. Looming over the man-creature, Zaren had not one thought of fear. He could break this man in a breath if he wanted to.

"Zaren, I will come back very soon," Jane promised. "But I must go for now." She stood on her toes to press a kiss to his ear and whispered, "We will leave when I return. This will be my last night away from you. Please…do not fight. I promise I will return."

Though Zaren trembled with rage, he allowed her to leave—but not without sending a dark, warning look at the man with cold eyes.

After Jane and the man left the hut, Zaren prowled about and investigated his surroundings. He was alone and had ample opportunity to find something that could be used as a weapon. He had no intention of waiting here until Jane returned.

The small nest—no, house; that was the word—had walls made of bamboo rods covered with tightly-woven dried grasses. Some animal skins, rubbed smooth and supple, also hung on the walls. There was a small opening in the roof for the smoke to escape, and one door where daylight filtered from beneath it.

A small fire burned in an enclosure in the corner, and there were jugs and trays on a table. A trio of bamboo poles had been arranged to hold up a pot, which hung over the fire. The floor was covered with dried grasses that had been woven into flat pieces. Two chairs were arranged near the fire, and he remembered the elderly healer woman sitting there. Animal skins and plaited baskets were piled in one area. His muscles bunched. Zaren was ready to break free of this place, and he growled in the back of his throat. *They will not keep me.*

And he would not wait. He'd find Jane and they would go. His jaw hurt, so tight from anger and pain. Whatever she was doing, he knew it was nothing good for her. He knew how to read the language of animals and man, and he knew she was just as unhappy as he.

Just as Zaren was about to break off a piece of the bamboo stand that held the cooking pot—it would make an excellent spear—he heard the softest sound of footsteps outside and smelled someone approaching. A moment later, the hut door opened and Zaren spun with a little growl.

"Have no fear," said the man with the cold eyes. He held up a hand as if to forestall Zaren's attack. "Your woman is being well cared for."

"Where is Jane?" he demanded, looking past the man and out into the light of dusk. He saw shadows of other people, the glow of the setting sun filtering through the trees and other jungle growth. But no nimbus of fire-gold hair.

"She will return soon. But in the meanwhile, I have brought you food and drink." In his other hand, he carried a small jug and a leather pouch. "I understand in England it is customary for men to sit and partake together."

Zaren didn't fully understand what the man was saying. The word *England* struck a shadowy memory that left a lingering pain in his head, and he had no idea what "partake" meant. But he was hungry and his throat was dry. According to Jane, he'd been ill for three days, and of course he must nourish himself.

Despite his wariness of the man, Zaren eased back. He understood enough from Jane that it was important to pretend not to want to leave, not to be ready to fight these people.

"You *are* from England, aren't you?" said Cold Eyes as he set the jug on a table and removed its stopper. "Never seen blue eyes on anyone in the jungle. But you've been here a long time. You don't remember any of it, do you?"

England. Again came that pain, now in the space above his eyes. Zaren didn't know how to respond. Instead, he took a small cup when it was offered to him and drank. The liquid wasn't cool and refreshing as he'd expected, but tasted sweet and heavy, like the sap from the anaharti tree.

"Drink," the man encouraged him when Zaren pulled the cup away and frowned at it. "See?" He lifted his own vessel to his mouth and tipped it up. All the while, those cold eyes remained on Zaren as if he were a wild animal, about to be uncaged.

He felt the weight of the man's attention as it traveled over his bare torso and flank, then down his legs, and Zaren realized belatedly he was still completely uncovered. He looked around for a cloth to put over himself, knowing most human animals preferred to do so. He did it only for convenience and protection.

"There was a story about a ship that wrecked," the man said. "Some years back. Fifteen? Twenty years, perhaps?" Now his eyes began to glitter, and Zaren felt an uncomfortable, hot sensation when the man looked at him. Like a tiger stalking its prey. "Drink." The man smiled.

Zaren wanted water, not this sweet, thick stuff. But he found if he tipped up the cup to sip, he could look around the room without being noticed. He was still searching for a weapon.

But now he began to feel a little unsteady on his feet. The room tipped a little, and Zaren touched the back of a chair to steady himself. Perhaps he was still weak from the fever.

"The ship was called the *Windstead*. It carried a well-known family from England." The man smiled at him. He was sitting in one of the chairs and he gestured for Zaren to take the other. "More?" he asked, offering the jug.

"Water," Zaren replied as he eased himself onto one of the seats. His tongue felt thick and his head heavy. Now the floor tilted and the air seemed soft and murky around him. He reached out to put his cup on the table and the table wasn't there…the cup fell to the ground with a soft thud.

"You drank it all. Excellent." The cold-eyed man bent to pick it up. "Did you say something about water?"

Zaren nodded.

"Of course. Whatever you wish. You'll need it to keep your stamina." The man smiled, and his grin was hot and dark and sent an odd shiver through Zaren. Then he stood and went to the door.

Zaren used the opportunity to blink hard and shake his head in an effort throw off this odd, blanket-like cocoon that seemed to envelope him…but instead of easing, it began to grow heavier and thicker and his movements became slower and more sluggish.

And then he slipped into shadowy darkness.

Something cold and wet splashed over him, and Zaren jolted awake.

"You asked for water," said a voice very close behind him.

Zaren was now wide awake and it took him only a breath to realize he was standing…facing a wall of the hut. His arms were spread wide and *tied to the wall*. And so were his legs, with thick vine-ropes that bit into his flesh.

A flash of panic rushed over him, then turned to fury. He growled and tugged on one of his arms. The wall of the hut shook and shivered, and little bits of dried grass showered down on him. He pulled again, harder, and still was unable to free himself.

"No," he ground out, and yanked at his other arm. Confusion was the only thing that kept him from struggling wildly. What was happening?

The man with the cold eyes laughed softly behind him. "Oh *yes*," he said in a catlike purr…*and touched him.*

Zaren jolted sharply and twisted, growling again, louder and with more warning. The man ignored him and smoothed a hand down over his hip and thigh, then slipped it between his spread legs.

Zaren roared in surprise as the man reached up to touch his sac, sliding his hand through from behind and fondling him. He jolted again, shocked and outraged…and yet he couldn't control the sudden surge of pleasure that shot to his rod. The man closed his fingers around him and Zaren began to pant and tremble as his cock surged full and hot, filling the man's hand.

Behind him, Cold Eyes was pressing his warm skin into his backside, rubbing muscle and hair and his own stiff rod against his arse. Zaren twisted and shook, trying to control the sensations blossoming inside him: dark and red and hot. He panted, losing his breath and his place, and fought against these strange and intense feelings even as he strained to pull his arms free.

"Beautiful," muttered Cold Eyes as he released him and reached to smooth his hands over Zaren's broad shoulders and bunching muscles.

His skin jumped and tingled beneath the man's touch as if burned with some hot pleasure, and he closed his eyes and tried to push the feelings away. Tried to pull and shift and work his arms free as the man's hands smoothed down over his hard belly and hips and flank. Prodding and poking, massaging and stroking everywhere.

The man stepped away suddenly and Zaren shuddered with relief. His rod was still stiff and protruding, nearly touching the wall when he leaned forward, and his skin still burned and shivered—but the man's hands were off him.

He gathered up his strength and tightened his arms, ready to pull: he'd tear himself from this wall and strangle the man.

But before he could do so, Cold Eyes was there again…in front of him. Zaren gasped a shocked groan as the man knelt before his throbbing cock. He couldn't breathe, couldn't move, as the man curved his fingers over Zaren's muscular thighs and pulled his hips closer as he leaned forward.

Zaren's mind went blank and dark and red as the man's mouth closed over his rod.

Nooo…

He couldn't think, couldn't even breathe as he was assaulted by the most unexpected, hot, slick sensation surrounding him. Crying out, he arched forward, then tried to twist away as Cold Eyes slid his throbbing rod deep into his tight, wet mouth, his lips full and his tongue jerking quickly along the bottom of the swollen length. The teasing tongue stroked and flickered along the most sensitive part of him, sending licks of heat and pleasure rushing over him. His cock strained inside that hot cavern, pulsing and throbbing painfully.

Zaren's knees gave away and he lost his place, nearly pitching forward. Lust and blazing pleasure roared through him even as he tried to fight his way free from the tight grip on his hips. This was wrong…*wrong.*

Jane. It was Jane he wanted…not this man with the cold eyes and the hot mouth.

But still the man sucked and licked, his lips and tongue fast and hot and hard, and Zaren felt as if he were ready to burst. He closed his eyes, curling his fingers into his palms, panting and shaking while the man held him in place, groaning and sighing against his cock as he worked up and down, up and down, licking and sucking and fondling his sac. The sounds of suction and fluttering licking filled Zaren's ears, the smell of man and sweat and something smoky and sweet…

He was wet and hard everywhere. Sweat trailed down his spine as he fought through the sensations and yet spiraling into the dark vortex of pleasure. All at once the man shifted, and Zaren felt something poking him, probing…his finger.

Zaren gave a low, guttural cry as the man slid a finger inside him and sucked his rod even harder, faster, tighter. The finger moved in and out, faster and faster, and the tongue flickered wildly around his turgid cock. He was a puddle of heat and raging blood, and the man's mouth tightened and pulled, dragged and sucked as if he meant to swallow him whole…and then Zaren went over.

His hips shot forward, jamming his rod deep into the tight heat that surrounded him, exploding with such force that he cried like a dying animal. He pulsed and shook and panted as he emptied himself, hanging by his wrists, his head tipped back, his hair clinging to his damp skin.

The man sucked one last time, swirled his tongue around his head as if in farewell, then pulled back and stood. His eyes were no longer cold, but burned dark and black. His lips were puffy and glistened and he looked at Zaren as if he were about to eat him. Meeting his eyes, he held Zaren's gaze as he swallowed heavily and thickly, then his tongue came out to lick his lips as if very satisfied. His smile was hot and the message there sent another unexpected bolt of lust through Zaren.

He closed his eyes, mortified and confused. He'd seen men and women in the mating act, but he'd not known men could do the same to each other. He trembled, thinking of Jane… what would she say?

He was still shaking, still lost in the vestiges of lust, when he felt the man standing behind him again. What was this?

The man's hands were on him again, stroking down his torso and hips, and then Zaren felt the prod of something much thicker than a finger behind him. He tensed, arching forward and away, pulling on the rope restraints.

But he was fixed fast, and the man's hands held him in place as he curled strong fingers tighter around his thighs. The probing became more insistent, closer, harder, and all at once Zaren realized what was happening.

He let out a furious roar, the sound of a lion attacking, just as the man shoved himself up inside him. Zaren cried out again as pleasure and pain coursed through him. Fury ripped through him as the other man's hard cock eased slowly in, deeper and deeper. He was full and tight, and the sensation was awful and yet horribly arousing…shocking and hot. His own rod lifted and shifted, beginning to harden once more. Pleasure grew like a starburst, spreading through his belly and limbs.

Zaren struggled desperately, pulling and twisting and trying to free himself of this invasion, but he was trapped and helpless.

The man panted behind him, his breath hot and moist on his shoulder. Full, wet lips brushed along Zaren's skin, making it prickle uncomfortably as the man pushed himself deeper. Zaren felt hard, hairy thighs pressing against his from behind, and he struggled anew, half-sobbing in desperation.

When the man gave a last hard thrust, burying himself deep, Zaren's vision turned red, and black fury roared through him. He bellowed and pulled with all his strength and outrage, and suddenly one arm whipped free.

Dried grass and bamboo rained down on them, and he reached behind him and dragged the man off him. He flung him away with one sharp movement, still roaring like a pained lion. With another hard yank he had his second hand free, but by then the man was lunging toward him.

Zaren grabbed him by the throat and effortlessly sent him sailing across the room to land in a heap near the fire. He tore off the bindings on one ankle, roaring and snarling. He was leaving this place and he was taking Jane with him.

ANE HEARD THE CRIES, and then the roar of a lion—much too close. She was, mercifully, not participating so closely in the fourth couple's mating process and merely stood in her position, trying to ignore them—and her body's response—as they fucked on hands and knees in front of her.

But the sound of the lion nearby, then again closer and more furious, distracted even the man and woman in the throes of passion. They disengaged themselves, bolting to their feet with frightened expressions and speaking in their native tongue.

Now they could hear the sounds of fighting, of destruction, mingling with the lion and Jane had a sudden stab of fear. It sounded as if the beast was tearing through the village.

Zaren.

Dear God, what if he was in the path of the creature? Unable to help himself, still weak and sleepy?

"Release me!" she demanded of the couple, who looked as if they were ready to bolt. To make her point clear, she shook her arms, causing the bed posts to shimmy violently.

For a moment, she feared they would leave her anyway, but even as the lion roared again—much too closely—the woman leapt over toward her with a sharp command to the man. They had just finished untying Jane's ankles and had moved to her wrists when the lion roared just outside the hut.

The woman screamed and the door burst open—and there was Zaren.

Jane cried out in surprise and relief, and suddenly he was next to her: naked and glorious and vibrating with fury. He looked at her, his eyes dark and angry, then he tore the bedpost away, cracking it in half. Her ropes slid from it and she was free.

"We go *now*."

Jane wanted nothing more than to crawl into his arms, crawl inside him, get away from here. "But there's a lion—"

Zaren roared, and it was as if the lion was standing in front of her…and she realized it was.

"We go *now*." He bit the words out and snaked an arm around her waist.

They erupted from the hut into the dark of night. If the villagers wanted to stop them, they didn't even try, for Zaren roared once more and clambered up a tree with an arm hooked safely around Jane's waist.

She didn't see Cold Eyes anywhere, but Devilish Grin peered at them from next to the village fire as Zaren grabbed a hanging vine.

With his bloodcurdling scream replacing the sound of the lion's roar and her arms locked tightly around his neck, they swung off into the night.

This time, no one shot arrows at them. Perhaps without Cold Eyes—wherever he was—egging them on, or perhaps since Jane had performed much of her "goddess" duties, they let them go.

Or perhaps they simply feared that the man who roared identically to a lion *belonged* with a goddess, and could turn into the wild cat himself.

She didn't care. She was safe, with Zaren, and they were going back to her papa and Effie.

They swung through the jungle for a long time until Zaren felt it was safe to stop. Or perhaps he simply knew of the massive tree with its trio of branches that made a nestlike bed high above the ground. A safe place to rest for the remainder of the night.

Jane curled trustingly in Zaren's strong arms, safe and secure at last. His head drooped onto hers, but not before he rained gentle, feathery kisses all over her temples and head.

"Jane," he whispered. "Jane. Only you. I want only you."

"Zaren." She curved her arms around his neck, tears filling her eyes. "I love you." She could hardly believe she was free and safe and could be with him forever.

She'd take him back to London with her. She didn't care what those biddies in Society thought.

Or maybe he'd want to stay here, in the jungle? But far from Cold Eyes and his goddess-worshiping people.

"I…love…you…?" The words were a question, as if he didn't quite understand.

Jane pulled away to look at him, their eyes meeting in the moonlight. She used her hand to make a fist over her heart. "I love" —she thumped her heart— "you. *Love.*" She thumped again and gave him her sweetest, most emotional smile, trying to get him to understand. "You. Only you. I want only you. Always."

His smile was a little wavery, but his eyes shone with comprehension. "Zaren *love* Jane." He reached out to touch her cheek, his fingers shaking with the same emotion Jane felt. Then he leaned forward to kiss her, ever so gently and slowly as if to impress her taste upon his mouth.

She felt a warm rush of beautiful pleasure billow through her—so different from the sharp, hard, intense arousal forced from her by the villagers—and she smiled.

Happy.

They slept, or at least she did, and in the morning they awoke with the first birds.

"Now we must go to my papa. Surely he is worried. And Effie too," Jane said as they drank from a nearby pool of water. Both were still naked, and she was uncertain how her father would react to her arriving at the treehouse, nude and accompanied by an equally-nude jungle man.

But that was assuming Papa would even notice. If there was a butterfly about, he surely wouldn't.

"Everett? Effie?" Zaren said. "Papa? Mama?" He pointed to Jane.

She smiled. "My papa is Everett, yes. The short man with the belly." She made the motions to describe him. "Effie is my—my nurse. The big woman. My helper." Jane shrugged. How did one describe a maid's duties to a wild man?

"They worry for you," Zaren told her. "I hear them talking."

"Then we must return as quickly as possible. But I should find something to wear." She gestured to her naked self.

The expression on Zaren's face—clearly he would prefer her *not* to cover herself—made her smile, and another streak of warm squiggly emotion spiraled through her belly. Tonight he would visit her in her bedroom in the treehouse and they would make love wildly and passionately *all night*.

She smiled at him with that promise, and he snatched in his breath, his eyes blazing blue.

"We go to my nest. Clothes there."

Jane nodded. She'd been there once before and had noticed the old trunks in the corner, likely from some shipwreck. Or perhaps they had even been Zaren's trunks—for surely he'd come to the jungle by ship. Perhaps even a shipwreck.

She'd never asked him, for their language barrier was still difficult. But if they went back to London—and even if they didn't—she would find out more.

It took much of the day for them to travel back to Zaren's "nest", which was only a short distance from the treehouse Jane shared with her father and Effie, and their guide, Kellan Darkdale.

When they arrived, Zaren found her an old—very old—shift from the depths of one of the trunks and Jane put it on. She felt odd being clothed again in the light cotton, despite the fact that it was loose and hung on her like a sack.

"I will go back to the treehouse and tell Papa I've returned," she said. "I want you to come, but I must have some time to explain what happened…and who you are. You come when the sun is…there. Touching those trees."

She didn't know how Effie and Papa would react to her return, let alone the fact that she would have a wild man in animal skins in tow. She would ease them into the explanation.

Zaren seemed to understand. "I must look," he said, a little frown appearing between his eyes. He gestured to the trunks to indicate where he was going to search.

Jane nodded. She could see the top of the treehouse from here, and knew she would be safe traveling there on foot. Aside from that, Zaren would hear her if she cried out.

With one last kiss that brought the heat back into his eyes—not to mention shuttling through her—Jane climbed down from Zaren's nest and made her way back to the treehouse.

But when she arrived, she found the place in disarray. Everything was strewn all over, as if there'd been some sort of fight or altercation.

"Papa?" she cried, rushing to the window to look out it.

Her heart surged into her throat. *A ship!* There was a ship just beyond the beach!

"Papa!" she screamed, clambering down the ladder. Was he leaving her? Had he thought her dead? Or had something worse happened? "Effie! Effie! *Zaaaaaren!*"

She screamed as she ran all the way down to the beach.

VIII

"THANK HEAVENS YOU'VE RETURNED!" Kellan Darkdale turned to Jane as she rushed onto the beach.

The ship sat a short distance away, sails at half-mast. A small rowboat rested just off shore and two sailors sat in it, ready with their oars.

"What's happened?" she asked, looking around for Papa and Effie. Something was terribly wrong. "Is Papa on the ship? Was he going to leave me?"

Darkdale took her by the arm. "It's horrible, Miss Clemons. I—we—feared you were lost for good in the jungle! That some wild creature had—well, that's neither here nor there. Now that you've returned, we have other, more serious problems."

"Where's Papa? There isn't anyone in the treehouse, and it looks as if there's been a struggle. Is he on the ship? Was he going to leave without me? Did he truly think I was dead?" She'd only been gone for a week!

"I have some terrible news, Miss Clemons. Please, brace yourself," he said, urging her toward the small dinghy. "We must get to the ship as soon as possible."

"What is it? Is Papa dead?" Jane didn't like the grave expression on his face, but at the same time, she couldn't help but remembering how he'd had his way with her in the hot bubbling pool…with Jonathan's permission. "What happened to him?"

"This ship has arrived…to take your father back to London. You see, he's been convicted of a murder. I am so relieved you returned before the ship left."

"A *murder*?" Jane halted on the sand. The bottom dropped out of her stomach. "Papa? When? How? *Impossible!* My father wouldn't hurt a fly!"

"That's why you must return to London," Darkdale said, easing her toward the dinghy again. "Immediately. They plan to execute him as soon as he sets foot on English soil."

"Papa!" Jane cried, terror sharpening her cry. "No. He would *never*…how could anyone even *think* that of him?" She no longer needed to be guided to the small boat—she was fairly running. Her father—her gentle, absentminded, brilliant father—must be terrified by now. Had they put him in the brig? Was he chained up?

And what about Effie? Was she with him at least, comforting him in Jane's absence?

"I will tell you all about it once we are safely on the ship."

"When did it get here? When is it leaving?"

"It's only by your good fortune you've arrived just in the nick of time, Miss Clemons. I had come back ashore one last time to make certain you hadn't returned—and that's the only reason we are still here. The ship is leaving immediately—as soon as we set foot on the deck. The captain has already pulled up the anchor." He helped her into the small boat, which rocked as she climbed in.

"Oh, my poor papa," she said, wiping away a tear as one of the sailors pushed them off.

Then with a horrified start, she remembered. "Zaren!" Jane bolted to her feet and the small boat rocked crazily even as the sailors began to row. "I must go back! My—there is a man…

he's an Englishman, he must return with us…I can't leave without telling him goodbye."

"I'm afraid it's too late, Miss Clemons," Darkdale said as the boat sped across the water. The men had put their muscles into the rowing, and the shore was falling away more quickly than Jane would have imagined. "There's simply no time to go back."

Just then, Jane heard Zaren's wild cry echoing through the jungle. He'd heard her call and came to find the disaster at the treehouse.

"Zaren!" she screamed, standing up again in the boat. "Zaren!"

"Sit down, Miss Clemons, or you will overset us," Darkdale said. "Who is this Zaren?"

"It's the Englishman I spoke of…please, can't we wait for him?"

By now—amazingly—their rowboat was brushing up against the side of the ship. As Darkdale urged Jane toward the dangling rope ladder which led up to the main deck, she looked back at the shore.

Just then, Zaren swung into view, landing on his feet in the center of the beach. "Jane!" he bellowed, staring after her.

"Zaren!" she cried, hesitating at the top of the wavering rope ladder. "I love you! I—"

"Hurry it up now," Darkdale said, pushing her none-too-gently onto the deck of the ship. She tripped over a coil of rope and fell onto her hands and knees; then he was behind her, nudging her out of the way.

Someone was shouting commands. The massive white sails rose, filling immediately with a healthy sea breeze and she felt the vessel shift.

"*Jane!*" Zaren's voice was louder and filled with distress.

She dragged herself to her feet and ran to the rail. "Zaren! I have to leave! They have my papa! I'm going back to London!"

She cupped her hands around her mouth, screaming as loudly and clearly as she could. "I will come back!"

"Come with you!" He was already past his hips in the water.

"Oh, yes! *Yes! Hurry!*" she screamed, hope rising inside her. "Wait!" She whirled, looking for someone to command. "Stop! Wait for him!"

Zaren had dived into the ocean, and she saw him swimming furiously after them. His powerful arms and legs cut through the water like a machine, and she stood, clutching the rail. "Please! Wait! Stop the ship!"

Darkdale was there next to her, and he seemed suddenly, inexplicably, satisfied and relaxed. "He'll never catch up to us."

"Won't you make them stop?" Jane begged, turning to face him. She reached for his arms, grabbing at them, ready to plead…but the expression in his eyes froze her.

"He can drown for all I care." Instead of pushing Jane away, he reached down and took her by the chin. "Either way, now I have you all to myself."

She wrenched away. "You do *not*!" Spinning back to the rail, she looked out again, anxiously searching for Zaren.

His bobbing head was so far away…becoming smaller and more distant by the moment. He had no chance of catching them. Her heart cracked and a wave of grief washed over her. *Swim back, Zaren. Don't drown. Please go back.*

"I'll come for you!" she shouted, knowing he couldn't hear her. "I love you! I'll come back for you!" She spun back to Darkdale, tears glistening in her eyes. "How dare you leave him. You will never touch me again."

He looked down at her with strange smile. "I feel quite certain you'll change your mind about that."

Jane's breath caught. "What do you mean? Never mind. I want to see my papa." She whirled away, but a strong hand yanked her back.

"Your papa isn't here."

"*What?*" she cried. All feeling drained from her body, leaving her cold and numb. "No! You told me—"

He was shaking his head. "I told you the ship came for him—and it did. But he was smart enough to escape deep into the jungle with that fat woman of yours. He knows what will happen if he gets back to London. He's already been convicted of murder, and it'll be the noose for him."

"You tricked me!" She could hardly breathe…it was as if the world was falling away beneath her feet. Why would he do this? "You told me he was here—being taken away."

"Not at all, Jane. You merely assumed he was on the ship. Everything I told you is true…and the one thing I didn't tell you is that I have the evidence to clear his name."

"You do?" Her heart thudded in her chest. Hope lifted her heart…just a little.

"I do. That is why I was going to return to London—but it's even better if you come with me. Together, we can prove he's innocent." He smiled down at her, then reached to brush away a curl that fluttered in the breeze. "You and I."

Jane swallowed hard. There was something in his eyes that made her uneasy. "Thank you, Mr. Darkdale. I—"

"But, of course, if I'm to save your papa from the hangman's noose, then you must do something for me." Now his eyes filled with heat and his fingers curved under her chin again. "I've become obsessed with you, Jane Clemons. Wholly enamored."

"I won't marry you," she said, stepping back, away from his hand. "I love Zaren."

He chuckled softly. "I don't require your hand in marriage, Miss Clemons. I merely require you in my bed, back in London."

"What?" Heat rushed up over her throat to her face, and all at once her knees felt unsteady. She gripped the railing. Her mouth had gone very dry.

"It's very simple, Jane. If you wish me to save your father's life, you will become my mistress. My very accommodating, very *submissive* mistress."

ENAMORED

Colette Gale

ONDON.

Jane stood at the ship's rail and watched details of the city take shape as the vessel navigated down the Thames. She didn't know whether to be more relieved or apprehensive about the unexpected, premature return to the city of her birth.

"It has been a long voyage," said a voice in her ear. "But now the real journey begins, does it not, Miss Clemons?"

She stiffened but didn't deign to turn her head, nor to reply. Kellan Darkdale had come to stand next to her—much too close—and slid an arm around her waist. His presence and touch was an unwelcome reminder of what awaited her now that they'd returned from the wilds of the jungle.

You shall be my mistress.

My very submissive mistress.

She drew in a long, slow breath tinged with the fresh scent of seawater and laced with the aroma of fish and coal smoke. After what she'd experienced at the hands of the jungle natives, Jane was certain she could survive anything Darkdale demanded of her in his bed.

Just as she had suffered the touch and titillation from Cold Eyes, Ulma, and the others for the sake of her beloved Zaren, she would willingly—even eagerly—succumb to Darkdale's demands in order to save Papa's life.

She would do anything for her brilliant, absentminded, naive father.

Thankfully he was safe—for the time being. As far as she knew, he was still back in the relative safety of the Madagascar jungle—along with Efremina and, she hoped with all her heart, Zaren as well. Would Zaren know to find them and tell them what had happened?

What little he knew and could comprehend?

A wave of grief clogged Jane's throat as the ship bumped into place at the dock. Her last sight of Zaren had been of him cutting smoothly and quickly through the water toward the ship as it set out to sea. His powerful arms sliced through the waves with ease, and his kicking legs left a trail of white foam in his wake. Though she begged for the crew to wait for him, her pleas went unheeded, and Zaren's dark head grew smaller and smaller as the ship sailed away.

Please, God, let him have made it back to shore.

Please, God, let him know I had no choice but to leave.

I will return to him.

"Missing the jungle already?" Darkdale asked, his voice low and husky in her ear. "Or are those tears of joy that you've returned to civilization at last?"

When she remained mute, his arm grew uncomfortably tight around her waist.

"Now this will not do at all, Miss Clemons. You will soon learn that, during our arrangement, I'll not suffer your impertinence. When I ask you a question, you'll answer it—"

Jane stepped brusquely away, disengaging from his grip. "Let me make one thing perfectly clear, Mr. Darkdale. Before we embark on any sort of arrangement, I require proof of what you claim: that my father is wanted—and has been sentenced to hang—for murder. And that you have the ability to clear him of all charges."

His eyes darkened and a little smile curled one side of his mouth. "I need only show you the newspaper wherein the court's decision is reported, Miss Clemons, and you will have all the proof you need that the moment your father sets foot in London, he will be taken to the hangman's platform. Unless I intervene."

Then, with elegant fingers, he took her chin in a firm grip and tilted her face toward him, tightening his hold until she met his eyes.

"As for our arrangement, Miss Clemons…I am very much looking forward to the challenge of taming your spirit and teaching you proper behavior. I suspect it will be quite pleasurable…for both of us."

Her chest felt tight, and her cheeks bloomed hot with fury…but even so, an unexpected quiver of heat caught her by surprise. Startled, Jane looked away, then, recovering quickly, turned back to him. "If you will clear my father's name, I will do whatever you wish."

"I know you will." His smiled turned cooler.

"But I will hate every moment of it—and every time you touch me, know that I will be shuddering with disgust, and my belly turning with nausea."

"What a challenge you will be, Miss Clemons. My dear Jane," he added, his voice dropping low and breathless as he took her hand. He raised it to his lips in a parody of a gentleman—which he most certainly was not—and pressed a soft kiss there. "I have been mad for you since Jonathan first told me about you, painting verbal pictures for me of your lustful passion, your glorious desires and beautiful body whilst we sat around our campfires in the jungle. That brief taste I had of your delicious self while we were in the hot pool has only served to increase my desire for you.

"You might protest now, but I promise you this, my dear Jane: there will be a time when you will beg for me to touch you…when you will plead for me to give you pleasure."

Jane stared unseeingly out the window of the carriage.

Darkdale had been as good as his word. No sooner had they disembarked from the ship and engaged a hansom cab than he directed it to the office of the *London Times*.

Shortly thereafter, he returned with a copy of a newspaper dated three months earlier. Although the headline wasn't the largest—nor was it even on the front page—it was bold and frightening all the same: *Celebrated Butterfly Scientist to be Hung for Murder of Mr. Gerald Carmichel.*

So it was true.

"How do you propose to see the charges dropped?" she'd demanded, staring at the article, willing it to disappear or for the names to change…or something.

"Why, it's very simple, my darling Jane," he said, his voice very silky. "Your father was with me—for we were making preparations for our journey to Madagascar of course—during the time of Mr. Carmichel's death. I need only testify that this was so, and his name will be cleared."

"And though an innocent man might go to his death, you will withhold this information unless I…unless I submit to you?" Fury tightened her voice and loathing rushed through her. She'd always known the man was a cad—from the very first night in the jungle, when he'd burst into her bedchamber high in the treehouse and attempted to seduce her.

And then there was the episode with him and Jonathan in the hot springs pool… He had done things to her she'd never have imagined. She shivered, and to her hot shame, it wasn't wholly a reaction of disgust.

"Ah, but my dear Jane," he said, his eyes glittering as he settled them on her from his seat across the carriage. "Unfortunately, I wasn't with your father at that time. But I am willing to perjure myself, to lie on the stand, in order to save him. Because, of course, he is innocent of the charges."

"What?" Jane's eyes went wide. "You would lie?"

"Oh, yes indeed. For I will have you, in my bed, as my mistress—and under my terms. I have waited too long for this opportunity, and now that Jonathan has met his fate—at the hands of a lioness, did you say?—there is no one to stand in my way."

Only Zaren, she thought. *Zaren*. But Zaren couldn't save her papa's life. Jane bared her teeth at him in a cold smile. "Sir, you are a snake of the very worst sort."

"No, my dear. I am merely an opportunist—and an excellent negotiator. You will receive something you desperately desire…and so will I. And, I posit, you shall even find pleasure with me."

Jane averted her eyes and focused her attention on the rows of houses lining the street. She dared not dwell on what awaited her once they arrived wherever it was they were going.

The fact was, she didn't have any idea what to expect from Darkdale. When he made his pronouncement shortly after her arrival on the ship—that he would clear her father's name if she became his mistress—Jane expected him to insist she begin sharing his bed immediately. It would have been more than convenient for him, for she'd had no time to don any clothing after her escape from the jungle natives—except a simple chemise that barely covered her and reached only to her knees.

However, he made no such demands. Instead, he merely treated her with the courtesy of a gentleman—finding some appropriate clothing on the ship, squiring her around the deck on his arm several times a day, insisting they dine privately with the captain, arranging for her to have a tub in which to bathe every few days, and even playing chess and gin rummy with her when she became bored.

If Jane hadn't known better, she would have thought he was courting her—a preposterous notion when one considered his demands.

Darkdale did insist they share a cabin, however. And when she was not with him, he kept the door locked from the outside—and the key on his person.

"Speak to no one, and do not attempt to contact anyone or to leave this cabin. If you do," he'd said, his eyes hard and cold. "I'll have you stripped bare and tied over a barrel for the crew. They would be happy to partake of your luscious body. And I would stand by and watch."

Jane was sufficiently cowed by his threat and had no intention of testing him. Aside from that, she saw no reason to leave the cabin without an escort anyway—the rough-looking sailors and their hot eyes were off-putting enough on their own.

And so she spent three weeks in a state of unease and apprehension, and yet relative luxury—knowing that at any moment Darkdale could come into their cabin and order her into his bed. The very thought made her both apprehensive and shamefully titillated, for while he was no Zaren in looks or strength—and definitely not in character—Jane had to admit Kellan Darkdale was a very handsome man. In other circumstances, she might even have been attracted to him.

But not now.

Not ever.

"I have spent the last three weeks imagining you sprawled beneath me on a bed...your glorious hair strewn about the pillows, your body bare and spread for me, your red lips open and begging," Darkdale said, watching her from across the carriage.

"I'll never beg—"

"But I have no reason to wait for such a pose, such a perfect position." He moved like a cat, swift and sleek, and was next to her, grasping her by the shoulders before she could react. "No, my darling Jane. There is no longer a reason to wait, to subdue my desire. Our arrangement has begun."

She held herself rigid as he covered her mouth with his, but his lips were surprisingly soft and warm. Full and sensual. She closed her eyes, squeezing them shut as he kissed her with possessiveness and skill. Her lips parted under his demanding ones, and when his tongue thrust deep into her mouth, she found herself matching it with her own. They tangled and tasted, their tongues dancing and twining until she realized what she was doing and wrenched her face away.

"No," she murmured, trying to even out her breathing.

Darkdale laughed softly and took her face in his hands. "Is that how you wish to play it, my darling? Nevertheless, you shall change your tune. I promise it."

His solid body pressed her into a corner of the bench seat, but he didn't attempt to kiss her again. Jane felt the firm muscles of his arms and thighs, as well as the solid ridge of his cock bumping her hip. His hands moved in lover-like fashion to pull her hair loose, combing through her long curls and over her shoulders as he kissed her, sampling her chin and jaw and then burying his face in the sweet spot beneath her ear. He nibbled on her lobe, gently biting her neck and sliding his strong tongue along her throat, sucking and tasting as he pressed himself against her.

Jane, whose body had been ignored and become dormant for weeks on the ship, couldn't dismiss the erotic sensations. She'd been aroused and pleasured multiple times on a daily basis at the hands of Cold Eyes and his people—most often insistently and against her will—and so she was unable to keep from responding to this sensual, almost tender, onslaught. It had been so long…

Darkdale's breathing was shallow and rough as he eased back to fumble with the buttons down the high collar of her shirtwaist. Then he wasted no time unlacing the corset beneath and releasing her breasts from its confines, tearing away the last bit of covering in the form of Jane's original chemise.

"Beautiful. So ripe and delicious you are, darling Jane." His voice was hoarse and his cock pressed even more insistently into her hip. "I did not have the opportunity to enjoy you thus when we were with Jonathan."

She bit her lip and couldn't help but look down as he gathered up her breasts as if they were the Crown Jewels, shifting them in his palms. Her nipples were already tight and ready, and when Darkdale bent to lightly kiss one of them, Jane felt a shock of real pleasure jolt through her.

She closed her eyes again, determined to hold up her end of the bargain and allow him to do what he would, but not to respond in any way. Still, as he kissed and lightly nibbled on her tits, it became more and more difficult to ignore the sensations. She fought not to shift or sigh or groan as the shivers of pleasure grew stronger and harder. His mouth was warm and wet, his tongue slick and smooth, and the tingling sensations grew insistent and hotter as he licked and sucked on each breast in turn.

Jane's heart was racing, her breath was out of sorts, and worst of all, she felt the familiar throbbing and dampness gathering between her legs. *No*, she thought. *I won't give in to him.*

She was thankful when Darkdale moved away, shifting to her skirts, and gave her the opportunity to recover herself. He hiked up the hem, bundling the fabric off to one side, and slid his hands along her thighs. The fresh air felt cooler now that there was only a thin layer of cotton covering her, and Jane realized she'd become warm and damp everywhere.

"By gad," he murmured, straddling her as he fumbled for the fastenings of his trousers. "I have waited for you for too long. Much too long. And this is only the beginning, my darling." His voice was rough and unsteady, and when she looked up at him, she saw the dark heat in his eyes and the way his nostrils flared gently as if he fought for control. His lips were full and they glistened, reminding her how busy they'd been just a moment ago, licking and sucking on her sensitive nipples.

She closed her eyes, relieved that the sensations he'd aroused in her had ebbed and her breathing was back to normal. The last thing she wanted was for Darkdale to give her pleasure.

Her breasts jounced gently as the cab trundled along. She felt the jerking motion as he unbuttoned himself, freeing his cock quickly and efficiently, and then he was on top of her again. Jane braced herself as he found the slit in her drawers, and knew she was wet enough that there would be no discomfort when he joined with her.

And then it would be over.

But then his fingers…they opened the slit, and slid in further to find her private, slick opening. He covered her moist lips with his hand, stroking firmly and sensually, teasing and fondling her tight little clit. She began to pant softly, trying to ignore his touch by gritting her teeth and squeezing her eyes closed. *No, no, no…* But her body had a will of its own, and she fell deeper and deeper into a well of heat and pleasure and need as his stroking continued incessantly. His fingers teased her, slipping in and around her hot juices as he bent to roughly nuzzle and kiss her throat.

"By gad, what a passionate woman you are," he muttered against her throat as his thumb moved busily over her clit, pressing down and rubbing the tiny little nib in a cross between pain and intense, hot pleasure. She felt herself straining against him, lifting her hips and pushing up to find more pressure, to find what she needed—then she forced herself to relax, to ease back, her heart thudding and her checks hot and damp. His mouth covered hers again, his tongue shoving past her lips to jam deeply inside, thrusting with a strong stroke that mirrored his fingers.

When he suddenly slipped inside her, thrusting three digits hard and fast, Jane couldn't hold back a cry of shock and response. He moved, fucking her with his fingers, in and out, using his thumb to play with her little pip as he worked and worked. She gasped beneath him, feeling her body draw up and swell, hearing the sounds of her thick juices as he stroked and stroked. He pushed in deeper, twisting and turning and stroking as she shuddered and swelled around him, her hips moving, bucking and shifting, her insides hot and fluttery and wanting.

She pulled away from his mouth, panting and gasping, wedged down in the corner of the carriage as his hand stroked faster and faster, twisting and pushing and screwing her like he was a machine. She had no control of herself; she couldn't fight the hot, powerful rise of pleasure as it grew and overtook her.

When she reached her peak, Jane cried out and arched up into his hand, shameful tears leaking from her eyes. She shuddered beneath him, mortified and yet sated, wet and throbbing and hot.

"For the love of heaven," he muttered, his voice taut as he shifted away. "I've never met a woman like you, Jane Clemons. By gad, it's going to be a thrill to tame you. To make you beg. I will master you."

She was still undulating inside, panting and twitching, when he moved, adjusting his position between her legs. She saw his cock then: long and purple, thick and turgid, huge and ready, gripped in his hand. She moaned in spite of herself, a wave of heat rushing over her at the thought of being impaled by such a rod. Of being filled and stroked and pleasured. Jane was panting again, hot and throbbing once more.

Darkdale noticed and gave her a breathless grin, his eyes so dark they were like black marbles as he fit himself against her swollen, wet quim. His mouth was tight, and with one smooth thrust, he slid…and slid…and slid inside. As he filled her, deep and long and fat, his groan was low and heartfelt, shuddering through his body so she could feel the depth of emotion.

"At last," he murmured, holding himself inside her, keeping her impaled on his massive cock. "At long last. You are mine, Jane."

Then he moved, fast and furious and hard, holding her hips in position as he thrust like a piston. He was so thick and hard and long…and Jane's well-trained body couldn't ignore the pleasure of such a tool. No sooner was he pumping inside her than the familiar pleasure filled her, roaring back into play. She couldn't keep from thrusting up to meet him, from gasping and panting for air as lust overtook her.

When the orgasm burst over her, it was even hotter and stronger than before. Jane cried out, bucking up into him, and he covered her mouth with his, drowning out the sound as he slammed inside her once more. She felt him go rigid and shudder against her, inside her, and then his body sagged against hers.

Closing her eyes, Jane let her head tilt back into the corner of the rumbling carriage. *How could I? How could I let go so easily?*

Could I have feelings for this man?

Then she shook her head. No. There was no sense in being ashamed for her body's reaction. She had no choice, no control over herself—she'd learned that while with the jungle natives. Her body was like a fine instrument, a mechanism, that if played correctly would respond a certain way. Her pleasure at his hands meant nothing.

Darkdale pulled away and looked down at her. His eyes glittered dark and hot. "Well then, my dear…I do hope you enjoyed that."

"I did not," she managed to say as he sat up and began to put himself right. "Not at all. I wouldn't even be here if you weren't blackmailing me."

"Indeed?" He glanced at her from the side. "Well, it matters not, for it shan't happen like that again. You see, my darling Jane, from the moment you set foot over my threshold, into my house as my submissive mistress, there are rules that must be followed. Laws, if you will, that you must adhere to.

"And if you break those rules or disobey me, the punishment shall be very severe."

R ULES.

What sort of rules could Darkdale mean?

Jane's heart thudded as the hansom cab turned through a gate and trundled down a short drive. A small brick mansion loomed in front of them. It was set on the outskirts of London, not very far from the Society area of Regents Park, but far enough away that there was a generous lawn—and a high stone wall all around it, to keep the vagrants out, and perhaps others in.

She drew herself up and straightened her shoulders. So there were rules. She could manage them. She could manage anything. This was all for dear, innocent Papa. She'd do whatever was necessary to save his life.

"Well then, my darling. Shall we?" Darkdale offered her his hand as the cab door opened. With the most gallant of manners, he helped her out of the vehicle.

As they approached the house, the front door opened and a very tall, elegant man stood there. He had a close-cropped, neatly trimmed mustache and beard, and his skin was smooth and darkly tanned. "Mr. Darkdale," he said. "Welcome home."

He bowed elegantly, his hand fluttering as he gestured them into the house.

"This is Jane," Darkdale said as soon as the door closed behind them. They stepped down three stairs from the foyer into a large antechamber.

"I see." The slender man perused Jane as if she were a racehorse. His almond-shaped eyes and dark skin gave him a hint of the exotic. "My congratulations, sir," he said after finishing his slow, openly critical examination of Jane.

She bristled at his rudeness then looked around for any other sign of life. Surely a house of this size must have a full retinue of maids and grooms, along with this man—whoever he was. Normally the entire staff would come out to greet the master on his return, but there was no hint of any other servants.

They were standing in a high-ceilinged, octagonal room with three other doorways that opened into corridors, plus the foyer through which they'd just walked. Several small windows, positioned high on the walls, allowed in the gloomy London light. A fireplace had been carved out of one wall, and two armchairs were arranged in front of it. Another wall was lined with shelves. The floor, made of smooth, planked wood, was covered by a fine rug in the corner by the chairs.

Appalled by the slender man's rudeness—not to mention that of Darkdale for not introducing her—Jane said, "And who are you? Are you the butler, then?"

"Ah." Darkdale turned to her suddenly, his expression glinting with something that made her uneasy. "And now we must begin. Trevor, you are dismissed. For now."

The elegant man bowed, but not before Jane saw a flash of amusement in his eyes. "Very well then, sir. Regardless…I am certain you will soon have things well in hand."

"Indeed." Darkdale watched until Trevor was gone, and then he returned his attention to Jane.

"Is he one of your servants? Are there others?" she asked before he could speak.

"That is none of your concern, darling Jane. Your only purpose is to please me; everything else will be taken care of."

She swallowed. "Yes, of course. I understand I'm to share your bed."

"When I require you to do so."

Jane relaxed a trifle. Perhaps this wouldn't be quite as difficult as she thought. "Of course. Will I have a maid—to assist me with my bathing and dressing, then? And perhaps you—or someone—could show me to my chamber?"

Darkdale smiled. But it wasn't a pleasant or charming smile. It was cool and hard. "Your chamber?"

"Where I will sleep when I'm not…sharing your bed." Even if he put her in the attic, three flights up in the servants' quarters on a small, lumpy pallet, it would be better than sleeping with him every night. Jane shuddered, imagining what it would be like slumbering beneath the blankets next to his muscular body and very impressive cock.

"When you are not sharing my bed, darling Jane, you will be sleeping there." He pointed to a shadowy corner of the octagonal chamber.

Jane looked, then turned back to him in confusion, then looked again. "But…"

"Yes, my darling?"

She swallowed hard and took a few steps toward the corner. There was nothing there but a small rectangular cushion, just big enough for a large dog—or a woman—to curl up on. "I'm to sleep there?"

"When you are allowed to sleep, yes, my darling. That is where you are allowed to rest."

By now, an icy feeling had begun to settle over her. "Why that's barbaric!" She'd had more comfortable sleeping arrangements in the jungle—even when held captive by the natives.

"Do you want your father's name cleared?"

Jane drew in a trembling breath. Yes, of course she did. And sleeping on the floor…well, it might not be very gentlemanly of him to shunt her off like a pet, but if that was what she had to do to in order to keep her papa from the hangman's noose, of course she'd suffer through it. She'd suffer through anything. "You know I do. And in regards to that, Mr. Darkdale, when will you be meeting with the barristers and the court to notify them of your intent to testify?"

"Very soon, my darling. As soon as I'm certain you've upheld your end of our arrangement. And we can start with the rules I mentioned in the cab."

"Yes, of course, Darkdale. Whatever your rules are—"

Thwack! Jane cut herself off at the sound of a riding crop… being smacked against Darkdale's hand. Where had that come from?

He smacked it again, his gaze suddenly flat and cold. "Then let me make them known to you, Jane, for the time of talk is over. You are now under my control, and our arrangement has begun. The first rule to which you must adhere is that I am Master in this house. Starting immediately, you shall address me as Master."

Jane's eyes widened and her lips parted in shock. "What?"

"What, *Master*," he said sharply. *Thwack!* "I shall have no tolerance for disobedience, Jane. The second rule is that you shall never speak unless you are bid."

"I—what?" She stepped back. "This is abs—"

He stepped closer, that crop in hand, and took her chin firmly. "I shall overlook your disobedience this one time, Jane, but that is only because you have not yet been apprised of all the rules. If you dare speak out of turn again—even just now—you shall find yourself at the very unpleasant end of a punishment." His eyes glittered as if he very much wished to punish her, then he pushed her away and stepped back.

She stumbled and caught herself, still shocked and quite overcome by this madness. What on earth was wrong with Kellan Darkdale? How could he think she'd agree to sleeping on a dog bed, let alone such tyrannical terms?

Do you want your father's name cleared?

Oh God, yes. Yes, she did.

"Very good, my darling. I see that you are indeed a fast learner. I will add one caveat to that second rule, however, now that I think about it. You may speak…but only to beg. You may beg me for pleasure whenever you like. In fact, my darling Jane, that is my fondest desire…my dearest fantasy. I shall have you begging and sobbing for me, willing to do anything for my touch, to give anything, to experience anything…hanging on my every movement, my every breath… Desperate for my very look. Begging. Hot and ready and desperate…" His voice trailed off, dusky and rough, and his gaze blazed as it scored over her.

No, Jane thought even as she quivered and burned deep inside, desire hot and liquid and roiling like a volcano. *Never. I'll never beg him.* He had enough of her, having her here in this house. *I'll never give him the satisfaction…*

Darkdale seemed to have collected himself, and he continued. "The third rule is even more simple than the others, and one I'm certain will come as no surprise to you: you must do as you are told. Without hesitation. Without question. If you understand, you may nod again, Jane darling."

Still utterly shocked and confused, Jane managed to nod stiffly. Her heart was thudding so hard she was certain it would burst forth from beneath her clothing.

"Excellent. The fourth rule is: you shall be completely unclothed at all times while in this house…which is why you will not be needing the assistance of a maid. Unless we go out."

Jane couldn't help but glance at the two entrances to the foyer and wonder if any of the maids were lurking about. She saw no one. Then she realized what he'd said: *Unless we go out.*

Did he mean to parade her through Society as his kept woman? Her throat went tight.

When she looked back, Darkdale was watching her. *Thwack!* The crop smacked his palm as his eyes fastened on Jane. They were black and cold, and his lips were parted slightly.

And then it dawned on her, like the rush of a cold draft. He expected her to disrobe, right here. Right in the grand foyer. Now.

"I shall wait no longer," was all he said. *Thwack!*

The threat was clear, and even though he hadn't struck out at her, Jane realized she had no choice—at least not at the moment, and not if she wanted to remain unpunished.

She bent to unfasten her shoe: all twenty tiny buttons. Without a buttonhook, it would be a long and difficult process, which would gain her some time. A chance to collect her thoughts and decide how to proceed. But she'd barely started when something fell next to her with a soft clatter. A buttonhook.

Jane didn't even look up; instead, she blanked her mind as she undid each button. At some point during the process, Darkdale took a seat in one of two armchairs by the fire, and she felt his attention focus heavily on her.

She removed her shoes, and then both of the knee-high silk stockings…and paused.

"Jane, darling…you seem much too eager to test my patience. Trust me when I tell you: I am more than eager to punish you." His voice was barely a breath on these last words, and for the first time, fear stabbed her, deep and low.

Her fingers hardly trembled at all as she began to unbutton the fastening of her blouse—the one Darkdale himself had undone only a short time earlier. It was foolish of her to be modest and shy; after all, not only had he seen her naked while in the hot springs pool in the jungle, but he'd also partaken of her body. Twice now.

She had nothing to hide. She had nothing but her pride… and she had already chosen to give that up for Papa. As Jane allowed her blouse to slide to the floor, she heard a distant chime. Moments later, as she was untying the skirt around her waist, Trevor entered the room.

He carried a tray that held a cut-glass carafe filled with brandy or whiskey, and a matching tumbler. He barely glanced at her as he served the drink to Darkdale, and when Jane paused in her disrobe, she saw Darkdale's hand flex over the riding crop. He looked up at her.

Heart shooting into her throat, she dropped her skirt, followed by the flimsy crinoline she'd borrowed on the ship. Now for her corset…

"You may take your time here, darling Jane," said her master. His voice was dusky and low. "For this will be the last time I'll see your lovely self thus revealed…bit by bit, like a gorgeous package."

He'd adjusted the chair, and now sat facing her instead of the fire, legs sprawled wide, glass in hand. Jane's breath hitched and she felt a sharp quiver of desire when she looked at him. She was shocked at her reaction, but he had never appeared so attractive: dark-haired and disheveled, yet frighteningly in control. He'd taken off his coat, tie and waistcoat, unbuttoned the top buttons of his shirt to reveal skin unusually tanned—at least compared to other men in London, who sported sickly white flesh.

She drew in a shaky breath, wondering where her mind was going…how it could even begin along this path when this man had manipulated her into such an untenable situation.

But she wasn't quite able to ban the memory of his hands over her breasts, and the sharp, hard sucking on her nipples…

and, of course, the feel of him filling her. The pleasure had been real even if she loathed the man and his "arrangement."

You will beg me.

No, she would not. He could take what he wished from her, but she would never give him anything.

Jane's fingers were clumsy as she began to unlace the corset, but she did as she was bid: taking her time, allowing the heavy, boned garment to sag away as it was loosened. Her breasts seemed more full than usual, eager to be freed, spilling over the top of the corset and filling out her chemise. Darkdale's eyes never left her, even as he brought the glass to his lips and drank of the golden liquid.

When the corset fell to the ground, and Jane was dressed only in her chemise, she hesitated only a moment…then she pulled the thin cotton shift up and over her head and flung it aside.

Darkdale hissed softly, his eyes avid and hot as he looked at her. "Turn around. Slowly."

Jane did as she was bid, making a small, tight circle with her feet on the bare wooden floor. Her long hair, still loose from when he'd unpinned it in the cab, brushed her skin like little curling fingers and slid over her shoulders and along her arms with every movement. She felt the weight of his eyes travel over her—down over the lower curve of her spine and arse, casting along the sweep of her hips, and then, as she came back full circle, lingering on breasts, and then at the patch of fiery hair that sprang at the juncture of her thighs.

Facing him, Jane stood there, obediently waiting for his next command. Her palms had gone clammy and her belly was fluttering as she tried to imagine what he would require of her next.

"We must now address the fifth and final rule, my darling Jane," he said. His voice was conversational, but his nonchalance continued to be betrayed by the avidity in his gaze. "It is the most important of them all, and is one that you have, unfortunately, broken twice already today." His lips stretched in a smile that was sensual in nature, yet restrained.

She remained mute, standing tall and proud, suddenly feeling even more apprehensive than she had when she'd been on display for all of the jungle natives. Perhaps Darkdale was more dangerous than Cold Eyes and his villagers had been, because the English gentleman was "enamored" with her. By his own admission, he'd been waiting for her for years.

My fondest desire…my dearest fantasy…

"But first, let us review: you must address me as Master, you must not speak without permission—except to beg—you must do as you are told without question or hesitation, you must not wear clothing, and last and most important of all, my darling Jane, for us to get on in our arrangement…you are never allowed pleasure without my permission."

HAT'S CORRECT, MY DARLING JANE. You mayn't orgasm, climax, or otherwise find satisfaction—unless it pleases your master."

Her eyes must have widened in shock, and her cheeks certainly flushed hot. The blaze of heat rushed down over her shoulders and breasts, and immediately Jane felt the familiar sharp, remorseful pulse of her clit. No.

It would be…impossible.

Wouldn't it? Suddenly, she was assaulted by memories and images from her experiences in the jungle. Her body had a will of its own. She needed pleasure. She craved it.

No. Please, no… Jane realized her lips were parted and she had begun to pant softly. Her knees trembled. How could he…

"I see that you understand me. Good." Darkdale smiled and crooked a finger at her. "Now come here, Jane darling, and let us begin."

She began to walk toward him, numb and yet hot and expectant at the same time, but suddenly he held up a hand.

"No. On your knees, darling. You must never approach me except on your hands and knees."

Jane eased slowly to her knees and, mouth dry, heart pounding, scooted her way to him. The floor was cold and unyielding beneath her knees, and her long hair threatened to catch beneath her hands. She paused, giving Darkdale a questioning look as she bundled the heavy mass into a loose knot that fell over her shoulder.

He said nothing, merely watched her as he held his whiskey in one hand and that sleek black riding crop in the other. She noticed for the first time that its end diverged into a shallow Y-shape, with two little prongs each tipped with a pea-sized ball.

When Jane approached his widespread legs, he beckoned for her to come between them. "Loosen me and take me in your mouth."

Once again, Jane did as she was bid—unbuttoning the placket of his trousers and freeing the turgid cock from its confines. He was warm and heavy, thick and straining in her hands, and she felt a responding pulse of awareness between her legs. *No*, she told herself fiercely.

Darkdale watched as she took him into her mouth, groaning low and deep when her lips closed around him. She tasted him: salty and musky, crisp and male, sliding his hot, hard length deep into the back of her throat.

He shuddered a little, his thighs trembling beneath her arms as she propped them on top of them and worked his thick length in and out, deeper, shallower, then impossibly deeper. The sounds he made, the taste and feel of the rod that had so recently given her pleasure, had lust traveling through her own body.

As she worked him, her mouth tight, her lips wet and full from the friction, Jane felt the flutter in her belly growing more intense, and the hot lick of lust moving to her hard little clit. It pulsed and throbbed, and her quim grew wet and more swollen, ready to be filled by the cock she sucked and licked and swallowed.

Her breasts were tight and her sensitive nipples brushed against his spread legs as she moved, and after a moment he reached forward to touch them. Jane gasped around his cock as pleasure shot through her; he pinched and tweaked, massaged and rolled the sensitive tips until she was fairly writhing against him. Juices trickled from her quim, and she was tight and hard and swollen as she sucked and sucked, faster and faster.

Darkdale suddenly stilled, then grabbed her by the head as he jammed himself up into the back of her throat. Jane gagged and coughed as he spurted into her mouth, hot and thick and salty. She felt the soft little shudders of his orgasm as he emptied into her mouth, and his firm hands held her in place as she swallowed his seed.

When he at last released her head, she pulled away, breathing heavily, her body humming and taut, ready and unfulfilled.

"Lick me clean," he said, settling back into his seat, whiskey back in hand again.

Jane moved forward to him once more, lifting his slick, softening cock and gently sucking and licking the last bit of salty ejaculate from it. She still quivered, for the scent of him, the musk and the pungent smell of sex, filled her nostrils and the heat of his body radiated against hers.

When she was finished, she released his now-flaccid cock and sat back on her haunches. Her sex throbbed, and she pressed her knees together in order to find some bit of relief for her pulsing clit, but *thwack!*

Jane gave a surprised shriek and reared back as the crop came down suddenly, just missing her shoulder.

"You will have no pleasure, no satisfaction without my permission," he snapped. "Keep your knees apart, Jane. I will not tell you again."

She bowed meekly, and now her little pip seemed even harder and more engorged, her juices even more slippery and abundant. Her breasts were tight and sensitive, nipples thrusting toward him in an ignored invitation.

Darkdale looked at her for a moment. "Spread your legs wider. I want to see your hot, red pussy."

Jane scooted her knees apart, and felt her quim swell even more, thickening and pulsing…ready. Very ready. Dripping.

Please. Oh, please…

"Lift your hips. You may rest back on your hands. I want to see your pussy. Is it ready for me?"

Oh yes. Dripping. And ready. But Jane refused to speak those words aloud. Instead, she did as directed, positioning so her hips were as high as possible and lifted toward him as she levered back on her hands.

"Hmm. Perhaps it would be best if you turned around." He sounded amused, and aroused. "And get on your hands and knees…" His voice was low and dusky. "Show yourself to me."

Jane's clit pulsed in response, lust stabbing her deep and low. Then she positioned herself as directed, her arse facing him, her knees spread apart.

"Lovely. Absolutely lovely," he purred. The sound of his voice—the low, velvety timbre of it—made her throb even more.

She heard him moving, sensed him rising from his chair. The soft clink of his glass on a table. The bare swish of his shoes brushing the hard floor. His scent came with him—something spicy and a little musky and warm.

Then something slender and cool on her back… The riding crop. Jane tensed as he traced the short, stiff whip along her spine, then brushed it lightly over her arse crack. She felt the thick, hard vee of its tip, where it spread like a Y and had those pea-sized knobs on each end. She imagined them sliding down over her…

Jane's skin prickled, her hair lifting everywhere. Her breathing became shorter and rougher. Moisture gathered between her legs, slick and hot, and when he slipped the tip of the crop down along her crack, she shuddered. The little knobs bumped along her arsehole and down, sliding through the juices of her quim, and then over her tight, pulsing clit.

A tiny ball caressed her sensitive, turgid little pearl, and Jane squeezed her eyes closed tightly as pleasure and need traveled through her. Darkdale laughed softly and slipped the crop's tip over her again, up and down, gently caressing her hot little pip, teasing it with those hard little knobs. Up and down, side to side, slick and slow and firm.

She smothered a soft cry and felt herself gathering up, tightening as lust roared through her. Pleasure grew, rose, hot and sleek, and she tensed, trying to blank her mind as she curled her fingers into the hard wooden floor. He stroked her over and over, slowly and languidly. As if he had all night. She swelled and throbbed, and sweat trickled down her cheeks, heat flushed over her skin. She was wet, dripping and slick, full and ready, and still he played with her…tapping and stroking her with those little knobs, slowly sliding along her arse and quim and bumping deliciously, tortuously, over the center of her sex.

No, she moaned inside. Jane bit her lip, struggling to fight off the blazing pleasure. It was even worse knowing she couldn't. She couldn't give in…she dared not give in to the sensations, the insistent strokes.

Her knees and elbows trembled as she held herself perfectly still. Her belly shuddered. Her breasts dangled, quivering as she fought to keep her breathing steady, to war with the desire lashing through her.

"My gad, you are easy," Darkdale murmured. His voice was so deep and rough with desire it sent even harder and sharper waves of lust through her. "Beg me, Jane. All you need do is ask."

No.

She wouldn't. She wouldn't!

The crop slipped up along her crack, and Jane relaxed a little as the intense pleasure eased. Then… *Thwack!*

She screamed in shock and surprise as the thin strip of pain radiated over her buttocks. Before she could collect herself, those nasty little knobs were back, poking and prying and sliding down into her quim, dancing around her thick, swollen lips as he moved the crop up and down, using the whip like a v-shaped tongue to stroke and tease.

Oh…oh…no, no…

She couldn't hold it off any longer. The lust was so hot and bold and strong, and the little black balls were so dirty and mean, slick and hard and insistent…and they went right where she needed them, right where—

"Ah!" she cried as the blaze of pleasure exploded over her, blossoming into heat and relief in a long, undulating orgasm.

Thwack!

Jane cried out as another streak of pain seared across her buttocks, and then a second and a third, even as she still quivered and trembled and throbbed from the peak of her desire. The thin, hot stripes over her buttocks mingled with the last licks of sharp, hard-won pleasure.

Thwack! Thwack!

"You must learn to control yourself, darling Jane," Darkdale muttered as he wielded the whip. "Not that I mind punishing you in the least."

She collapsed on the floor, shuddering from an unsettling combination of pleasure and pain, warmth and searing heat. Tears mingled with sweat, and her arms and legs trembled.

Suddenly, the whipping stopped and the next thing she knew, he was forcing her back up onto her knees. Hands on the ground in front of her, face angled down so she stared at the wooden floor, knees spread wide.

Jane cried out in pleasure as much as surprise when he rammed himself inside her. Darkdale groaned, low and deep, and filled her with his long, thick cock. She was so wet, he moved easily, sliding madly in and out, in and out like a piston. The sounds of wet suction filled her ears, along with her heartbeat and the noise of her own breathing as he grasped her by the hips and began to move even faster and harder.

She gasped as lust shot through her once again, her channel closing tightly around his girth as he rocked and pumped, slamming her so forcefully she could barely remain upright. Fast and deep and hard, over and over, and Jane couldn't hold back the rise of pleasure once again.

"Ah!" It was his turn to cry out, triumphant and loud. He shot into her, one last, hard stroke, and Jane felt him pulsing long and strong inside her.

She whimpered softly, tears stinging her eyes as her quim tightened and quivered around him. Her hips moved, sharply, desperately…for she only needed one more stroke…just one… more… She twitched, shifted—

"No!" he roared, and shoved her away.

Jane tumbled face first onto the floor, arms and legs akimbo and skidding painfully over the hard wood. Panting, gasping, she sobbed as she lay there, hot and throbbing and needy.

"By gad, you are a lusty bitch. I cannot wait until you are fully mine, darling Jane. Until I can have you in my bed, at my every beck and call." Darkdale's voice was rough and dark and satisfied as he pulled swiftly to his feet. "Now, you disobedient cunt—on your knees, and keep them wide, or I will whip you into a pile of skin and bones and then fuck you until you faint."

Jane's arms trembled as she pulled herself up onto her hands and knees. Her buttocks were red and sore, and at the same time, her quim throbbed, slick and so full that even with her knees apart she could feel the straining, pulsing need centered there.

She braced herself, waiting for another stripe of searing pain over her arse, trying to keep from sobbing audibly. But the pain didn't come.

Instead, Darkdale walked slowly around and stopped at the front of her, his shiny black shoes halting in front of her face. She dared not look up, dared not relax. It was all she could do to bring her rough, panting breaths soft and under control, and to keep her knees from giving away.

He stood there for a long moment, saying nothing. Then she felt the familiar stroke of the ball-tipped crop sliding slowly down her spine. Jane gasped, starting to pant again as her skin tingled and her body turned hot as the little knobs stroked her, down…down…down…

When those teasing pea-shaped balls slipped down into her moist arse crack, Jane tensed, biting her lip, struggling to keep herself still. But they were insistent, dancing around and prodding her in the arse, then in her dripping wet quim…

She began to sob as lust built painfully inside her, centered there at her turgid little sex and all around her sensitive, full lips. Her breathing became ragged and shallow and she tensed, tightening, waiting for the blow to come.

But it didn't.

All at once, those teasing black knobs lifted away. Then Darkdale's shoes turned and they walked away…out of the chamber.

Jane was alone. Full and needy and painfully hot and engorged.

IV

JANE DIDN'T KNOW HOW LONG SHE STAYED there on her hands and knees in the center of the chamber.

Time crawled or slid by—she wasn't certain. Shadows lengthened. Her knees and palms ached from being slammed against the unforgiving floor, and from pressing into it for hours.

It had to be hours.

She'd stopped sobbing. Her buttocks had stopped burning, though they still twinged occasionally. But her sex was still swollen and ready, painfully engorged and needy.

I should have begged. I should have asked.

No. Doing so would give him too much power over her.

But he has all the power already. What difference does it make now?

Your pride, Jane. Your own mind.

I don't care. I've had worse. All I want is to save Papa. And to end this torture!

Jane's mind bartered with itself, arguing and pleading in an exhausting whirlwind. Her knees were trembling, her shoulders ached, and she was tempted to allow herself to sink to the floor.

No one was around. She'd heard nothing, not one sound for hours. No one would see.

He wouldn't see.

And what if she eased her knees together, just a little. Just enough…

Or if she slipped one hand back there to touch herself? It would only take a moment. One quick jiggle, one well-placed stroke, and the torture would be over. Relief.

Jane was breathing hard again; all of her thoughts focused on the possibility of relief. She felt herself grow even more huge and ready, hot and throbbing, as if her sex was attempting to lure her fingers into the temptation. She could do it in a trice… He'd never know.

She eased forward slightly, heart pounding. A swath of hair fell from where it had been loosely bundled at the nape of her neck and dangled from her shoulder. If she was lucky, if someone was watching, it would obscure the fact that she was moving one hand from beneath her shoulder…and back.

Stealthily, slowly, as her body twinged in anticipation…

Jane touched herself, found her wet, swollen folds, and swallowed a sigh of relief and pleasure. Biting her lip, she closed her eyes and thought of Zaren.

The barest touch of a fingertip on her tight little nub sent waves of hot, sharp lust through her. Yes. Jane jiggled it, stroked, and then she exploded. Waves of pleasure rocked her, traveling through her body as she muffled a groan of triumph and relief.

Panting, half sagging in a heap onto the floor, she opened her eyes a moment later, still warm and flushed and shuddering.

There was a pair of shoes. Right in front of her.

Jane gasped and looked up. A shock of cold fear rushed over her when she saw Darkdale's expression.

"Apparently," he said in that low, exotic voice, "you like to be punished. You want to feel my wrath. Don't you, Jane darling?"

"No," she pleaded before she could stop herself. "Please… no!"

He lifted his dark-winged brows. "Are you begging for pleasure? Or are you speaking out of turn? Either way, my darling, you've already garnered a new—and delicious—punishment."

Jane's breath clogged and she closed her mouth, trembling and hot. *Please*, she wanted to say. What would he do to her now?

"There are so many ways I could punish you, my dear Jane. I could whip you until you beg for mercy. I could hang you from the ceiling and let you dangle for hours, naked and untouched. I could turn you over my knee and spank and spank until your arse was blazing hot, and your cunt red and dripping. And it would be, wouldn't it, Jane? You'd like that…perhaps a bit too much. But I think," he said, taking her roughly by the arm, "I have a more pleasurable way to punish you."

He yanked her to her feet, and her hair swirled about even as she staggered on weak knees. Her heart thudded and her mouth was dry, but she dared not speak.

Darkdale pulled her from the chamber and she walked as well as she could, stumbling and trembling as they made their way down an empty corridor to a set of French doors. He flung them open and dragged her inside, entering a large bedchamber.

A massive four-poster bed sat on one end, piled high with red velvet coverings and pillows. Its curtains were tied back at each ceiling-high post, thick rugs covered the floor, and a fire roared in the fireplace. Decorated tastefully and lit with the yellow glow of lamps, the chamber was amazingly warm and inviting.

Jane hardly noticed the other furnishings as Darkdale shoved her toward the massive bed. She fell into the side of the high mattress, then turned to face him in trepidation.

"You want pleasure, my darling? You cannot wait for me to grant permission? Very well, then, my dear…you shall have it. You may have as much pleasure as you like." Though his words threatened, his eyes burned with that familiar heat, avid and intense as they swept Jane's naked body. "Indeed. I look forward to hearing your cries and sighs and moans. Please…be as loud as you like."

Her palms were sweating and her belly roiled. What was the catch? What was the trick?

"Now come here, Jane, and kiss me. Seduce me."

She balked, but only for a moment. Better to obey than to risk the wrath of yet another punishment. Swallowing hard, forcing her trembling legs to move, she moved toward him.

Instead of grabbing her, taking her by the arms and pulling her up against him for a hot kiss, he stood passively. Despite the lecherous glitter in his dark eyes and the slight rise of his breathing, Darkdale remained still as Jane approached.

He didn't move when she came close enough to feel his warm breath and the heat emanating from his body. She lifted her face to find his lips, pressing her mouth against his.

A surprising flush of heat shuttled through Jane as she tasted him. But when he didn't respond, she stepped back and wondered if she'd done something wrong.

"That's all?" he said. "Perhaps I should have been more clear. Jane, you are to kiss me. You are to undress me and seduce me, and you are to make me want you. But…you may use only your mouth. No hands." He looked at a small hourglass on the table next to the bed, and his handsome lips curved. "To make it more interesting, and to increase your investment in the outcome, my darling Jane, you have until that glass empties to make me come. Twice." He smiled and flipped the hourglass over so that the grains of sand began to trickle down in a narrow stream. "If you succeed, you may share my bed tonight. If you do not…well, I have a gathering planned for tomorrow, and I suspect my companions would be more than delighted to help me punish you for your disobedience."

Jane's heart thudded, and she felt hot and a little dizzy at the thought of some unknown number of men punishing her. She drew in a deep, steadying breath and stepped toward him again. She was just about to reach for his head to pull him close for another kiss when she remembered: no hands.

Instead, she wet her lips with her tongue, feeling a stab of desire and satisfaction when she noticed his attention had fixed there. She moved her tongue slowly and sensuously over her lips, then eased up and into Darkdale.

Making certain her naked breasts brushed against his shirt and vest, she licked the seam of his lips, then tilted to brush her mouth against his. His lips parted slightly and she thrust her tongue inside, deep and strong, swiping and tangling with his. When he made a soft sound in the back of his throat, she knew she was doing something right. *He has a weakness*, she realized suddenly. *And it's me.*

"Undress me, Jane," he murmured, pulling away from her increasingly confident and passionate kisses. "My boots first."

She'd become warm because of the proximity of his body, and now as she knelt at his feet to obey, Jane felt a little colder. Her hair swung over her shoulders, falling in a lush pool on the floor on and around his booted feet.

How was she to take off his footwear without using her hands? Jane felt a rush of nerves and glanced up at the hourglass. The upper half was still full, and only a trace of sand had begun to pile in the bottom vessel. Still, the grains poured inexorably through the slender opening, and her time was limited. She had no doubt that, obsessed as he might be with her, Darkdale would mete out any punishment he deemed necessary.

Kneeling at his feet, Jane bent over and nudged away the hem of his trouser leg to see what sort of fastenings there were on his shoes. She felt a wave of relief to find a single large buckle near the top of the ankle-high boot; it would have been impossible for her to simply tug off one that didn't loosen.

As she nosed the edge of his pants out of the way, Jane felt her arse lift high and her breasts bump and jolt against the floor. Her hair was in the way, and she felt vulnerable and exposed as she used her teeth and lips to unbuckle one of the straps. When it was loose, she didn't know what to do, for of course she couldn't pull it off while he was standing…and Jane didn't know if it was permissible for her to speak.

Other than to beg.

So she looked up at him and then nudged against his leg in an attempt to make him sit down. Then, feeling like an insistent dog, she moved to the other boot and began to work on its buckle. The metal and leather felt odd in her mouth, hard and pliant, dusty and cold, and Jane couldn't help but wonder what Darkdale himself would taste like once he was unclothed.

To her mortification, she found she was almost looking forward to finding out, for the kisses she'd given him hadn't been altogether unpleasant.

When she finished with the second boot, she nudged him again, harder this time, and sat back on her haunches to look up.

"You magnificent, lovely bitch," he murmured, reaching out to caress one of her breasts. She arched into his palm like a ready cat, and he stroked her taut nipple with a nimble thumb. Jane shuddered with need, lust blasting through her as her body gathered up hot and moist and ready. Then, as if catching himself, Darkdale quickly removed his hand and stepped back. "You've managed to do nothing but unbuckle my boots and get yourself hot and ready, darling Jane. But my pleasure should be your only focus, and time is running out, my dear."

"If you would sit…Master," she whispered, looking up at him with parted lips and as much of a sensual expression as she could muster. "I will commence with your seduction."

His eyes flashed dark and hot, and she felt him give a little shudder. Darkdale was most definitely enamored with her—possibly even weak around her—and that could only work in Jane's favor. She licked her lips slowly once more as she positioned herself on her haunches, thrusting her breasts forward prominently.

He sank onto the bed, his cheeks flushed and his eyes fastened on her as she shifted herself in place to work off his boot. It was nearly impossible to pull it off using only her teeth and mouth—plus her jaw was sore, and the grains of sand in the hourglass were running out faster and faster…

Jane found herself fighting tears of frustration until she figured out to nudge his heel loose inside the boot by using her chin. After that, it was relatively easy to work it the rest of the way off his foot, employing her teeth and chin in turn to tug and shift it out of place. Her breasts swayed and bumped against each other, her sensitive nipples brushing the floor, his trousers, his leg…

By the time she divested him of both shoes, a much-too-large pile of sand had formed in the bottom of the hourglass, and Jane fought back a surge of real apprehension. A little frightened now, she set to pulling off his stockings, tugging with her sharp teeth as her cheek slid along his hairy, muscular calf. Tasting the essence of salt and man, she hurried to tug off the second stocking…and then, finally, she was able to get more serious about her goal.

When Jane looked up from her position at his bare feet, she found him watching her with a languid, haughty expression. That edge of obsession was gone from his eyes, and he seemed prepared to make her work for her reward.

But she really wanted to sleep in a bed tonight, not on the cold, hard floor. And she certainly didn't want to be involved in any "punishment" tomorrow night. So Jane made her eyelids droop just a little, and she bit her lip, sliding it between her teeth so it puffed out, full and wet, when it popped free. He looked down at her. When he reached to brush a thick lock of hair from her face, she saw hot, bold lust in his eyes. And something else. Need?

Galvanized, she edged between his legs, as she had done in the other chamber, and the memory of his throbbing, ready cock between her lips, sliding deep into her mouth—and elsewhere—had saliva pooling around her tongue. Taking her time, ignoring the incessant drain of sand down the hourglass's funnel, Jane used her teeth to unbutton the placket of his trousers.

She felt that magnificent cock shift and rise beneath the fabric as she brushed against him, and she took every opportunity to rub or press against it. His breathing changed and she felt the tiniest quiver beneath his skin, as if he too anticipated what would come next.

When she pulled the opening of his pants wide, then adjusted her position and went back up for his drawers, Darkdale stopped her with a firm hand on her head. "Undress me, Jane darling. I want to be skin to skin with you."

Biting back a curse of frustration, she hurried to do his bidding. Darkdale was accommodating, and rose to his feet as she worked the woolen fabric down over his hips and legs, using only her teeth. It was slow, tedious work, but she was determined. Once, she dragged her moist lips down the inside of his thigh and he tensed and shuddered beneath her touch. Emboldened, she nibbled the soft, hairless skin at the back of his knee, tasting warmth and salt, and feeling a brush of the dark hair that grew elsewhere on his legs.

When she rose to do the same on the other leg, Jane glanced up and saw that his jaw had gone slack and his eyes were half closed. *I can do this.* She glanced at the hourglass and saw that the bottom vessel was still more than half empty, but filling steadily. *He is ready for me.*

Now that he was divested of his trousers, she rose back up on her knees and tugged at the drawstring of his bulging underdrawers. When she pulled them away, Darkdale's cock sprang free, tall and long and eager. It looked delicious: thick and red and fairly quivering with readiness.

Jane couldn't subdue a quiver of anticipation, and she lunged forward to take him in her mouth. Her lips closed over the soft, velvet-skinned head that looked ready to burst. But no sooner had she tasted the droplet of saltiness gathering there, flickering her tongue over the tip, than Darkdale was once again forcing her face away from him.

"Jane, I will not tell you again. You are to undress me. Completely." His voice was taut and dark and his fingers dug into her scalp painfully, twisting a lock of hair for emphasis.

She swallowed a soft moan of disappointment and impatience and released the heat of his erection. With a tight half-smile, Darkdale eased back into a supine position on the bed as Jane began to work his underdrawers down over his hips, then muscular thighs and knees and to his feet. He did nothing to assist—obviously willing to prolong her efforts as much as possible—and she found herself kneeling on the floor in order to pull the cotton clothing completely free of his ankles and long, narrow feet.

Then, breathing from exertion and frustration, breasts swaying and hair tangling, Jane finally climbed up onto the bed next to him. He wore only a shirt and vest, along with a loosely tied neckcloth, and she set to working free the knot of his cravat—but not before she impudently straddled him at the waist, settling her moist center over his bare belly.

Pressing down into his abdomen, Jane felt her little pip quiver and swell, eager for pleasure. She slid up his torso with a sharp jerk, using her juices for lubricant over his warm skin as she bent to take the neckcloth in her teeth. Darkdale made a soft sound beneath her, and she felt his stomach muscles tighten as she shifted and moved on his belly under the guise of working his tie free.

In other circumstances, Jane might have been smug about his reactions, but she wasn't foolish enough to become complacent. The grains of sand kept falling, and she had not even brought him to one orgasm yet. She was acutely aware how easily her needs might come to fruition, but she had a difficult task ahead of her.

At last the tie slid free, and she set to work on his shirt. By now, her jaw had become sore from clenching her teeth and shifting about, and her movements were slower and clumsier.

Finally, his vest was open and his was shirt unbuttoned. All she had left to do was get his arms out…

"Master," she whispered, settling back on her haunches on his belly. "If you would sit up, I would remove your shirt. And then, with your permission, we could be skin to skin." Her voice dropped low and husky at these last words, and it was, shamefully, due more to her own anticipation than any acting on her part.

"Very well, darling Jane." He sat up and she scooted behind him to take the collar of his shirt in her mouth. His dark hair brushed her face as she tugged it free of his broad shoulders, and then pulled each sleeve down his arm.

By the time she was finished, and the shirt and vest were gathered in a pile on the bed, Jane was panting and frustrated. But it was finished. He was naked at last, and now she could attend to the more pleasurable aspects of her task.

A worried glance at the hourglass had her heart spiking with fear. More than half her time had elapsed!

Jane maneuvered herself back to the front of Darkdale, noticing for the first time the pelt of dark hair over his chest, and that his body was well-muscled and lean. He wasn't nearly as beautiful as Zaren—*oh, Zaren! Will I ever see you again?*—but she could not allow herself to think about her jungle-man lover right now. She couldn't be distracted.

Not yet. Not now. Later, she could dream about him, and pray he was safe and whole, and that one day they would be together again, but now she must concentrate and put her fear and sadness away.

Thus Jane wasted no time straddling Darkdale once again. His cock was full and ready, and she was so wet and throbbing that he slid easily inside her. She heard him muffle a groan and felt his body tense as she impaled herself. A shock of lust whipped through her and she couldn't control a gasp of her own. *Oh yes. Oh gad, yes!*

She'd diddled herself in order to find relief, but the sensation of being filled and stretched, the weight and heat of his cock quivering inside her, was so much better than anything she did on her own.

Darkdale seemed to agree, for his face had gone taut and his eyes burned up at her, dark and hot. "Are you going to fuck me, then, darling Jane?" His voice was as tight as his face, and laced with desperation.

For that one moment, Jane felt completely in control. She began to move, first slowly, rocking her hips, feeling his broad cock bump and shift inside her channel. But that wasn't enough—not nearly enough—and the next thing she knew, she was pumping up and down, bucking and riding him as if she were a madwoman.

She was a little mad, desperate, crazed, blinded with lust. Her legs shook as she rolled her hips, undulating them as she stroked him inside herself. She rose and fell over him, faster and faster. The sounds of flesh slapping against flesh and slick suction filled her ears, along with the soft pants and moans and sighs she couldn't control. The essences of musk and sweat and man filled her nostrils, and the sensation of his hot skin burned against her thighs. His body was hard and warm beneath her hands—yes, somehow her palms had found their way and become planted on his chest as she used them as leverage for her manic ride.

Jane reached her peak first—fast and easily—and cried out as it ratcheted through her, hot and hard. Exhausted, she slowed for a moment, shuddering and quaking, weak in the knees and elbows…and then she started up again, sliding and pumping and shifting and rolling.

Now she wasn't quite so blinded with lust, and she watched his face, watched for his reactions and responses so she could gauge how close she was to fulfilling her task. But as Jane rose and fell in a strong, true rhythm, Darkdale remained stoic and still. She glanced at the hourglass and her pulse ratcheted up. Not much time, not much time at all remained, and he hadn't even come once!

Hiding her apprehension, she sat back on her haunches, lifting her hands high so her breasts lifted and jounced as she made little figure-eight circles around and over his cock. Teasing its burgeoning head, she tightened herself around him, squeezing as she slowed her rhythm, then lifted her hands to play with her breasts, pinching and stroking her nipples, hefting and sifting the heavy globes in her palms, shifting and speeding and then slowing her rhythm. Pleasure spiked through her once more, as always shooting in hot, delicious licks to her core. But it was Darkdale on whom she must focus.

Come on…come on!

But still Darkdale remained still and cool, watching her from his position on his back, though his eyes were anything but frigid. More than a little nervous now, Jane moved faster and faster, and her own body tightened, growing wetter and throbbing with need. That familiar feeling of climbing the peak to orgasm gathered inside her once more, and she leaned forward so her breasts brushed his chest as she jerked her hips up and down over him.

"Oh!" she cried in surprise when another orgasm washed over her—strong and sharp, sending her collapsing onto Darkdale's torso as the pleasure trundled through her.

But still his cock remained hard and raging inside her.

Weak and growing more desperate by the moment, she dismounted from her position and took him in her mouth. His massive erection was full and turgid, slick with her musky juices, and it seemed to quiver in her hand. She slid him deep in her throat and felt a faint sizzle along his length, as if his seed was moving up and ready to explode.

Though her jaw was sore, she opened wide and thrust her mouth down over him, taking him deep and long, sucking and licking and stroking until she grew lightheaded and out of breath. His fingers gripped the bedclothes; she could see the white cast of his knuckles, and that was when Jane realized Darkdale was fighting his pleasure with every bit of his strength.

He didn't want her to win. He wanted her to lose.

He wanted to punish her.

NO. SHE HAD TO WIN.

Desperation spurred Jane, and she shifted around—still sucking and licking, spinning her tongue and herself over his cock—until she was positioned with her quim above his face. Her knees straddled him at the armpits, and now she dove low and long, jamming his cock so deep in her throat she gagged. Her breasts brushed his belly, and she lowered her hips over his face, bringing her wet, red, pulsing self just over his mouth.

Take that, she thought, concentrating on sucking every last bit of seed from his cock. She sucked and stroked and moved her hips, and she felt him gathering up at last—at last—and finally, he arched beneath her.

Darkdale grabbed her hips and pulled her down to his mouth, and his tongue thrust deep inside her slick, swollen cleft just as he slammed up into the back of her throat. The shot of hot, salty ejaculate gagged her, filling her mouth and then coating her tongue. But she hardly noticed as she swallowed the thick stuff, for his mouth and tongue were mauling her quim, sucking and licking her tiny pearl into submission.

Jane's cry of completion was muffled by the half-mast cock in her mouth, and she pulled away as the sharp, hard orgasm shocked her. It blasted through her body, more painful than pleasurable, and left her wrung out and weak.

After collapsing on the bed next to him, she lay there, panting and gasping, sated and yet desperate for more. Darkdale was unmoving, his own breathing rough and coarse, his hands still possessively over her hips.

And then she looked at the hourglass.

The top chamber was empty.

She had lost.

Jane scrambled to her hands and knees, lunging toward the table. She bumped against it purposely, hard enough to send the hourglass tumbling off and onto the floor…and it shattered when it struck the marble fireplace hearth.

The dark, deep roll of laughter had her turning to see Darkdale watching her. His eyes were black with victory and lust.

"You think you're so clever, don't you, darling Jane," he murmured as he slid his fingers around her arm. "Trying to hide the fact that your time was up." With a rough yank, he pulled her so she fell against him, facedown over his lap.

He pressed her head toward the bed as his fingers slid down around the cleft of her arse and found her dripping folds. "As it happened," he said, sliding his clever fingers around inside her, stroking and teasing, "you had already lost before even bringing me to my peak once. Which means"—he shoved two fingers deep inside her, and Jane couldn't control a heartfelt moan against the blanket—"you must be doubly punished."

"Please," she whispered as he fit a third digit inside her, pushing in and up as far as possible. He pressed against her sensitive, sore little clit, trapping it between his leg and his fingers. A sting of lust shot through her even as she licked her lips, willing it to dissipate…wanting peace. To rest and recover.

"Oh, yes, my darling Jane," he said, stroking her firmly, pumping long and slow with his three fingers. They slid along her pip, filled her opening, long and slow and sure. Tortuously slowly and unbelievably long. "Beg me, Jane…'tis music to my ears."

No, that wasn't what she meant. But Jane couldn't fight her body's desires. She sighed and shuddered deep in her core as he stroked and slipped and caressed. Her nipples were tight and hard, brushing against the rough bedclothes, and her face was half turned so she didn't smother in the blankets.

His thumb found the opening of her arse. Before she realized what was happening, he used her own juices to help it inside, filling her with the short, thick stub of his digit.

Jane gasped with surprise and her eyes flew open. The pressure on the back of her head eased, and she craned her neck to find Darkdale watching her. His lips were parted, his jaw tight and his nostrils pinched as if he fought to control his reaction.

"Come with me now, Jane," he whispered, pivoting his fingers inside her. Shoving them deep, he worked his hand rhythmically, rocking it back and forth inside her two openings…deeper and faster, shifting his wrist as she writhed and bucked beneath his hand.

The sensations felt odd—dark and intense—but Jane had no choice but to succumb to them. Her body was too well trained, too needy. Too lustful. And his hand was slick and fast—too cunning and deliberate. As she filled with heat and lust, Jane felt his cock swelling against her belly—hot and hard and damp. Her pleasure grew, soaring into something strange and unfamiliar, and just as she gathered up to explode, to reach that strange, dark peak, he gave a great shout and shoved her away.

Jane tumbled off the bed, landing on her hands and knees next to the broken hourglass. Before she could recover herself, Darkdale was there, standing in front of her. His cock raged in her face. He took her head with powerful fingers and shoved himself inside her mouth.

She gagged and gasped around his hot, salty length, grabbing on to his legs for support as he pumped deep in her mouth—once, twice—then he exploded with a strangled cry, surging deep into her throat, pulsing with long, strong undulations as his thighs trembled against her.

Jane sagged into him, weak and confused, her body still pulsing with pent-up desire and arousal. She felt her juices in and around her quim and arse, slick and thick. Her overripe clit pounded with frustration, and the rest of her felt too full, too thick and hot and needy. Darkdale released her then stepped away. She sobbed softly, leaning against the bed. She needed release. She needed—

"Keep those naughty little fingers away from your pussy," he ordered. His voice was cold and a little breathless. "I believe you've had enough pleasure for today."

Jane submerged a soft moan and closed her eyes, fighting to ignore the pounding between her legs.

"Now, you shall clean up your mess, darling Jane. Remember: no hands." Darkdale sounded almost gleeful as he knocked a piece of the hourglass toward her with his foot.

Taking care not to kneel on the pieces, Jane used her nose, chin, and cheeks to carefully scoot the shards of glass across the wooden floor and into a corner. The hourglass frame was a brass affair, and she was able to pick it up with her teeth and, scurrying on her hands and knees, bring it to rest upon the hearth. The sand, however, was a wholly different matter. At first she had no idea how to attend to the scatter of tiny grains until she realized she could gently blow them into a pile—or under the high-mounted bed.

As Jane set to work, Darkdale pulled on a dressing gown and sat in an armchair in front of the fireplace. She heard the soft clink of glass and the soft swirling sounds of brandy or whiskey being poured, followed by a quiet humming from the back of his throat. His contentment was obvious.

Jane felt his attention on her as she worked, but even more than that, she was uncomfortably aware of the need pounding at the apex of her thighs. Even as she exerted herself in this awkward, tedious task, Jane couldn't escape from the constant throb of lust simmering in her body. And every time she turned to present her arse to Darkdale, she knew what he saw: a swollen, slick quim—red and pulsing and ready.

Needy.

And every movement, every time she shifted or crawled or scooted, her legs rubbed together and put the slightest bit of pressure on her sex. There was pressure…oh, but it wasn't nearly enough.

The fleeting brush of sensation was nothing more than another constant tease—a reminder of how much she wanted and needed, and of how she was unable to get it. Her clit was hard and full, swollen and, she imagined, shiny as a ripe berry, ready to explode at the slightest touch. Jane's breasts swayed, brushing constantly against the cold, hard floor as she used her face and mouth to nudge the broken hourglass pieces into a pile. Her hard, sensitive nipples dragged lightly over the wooden slats, and the sensation only added to her discomfort.

She was carefully nosing aside a pile of tiny glass shards when he bolted to his feet behind her. The air stirred with his sudden movement, and before she could prepare herself, Darkdale grabbed her by the hips and buried himself deep inside her.

Jane cried out with shock and pleasure, and hot, prickling, relieved sensations trundled through her body. She shifted backward, hard and sharp, meeting his next thrust, desperate for release.

"Ah!" Darkdale cried as he came. His cock pulsed inside as he held Jane immobile, keeping her in position even as she twitched and wriggled and writhed against his rod. Then, "Be still!" he ordered.

"Please," she moaned, her cheek against the floor. "Oh, please…" The prickle of tiny glass shards biting into her face did nothing to detract from the angry pulsing between her legs, the painful, unsatisfied throbbing.

He pulled out and released her with an abrupt shove that nearly sent her sprawling on her belly. But Jane caught herself in time and struggled back onto her hands and knees. Tears fell from her eyes, and she trembled and panted as she attempted to gather her wits.

His bare feet appeared in front of her, but she dared not look up at him. "Finish your work, Jane darling. And then you may sit on my lap and I will feed you."

Blinking back tears and sniffling, she returned to her task. Some time during her exertions, Darkdale rang the bell for a servant, and shortly thereafter, Trevor came into the chamber with a platter of food. The smells were delicious, and Jane felt a very different sort of pang, this time in her belly, reminding her she hadn't eaten since leaving the ship this morning.

After she scooted every bit of sand and glass to a corner, Jane was nearly finished. She held a dustpan in her teeth and carefully prodded the pieces against the wall so they tipped into the pan.

Finally, exhausted, hungry, and still painfully aroused, Jane completed her task and approached Darkdale's chair on her hands and knees. He reached down to stroke her head, then murmured, "Onto my lap, then, my dear Jane."

She climbed up as bid, the silken dressing gown he'd donned slipping sensually against her bare skin. She brushed his muscular thighs and then eased against the opening of the robe, her palm against his dark-haired chest. Darkdale was warm and he seemed almost affectionate when he curved an arm around her waist. Jane settled into place, realizing how much warmer the area by the fireplace was, and leaned her head against his shoulder as he idly cupped one of her breasts.

"Here, my darling. You may drink this." With his free hand, he offered her a small glass filled with a sparkling pink liquid, and Jane took it gratefully. She sipped and felt the sherry's warmth flood her limbs and veins, even as Darkdale's smooth fingers stroked the sensitive underside of her breast.

When he offered her a piece of cheese, she lifted her hand to take it, but Darkdale tsked. "No, my love. I shall feed you."

She accepted the food when he slipped it between her lips, his fingers lingering there longer than necessary. Jane didn't think she'd ever tasted anything so delicious as that piece of cheese, and she eagerly opened her mouth when he presented her with another piece atop a small square of bread.

"My lovely little bird," he murmured, nuzzling her throat as she ate. "My delicious little pet." He continued to fondle her breast with one hand while feeding her with the other, and Jane slipped into a world of pleasure: delicious food combined with the soft allure of the sherry's intoxicant, plus gentle, skillful titillation.

Darkdale offered her grapes and dates, cheese, bread, slices of apple, and tiny little squares of fig cakes. He kissed her neck and throat, using his strong tongue to stroke her along the sensitive tendons beneath her earlobes, and his teeth to nibble at her skin. He'd teased her nipple into a rock-hard state, swirling his thumb over the tip of it as a constant reminder of her unsated lust.

The more her hunger for food was vanquished, the hotter and more aroused she became once again. When Darkdale eased his hand between her legs, sliding up along the inside of her trembling thighs, Jane couldn't hold back a surge of hope and desperation.

Please. She dared not speak the word aloud, but her entire body tensed and burned as every bit of her awareness shot to the swollen folds of her sex. His fingers moved wetly through her juices, the sounds of slick stroking arousing her just as much as the firm, teasing touch. Jane trembled in his arms, her body gathering tight and hard as the pleasure built. His cock rose beneath the dressing gown, bumping against her hip—hot and hard and ready. *Oh, yes…please…*

"Remember the rule," he murmured in her ear, then darted his tongue deeply inside, wet and strong. "The fifth rule, darling Jane."

She moaned aloud, biting her lip, unable to keep from twitching and shifting beneath his insistent fingers. Her own digits curled into the satiny collar of his dressing gown, and she buried her face in his shoulder, pressing his hard cock between her hip and his belly while fighting to keep herself from tipping into the hot volcano of pleasure.

"Please," she whispered, hardly able to form the word. "Oh, please…may I…please…?" She was panting and tight, dripping wet and swollen to burst. At any moment, she would explode—whether he gave her leave or not.

"Oh, my lovely Jane," he whispered against her ear. "You are so delicious. But I must yet withhold my permission."

She moaned in desperation as he fingered her quim with one hand while using the other to turn her face firmly toward him. As he covered her mouth with his, he thrust his fingers deep inside her pussy and began to stroke, long and slow.

She shuddered against him, accepting the thrusts and stroking of fingers and tongue alike, kissing him back and writhing against and on his hand even as she knew she courted danger. She must hold back, she had to keep herself from going over; she must think of something else, anything other than this insistent, titillating torture…

Her eyes were closed, and she could hardly breathe other than desperate little gasps. Her entire world was centered on his fingers, on the overripe little pearl he slipped by and around, teasing and stroking and sliding against. She fought it, fought what she needed with everything she had, gasping and panting and yet writhing and grinding against him. Tears slipped from her eyes as he kissed her, eating her tongue and lips, swiping his own tongue as deep and long as his fingers.

Just as she was about to lose the battle, he pulled his hand away. With a swift, shocking movement, he lifted her by the hips and slid her *slooooowly* down onto his ready cock.

Jane nearly screamed. Her eyes flew open as her body began to constrict around him, uncontrollable and ready. Pleasure traveled through her, mixed with fear and pain. He filled her, deep and thick and hard…so hard.

No, no, noooo…

"You may take your pleasure, my darling Jane," he said. His voice was a caress, but she hardly noticed, for at his words, she let herself go, ready to explode.

And then he thrust up, sharp and hard inside her.

Now she did scream, but it was a sound of triumph and release. The orgasm rocked through her, strong and hot and hard—painful in its intensity, yet delicious and long, like a glossy liquid river of pleasure.

She came, and she came, and she came. Her world was red and warm and wet, and she trembled and shuddered and moaned. Her toes curled, her belly dropped, and at last she heaved against him one last time, exhausted, sated, wrung out like a cotton rag.

He stroked her hair, his hand running down the entire length of her curling red tresses, and he pressed a kiss onto the top of her head. "You are magnificent," he said into her forehead. "Jane, you are beyond compare. I shall never let you go."

Somehow, his words and their meaning penetrated the hazy fog of exhaustion and pleasure. A shock of worry trundled through her, but she was too weary and weak to attend to it now.

Tomorrow.

For now…she was content.

ZAREN HAD NEVER BEEN on such a massive vessel before. A "ship," it was called, and it sailed through the ocean day after day after interminable day.

When he wasn't busy with his "studies," he paced the long expanse of ground—"deck"—day and night, hardly taking time to sleep or eat. With the ease of a monkey, he climbed the branchless trees called masts, up to the very tips, peering out over the horizon. There was nothing to see but water…forever and ever.

The world was so much larger than he'd ever realized. Would he ever see Jane again? How could he ever find her in such a world?

He knew he must have come to the jungle on a ship like this, but of course he couldn't remember it. He didn't know how old he'd been at the time, but he must have been very young. Five summers, perhaps, or even four?

It mattered not. Nothing mattered—how he came to the jungle, why, or from where. All that mattered was finding Jane.

His last glimpse of the woman he'd come to think of as his mate was of her standing on a ship like this. Her fire-gold hair billowed around her, blazing in the sun like an aura of flame.

I love you! I'll come back for you!

Her words had carried over the splash of waves, over the rhythm of his own limbs sliding smoothly through the ocean. Zaren swam as fast and as hard as he could, but as fast as he was, the ship had outmatched him. It sped off into the distance, as unreachable as a cloud moving across the sky.

"We should see land late today or early tomorrow, Zaren."

He turned from his pensive contemplation from the railing. A short, round, balding man stood there, the wisps of his gray and white hair fluttering in the breeze. The sunlight glinted off his round eyeglasses. Everett was his name—although it had taken Zaren some time to realize he was called "Everett" and not "Darling"—and he was Jane's father.

If it hadn't been for him, Zaren would still be in the jungle, still dressed in animal skins, devastated by Jane's unexpected and abrupt departure, and helpless to do anything to find her. Now, he wore clothing more like that donned by Everett and the men on the ship—sailors, they were called.

And because of Everett, Zaren was traveling to the far-off place called London where they—along with the warm, motherly (but very loud) woman named Effie—would find Jane.

They must find her.

"When will we see London?" Zaren asked, aware of how much more easily the words of his native language tripped off the tongue now.

Although he had spoken to Jane when they were together, they hadn't spent as much time in those sorts of activities as he had done for these last weeks while at sea. Everett called it his "studies," and insisted they spend several hours a day reading, writing, and conversing about life in England.

No...the short time he was with Jane—before she'd been taken by Cold Eyes and his people, and held captive—he wanted to touch and taste her. There was time for talk, but they often communicated with few words. He spent time showing her the world he knew, gliding through the jungle from vine to vine, and taking her to his favorite places. The beauty of his environment didn't need conversation. And the rapture in her eyes, and the way she touched him, told Zaren all he needed to know about her wonder.

But since he met Everett and Effie, Zaren had put more effort into relearning the language he had once known, at least at some level. And although he was by no means perfect, and many times still searched for the correct word, he now communicated well enough that the sailors had no idea he'd been raised by animals in the jungle.

"Two more days. Perhaps three." Everett tried unsuccessfully to plaster down his flyaway hair, but it wouldn't cooperate.

"And when we arrive in London, what do—shall—we do?"

"Well, there is the matter of Everett and the murder charge," said a strident voice behind them.

"Hush, Efremina," said Jane's father, glancing warily about as if to ensure none of the sailors heard her.

"It's in the newspaper, darling," she replied, patting his cheek fondly. "It's hardly a secret." She was a large, soft woman who stood more than a head taller than Everett, but that hadn't stopped the man from taking her onto his lap.

Zaren tried to block from his mind the first time he'd caught a glimpse of Effie and Everett—she'd been riding him on his chair, and they were mating, loudly and energetically—but he wasn't successful in pushing the memory away. And for some reason, the mental image made his cheeks feel warm even now, and his loins shift and stir.

Jane.

Why had she left? As he was splashing into the water toward her ship, trying to reach her, Jane had shouted, "They have my papa! I am going to save him!"

But that wasn't true. Everett—or Professor Clemons, as he was also called, because he knew a lot about butterflies (so did Zaren; he wondered if he was a professor too)—was Jane's father and he was still in the jungle. She had even left him behind. It was this realization that turned Zaren terribly cold and terrified about her fate. Someone had tricked her and then took her away, and he knew who it was.

The dark man standing next to her on the ship.

He'd seen the man before, and like a jungle cat trained to honor his instincts, Zaren immediately knew the man was bad and violent. He would hurt Jane.

Even Cold Eyes, who'd taken her for the use of his villagers, hadn't exuded the intensity of danger and desperation as the man on the ship.

"My name being blacklisted might be in the newspaper, but there's no need to draw attention to it, Effie," Everett grumbled. "If you don't take care, the captain'll slap me in chains and put me in the brig as a murderer."

"That's bloody ridiculous and you know it!" Effie said. "Captain Morrow knows you're no more a murderer than that gadfly there buzzing 'round the fish barrel. Once we get to London, you'll clear this up quick as a trice. How can a man stand trial if he ain't there to defend himself?" She glanced at Zaren, her brown eyes softening with concern as she patted his arm. "There, there, young man. We'll find our beloved girl. I always knew you would help us, even way back when the first time you brought Jane back to us."

"What nonsense are you talking about, Efremina?" Everett blinked behind his spectacles. "Brought who back when?"

"I warned her about snakes, I did," continued the woman, nodding sagely. "There are snakes, and then there are man-snakes. And that Mr. Jonathan was a man-snake. And so was that Mr. Darkdale!"

Zaren didn't fully understand what the woman was saying—and from the look on Everett's face, he didn't either—

but he knew the name Jonathan, and by now he knew who Darkdale was.

There had been a time when Zaren believed Jane wanted Jonathan to be her mate, and so he'd left her alone. But that separation was short-lived, for he'd been lurking outside Effie and Everett's nest—no, "treehouse" was the word—and heard them talking one day after Jane disappeared.

Someone must find 'er, and bring Miss Jane back. Get th' girl away from the snakes and bad 'uns in the jungle. Someone must bring the poor chit back to us, Everett. Someone must bring her home.

Zaren remembered the way Effie had spoken, looking out into the jungle, directly at the tree in which he was perched.

As if she knew he was there. As if she knew he would save Jane.

And that was why, after he'd sloshed back to shore many hours after Jane's ship had disappeared, when he came upon Everett and Effie in the jungle, he told them what happened—at least, the little he'd understood.

Effie believed him immediately, and it took little prodding for her to convince Jane's bewildered father of the same. "I allays knew he was a bad 'un," she said, her round face tight and serious. "I never trusted 'im."

It wasn't until they boarded the ship of Everett's old friend Captain Morrow—who'd come to drop off supplies and check whether the professor had finished his study of the elusive triple-spiked indigo butterfly—that Zaren learned the whole story.

Effie had been down by the beach when she saw a ship that didn't belong to Captain Morrow. She hid in the bushes when Darkdale appeared, and listened as he spoke with the men who came ashore in a small boat. She heard them talking about a murder, and how they were coming to take Everett back to London, and she ran off to warn him.

("Murder" was a word unfamiliar to Zaren, but Effie described it to him with great vigor and enthusiasm. Then she followed up the definition by acting out the fate that awaited Everett with the hangman's noose—an activity the professor didn't seem to appreciate.)

Everett and Effie hid deep in the jungle for two days. Jane had gone missing, and they weren't about to leave her abandoned in the jungle. The professor took the opportunity to search for the mating ground of the triple-spiked indigo and make copious notes, while Efremina stole back occasionally to see if the ship had left or if Jane had returned. Neither of them had any inkling that Jane was on board with Darkdale until Zaren found them and explained.

"Do you believe it will be simple to uncover your name?" asked Zaren, choosing his words carefully.

"Uncov—oh, you mean clear my name?" Everett replied. "Of course it will, my boy. I am innocent of the crime of which I'm accused, and I would easily have been able to produce an alibi and witnesses to support it if I had been present for the trial. They might think of me as a cloud-headed lepidopterist, but when I put my mind to a problem, I'm sharp as a tack."

"Of course you are." Effie patted him once again. "And it's Jane we must worry on. The poor mite's probably beside herself with worry over you, Everett."

The professor's round face tightened, and Zaren could see the reflection of his own worry in the man's eyes. "I'm afraid, Effie, that clearing me of a murder charge might be the easier task ahead of us."

For the first time, Effie's demeanor changed into one not very different from a female tiger whose cub was threatened. "That Darkdale man won' stand no chance once I get my hands on him."

Zaren gritted his teeth and looked out over the infinite ocean. Miss Efremina was going to be very disappointed if she thought she'd be the one to deal with Darkdale.

JANE WAS JOLTED AWAKE by a sudden pain in her hip. Her eyes flew open and she looked up to see Trevor looming over her. When she didn't move immediately, he kicked her again—this time, narrowly missing her breast in favor of planting the toe of his boot into her ribs.

"Get up," he said, and when Jane saw his foot rear back a third time, she rolled away and stumbled to her feet.

Her body ached, and she bumped against the wall of the corner where she'd been sent to sleep, which sent another rattle of discomfort through her limbs. Her tangled hair fell over her shoulders, obscuring some of her torso but leaving most of her body bare. She glanced over to see if Trevor seemed to notice.

However, his expression was one of irritation rather than lasciviousness. "The master is waiting for his breakfast. Move!" Before she could ask where to go or what to do, he smacked her sharply on the arse.

Jane squeaked and looked around for some idea of what she should do, but she was saved from having to ask when Trevor pointed down a corridor. "This way. Let's go!"

Breasts swaying and hair fluttering, she hurried in the direction he'd indicated. At the end of the hall, she entered a large, well-lit kitchen. Although it was empty of a cook or any other servants, Jane was relieved to find a tray prepared with a generous breakfast—presumably what she was to deliver to Darkdale. But she looked at Trevor to be certain.

"Take that to him! He's been waiting. You slept through your bell," said the manservant through gritted teeth.

Jane blinked. *Bell?* Maybe she had remembered hearing a soft tinkling noise, but she'd been sleeping so heavily she dismissed it as the remnant of a dream. Unsure whether her ban on speaking extended to Trevor, she opted to remain silent and instead picked up the tray.

She nearly got lost navigating back to the main octagonal room (where she'd slept) and then on to Darkdale's bedchamber. And just as she approached the door—which was cracked open—Jane suddenly remembered and dropped to her knees.

Heart pounding from her near-oversight, she entered the room by scooting on her knees with the tray held upright. The smells of cooked eggs and fried ham made her stomach growl, and the pot of tea sloshed a big drop of hot liquid on one of her hands, but she managed to make her way to the bed without any mishap.

Darkdale was sitting up, propped against a collection of pillows. His muscular chest and sleek arms were bare, and Jane couldn't help but notice that a trail of dark hair led down his belly and beneath the blankets…where a pole seemed to rise from between his legs. Her mouth went dry at the memory of just what that "pole" portended, and, despite its exhaustion, her body twinged in anticipation.

She offered the tray wordlessly, sliding it carefully onto the bed next to him, and sat back on her haunches to wait for further instruction. And possibly a piece of ham.

"Good morning, my delectable Jane." He picked up a piece of toasted bread and spooned a generous amount of strawberry jam onto it. "I trust you slept well?"

She looked down to hide the flash of fury that surely blazed in her eyes. *Bastard.* The only reason she'd slept well was she'd been exhausted. The pallet in the corner to which she'd been banned was thin, and the single blanket she'd been provided hardly covered her.

"You may answer me, Jane," he chided. "When I ask you a direct question, you may answer me."

"I slept well enough."

"I slept well enough, *Master*. Surely you haven't forgotten yesterday's lessons already?"

"No, Master. Not at all, Master." Jane had to struggle to make her voice sound plausibly sincere.

"Very good, darling Jane. Now, if you would like a bit to eat, come closer and I will feed you."

As much as she despised the thought of being fed like a dog, Jane wasn't foolish enough to dismiss an opportunity for sustenance. She must keep up her strength for whatever he might have in mind for her today…and tonight. For she hadn't forgotten his threat to have his guests assist with her punishment.

She subdued a shiver and ate everything he offered her, finishing up when he allowed her to actually use her hands and drink from a cup of tea.

When the tray was cleared of food, Darkdale set it aside and looked at her. "As much as I would like to partake of your deliciousness this morning, my darling, you are in need of a bit of washing up before our guests arrive, while I…well, I have some business to attend to."

Jane's attention perked up and she opened her mouth to speak, then caught herself and snapped it closed. Her intent clearly showed on her face, for Darkdale smiled and petted her affectionately. It was all she could do to keep from ducking away from his condescending touch. "You are wanting to ask me a question, aren't you, my dear? Perhaps whether my business is related to that of your father's conviction?"

She nodded, her eyes wide and pleading.

"Unfortunately, today's business does not take me to the courts or to the offices of the barristers or judges. However, I am confident if you continue to please me as you have done—and be proper and obedient—I will soon have cause to make a call on them."

Jane wasn't able to keep her disappointment and frustration from her expression, but to her relief, Darkdale made no comment. Instead, he flung the sheets and bed coverings aside to reveal his bare legs, uncovered torso, and magnificent erection.

Her mouth began to water at the sight of his purple-red cock, its head smooth and proud and ripe. She felt her heart pounding so hard her breasts thudded too, and that telltale moisture began to gather between her legs.

Darkdale didn't say a word. He merely perched on the edge of the bed, spread his legs, and leaned back on his elbows.

Jane took that as the invitation it clearly was, and scooted into position between his knees. She scooped him up in her hands, gathering his heavy, tight bollocks into her palms and gently fondling them as she scraped her fingernails over the hair growing there. He sighed and shivered, and once again Jane was reminded that she did indeed have at least a modicum of power and influence on the man.

She just had to learn how to wield it to her advantage.

One way to begin was to take his cock in her mouth and slide down, all the way down, until he bumped the back of her throat. His velvety length was heavy and hot, and its girth stretched her mouth and jaw as she worked up and down, slowly and deliberately.

Her saliva coated him, allowing her to move faster and with the same slickness he enjoyed from her quim, which was becoming hot and wet all on its own. The wetness from her mouth dripped and pooled at the base of his rod, where she fondled his stones. Jane curled her fingers tightly around the bottom of his cock, stacking her fists on top of each other beneath her lips, and used all three to stroke, faster and faster. She sucked and pumped, her hands tight and slick, her mouth sliding along in rhythm with them until he gave a sharp groan. Darkdale arched up abruptly as he shot a hot wad into her mouth.

When she was certain he'd finished, she licked him clean and sat back on her haunches. Her lips were puffy and throbbing, and her nipples were tight and thrusting with readiness. Her own juices dampened her inner thighs, and her sex pulsed softly…waiting.

Darkdale rose from the bed, patted her head, and reached to ring a bell. Despite her best intentions, Jane couldn't keep her attention from following him. She wanted him to touch her, to penetrate her, to taste and lick and suck her into the same frenzy she'd just done to him.

But she was bound to be disappointed.

The bedchamber door opened and Trevor entered. Behind him was an elegant blond woman. She appeared to be in her late forties, and her hairstyle matched her stylish and expensive clothing. She looked like a wealthy woman of the gentry making a social call—a woman who'd just dismounted from her mare, if one were to judge by the riding crop in her hand.

"Good morning, Kellan."

"And good morning to you. You're prompt as always, Marcine."

"Naturally. And you must be Jane," said the woman, reaching to take her by the chin. Her grip was hard and cruel, and even though she wore gloves, her nails dug into Jane's skin. "You are a lovely one, I'll grant that. She appears an excellent choice, Kellan," she added, sounding dubious as she released Jane's chin.

"There is work to be done, to be sure." Darkdale stood passively as Trevor buttoned up the shirt he'd just donned. "I trust you'll do your part."

"It will be my pleasure." She transferred her attention back to Jane. "Come with me."

She made move to rise, but Marcine reacted immediately, and the riding crop snaked out. Its slender tail whipped sharply into the side of Jane's hip, and she reared back in shock and pain.

"Have you not taught her even the barest of humility, Kellan?" she exclaimed, then struck out again with the crop. This time it striped down her arm, and Jane couldn't mask a whimper of pain. "Who gave you leave to rise?"

Jane bowed her head, fighting tears and the sharp stinging on her skin.

"She is a clever one, and more than a bit stubborn," Darkdale commented as Trevor tied his neckcloth. "My darling Jane has already been punished several times since our arrival—which, I might remind you, Marcine, was only yesterday."

The woman made an exasperated sound. "Well, the more clever and stubborn ones usually turn out to be the most worthwhile. Still, I have no patience for impudence, girl. You had best mind your manners when you're with me. The last thing I wish to do is mar that beautiful skin of yours—but make no mistake. I have forms of punishment that will leave no marks. Now come with me. I expect utter obedience and obeisance." With an angry huff, Marcine swished out of the bedchamber, leaving Jane to keep up with her fast pace.

She glanced at Darkdale as she left the chamber, but he seemed to be paying no attention to her…and for some reason, that made her even more apprehensive.

Jane scurried down the corridor in Marcine's wake, trying to ignore the discomfort of her knees traveling over a variety of bumps and sharp edges. The woman led her toward the back of what turned out to be a house that was much deeper than it was wide.

"In here." Marcine flung open a set of double doors.

Inside were two women wearing simple gray frocks that could only be described as uniforms. Judging by their gray hair and facial lines, they appeared older than Marcine by at least a decade. Each had hair that was scraped back into a tight bun high at the back of the head, and they stood as if at attention, waiting for a command.

The room was furnished in a manner Jane had never seen before. There was a large square tub made of tile situated in the center of the chamber—large enough to hold three or four people. It was filled with water so hot steam rose from it. Piles of fluffy white towels sat near one edge, and at the other was an array of small pots, jars, brushes, tubes, and other items she couldn't identify. Some pleasing, musky scent wafted from the pool and filled the room.

Elsewhere in the chamber were trunks and wardrobes, mirrors lining one wall, and a large platform-like bed draped with blankets, cushions, and furs. One wall was lined with cupboards, drawers, and shelves.

"You may stand now," Marcine told Jane, then took a seat in a large, plush chair that looked more like a throne than a mere resting place. She gestured languidly as she picked up a notebook and pencil and began to peruse the open page. "It makes it easier for Belinda and Bernice to attend to you. And, I would say, they most certainly have their task cut out for them. Wouldn't you, ladies?"

The women—possibly twins—made assenting sounds as Jane pulled to her feet more slowly than she would have liked. She was sore. She wondered if the tub was for her, and recalled Darkdale's words that she needed to be bathed. A bath would be welcome, as long as it didn't entail the sort of ministrations she had been subjected to while being cared for by the women of Cold Eyes's village.

She shuddered at the memory just as Belinda and Bernice approached. Uncertain what was expected of her, Jane waited passively. No one would be shy about telling her if she was wrong.

The twins walked around her as if she were a prize mare—or a statue—and examined her from head to toe. They lifted her hair and tsked over the slender red welts from Marcine's riding crop, and the less noticeable ones from Darkdale. They pored over her hands and toes then poked and pinched her in more than a few places.

"I've half a mind to cut it all off," said Marcine when she noticed the two women using their fingers to comb randomly through Jane's tangled curls as if to sort it out. "But I suppose Kellan would be annoyed. So I'm afraid you'll have to work through it. I'll be certain to charge him extra."

"Into the bath with you, then," said one of the maids. "And don't slip on the tiles. 'E wants to be the one to put any bruises on you 'imself."

Despite those foreboding words, Jane eagerly climbed into the tub. Even though she hissed at the bold heat, she sank in as quickly as possible. The aroma was that of lavender and sandalwood, and it was soothing and relaxing. For the first time since arriving at Darkdale's home, she felt blissful as her muscles loosened and she warmed up pleasurably.

However, her contentment lasted only a short time, for no sooner had she submerged up to her shoulders than the two women were "attending" to her.

One began to work on her hair, shoving Jane's head unceremoniously beneath the water and holding it there longer than she would have chosen. Then the maid scrubbed and soaped, rinsed, then scrubbed and soaped again. After that, a thick, sweet-smelling paste was massaged into her hair from scalp to ends, and Jane's head was wrapped in a cloth with all her hair tucked up into it.

Meanwhile, the other woman bustled around, laying out items on one of the tables, showing options to Marcine, who either approved or declined as she sat in her throne chair and sipped tea—which had been brought to her by an unusually subservient Trevor.

Once she was thoroughly washed and her hair was rinsed of the paste, Jane was brought from the tub and settled on a far less comfortable chair than Marcine's. Still, it was better than being on her knees, and she knew better than to complain—even mentally.

Here, her hair was combed out (none too gently), her toenails and fingernails clipped and lotioned, her skin buffed and moisturized. During this process, Marcine deigned to rise from her seat and walked over to check on the progress.

"She cleans up well, I'll grant him that." She pursed her lips as she circled Jane, then finished by standing in front of her and pointing directly at the bush of hair between her legs. "That must be attended to. And beneath her arms, and her legs as well. And then you'll have just enough time to do the bejeweling, for Kellan bade me to have her prepared by six o'clock."

Jane's eyes widened at her words, but she had no time to speak or otherwise respond. Bernice and Belinda ushered her from the chair and directed her to a narrow, backless sofa. She was directed to lie on her back, and while Bernice arranged her newly combed hair so it wouldn't tangle, the other twin pulled her legs apart.

Jane tensed, prepared to be manipulated, teased, and mastered as she had been in the past, but Belinda's touch was utterly impersonal—even detached—as she began to do… *something* down there.

At first, all Jane felt was a little bit of tugging and prickling. When she was finally able to lift her head, she saw that the woman was snipping off the bright red hair that grew at the apex of her thighs. Quickly and with cold efficiency, Belinda cropped the tight, coarse curls until they were short and neat.

Meanwhile, Bernice roughly lifted Jane's arm and applied some sort of thick, sticky paste over the hair growing there. Then she placed a strip of cloth over the paste and ripped it away. Jane gasped in shock and surprise, but before she had a chance to react (really, what could she do anyway?), Bernice moved to the other side and did the same there while Belinda conducted the same process on Jane's legs. This was more painful, and by the time the twin was working on the second leg, Jane was blinking back tears of pain. The last two strips of cloth were the worst, for they were aligned over paste that had been painted onto the outside of her labia. Thankfully, Belinda and Bernice each pulled one strip at nearly the same time, which left Jane nearly sobbing with shock and pain, and completely denuded of hair except for a narrow strip down the center.

She wasn't certain whether she preferred this form of torture, or the one she'd succumbed to at the hands—and mouths—of the women in the jungle.

"Much better," mused Marcine when the two maids finished their task. "Now, I suggest you take some time to rest whilst your hair dries and your skin settles. You shall need all of your strength for tonight, and in the meanwhile, we have other preparations to make."

She gestured to the large bed and Jane gratefully went over to it, surprised that she should be afforded such a luxury. Without a backward glance, Marcine left the chamber, taking her two maids with her. At the door, she paused. "Lest you should entertain any thought of leaving, I shall lock the door. So do yourself a favor and rest when you can."

The door closed behind them and Jane heard the ominous sound of a heavy bolt being thrown. As she lay on the soft bed, she looked around the chamber, wondering if this was some sort of test or trick. But after a while, her eyes drooped and she did ease into sleep.

It was a light, restless sleep, for at some level she feared being tricked or otherwise disturbed awake…yet it was a repose filled with images and thoughts she'd tried to protect: worry, fear, and love for Zaren and her papa.

But Zaren would not be banished this time, and his amazing blue eyes cast upon her, filled with love and warmth. Though he desired her, his gaze was not at all filled with the bald lust and cold lasciviousness of Darkdale's. In her dreams, Jane reached for Zaren, begged him to save her, wondered if he still loved her after all she'd given up and all that had happened to her…but he was always just out of reach.

She cried in her sleep and in her dreams and despaired of ever seeing him or her papa again.

∾

Jane startled fully awake when the door's bolt was thrown open. Marcine and her companions paraded in as Jane noticed that the light outside had dimmed. It was past afternoon and into the evening, and she was surprised she had slept at all.

"Now," said Marcine briskly, "let us see what we can do to make you even more lovely."

They prodded Jane to her feet and gave her a spoonful of mint leaves with which to chew and clean her teeth. As Belinda began to do something to her long tresses, Bernice came to stand next to them. She was holding a silver tray with a variety of jewels, tiny pots, and brushes arranged on it.

As Jane stood silently, Marcine used a brush to dab some sort of clear liquid onto one breast, making several dots around the edge of her areola. Then, using tiny forceps, she picked up jewel after jewel and affixed tiny, lentil-sized gems to the dots she'd made.

When she was finished, there were six tiny emeralds winking in a circle around Jane's left areola, which had shriveled and tightened beneath the woman's ministrations. Marcine moved on to do the same to the other breast, taking her implements and supplies from Bernice's tray. Jane's nipples thrust strong and hard from inside the glittering circles, and when she finished her task, Marcine used the tip of a different brush to stroke over one of them.

Jane jolted and shivered at the unexpected sensation, and her nipple tightened even more. With a faint sound of satisfaction, Marcine flickered the brush over the other nipple, lighter and in a more prolonged fashion. She glanced up at Jane, amusement lighting her cold blue eyes, stroked slowly and carefully around the nipple, and then flicked the soft sable brush hairs across the sensitive tip, over and over, back and forth, ever so lightly until Jane had to bite her lip to keep from moaning.

"It's clear why he chose you," Marcine commented, resting the brush back on the tray. "You're not only lovely to look at, but you have a responsiveness most men would kill for—in themselves as well as their women." She tilted her head to one side, a little smile curving the corners of her mouth.

As she looked at Jane, holding her gaze, she reached forward and slid her hand down along the gentle swell of Jane's belly. Her fingers brushed lightly over her soft, perfumed skin, trickled through the patch of short, trimmed hair and over the sensitive bare skin of her mound, and then moved down to cup her quim. Jane tensed even as the familiar rush of pleasure surged to her sex, and she couldn't control a little quiver.

Marcine's hand remained there, warm and steady and still, with just the slightest bit of pressure upon the lush folds there.

She watched Jane, her gaze critical and cool, as she held her there—literally in the palm of her hand.

Jane's heart began to thump harder, and she couldn't control the reaction of her body to that soft, steady, confident pressure. Her breath grew rough, and all of her concentration, all of her awareness, focused on Marcine's hand. She was aware of herself swelling and tightening against the woman's palm and fingers, of growing damp and hot, and of the deep-seated burn of lust building and building until she needed to move and writhe and shift…

When Marcine at last adjusted her hand, sliding it softly and slowly down and over the full, wet folds, her fingers were slick and wet. Jane shivered, shuddering with restrained need. Then one digit moved, sliding just the barest tip inside her, and found the underside of her tiny, ripe pearl. Then, leaning a little closer, her expression passive, Marcine pressed hard, up into her as the pad of her finger twitched once against Jane's burgeoning clit.

A single stroke. And all at once Jane's body let go, and she came, a flood of heat and pleasure washing over her as she stood there, cupped by Marcine, helpless to deny the convulsions of her body, hot and weak and wet.

"My goodness," breathed the other woman, whose eyes had never left Jane's face. "You are a delight." She removed her hand and Bernice offered her a cloth to wipe her fingers. "It's no wonder Kellan wanted you—and for so long." She paused, looking at Jane with consideration. Then she smiled, still cool and amused, but now with a layer of heat in her eyes. "I look forward to further exploration."

She turned back to the tray and selected another brush, then gestured for Jane to step up onto a stool Belinda had brought over. Still a little trembly in the knees, Jane nevertheless climbed onto the stool. This position put her hips and belly at Marcine's eye level, and for a moment, Jane felt weak. The woman's mouth was right…*there*.

She looked down and saw Marcine watching her, a knowing light in her eyes. But apparently the blonde had other plans, for she nudged Jane's thighs apart a little and began to paint another set of small adhesive dots on the bare skin of her nether lips. More jewels followed there, and then Marcine directed Jane to bend over.

She walked around behind her as Jane obediently put her hands on her knees. Jane tried to keep her mind away from the image she must present to Marcine: her full, wet, red pussy, on display and eager for more pleasure. It was all she could do to keep her self from growing full and wet again at the thought of what the other woman might do.

When Marcine touched her, Jane flinched…but it was only the damned brush again. This time, Marcine made feather-light dots on the backside of her quim, and affixed the tiniest of diamonds and rubies there, around the edge of her opening.

"There. Quite delectable, you are. Kellan will be pleased. Belinda, you must finish her hair and eyes, then it will be time to deliver our lovely Jane to her master."

As Jane was helped down from the stool—it would do no good for their handiwork to be ruined if she fell or moved awkwardly—Marcine eyed her once more. "'Tis a pity I won't be there to enjoy the entertainment tonight. I'll have to speak with Kellan about changing that in the future. Oh, and Bernice—the gloves and stockings, please."

Jane was positioned in front of a long mirror as the final touches were attended to: her hair braided in one long, loose braid that hung over her shoulder or down her spine, black liner drawn thinly around her eyes, then their lids painted green and blue in a design not unlike butterfly wings. Marcine added two more diamond crystals, one at the corner of each eye, and then a single, fingernail-sized one just below Jane's left collarbone. She brushed soft pink color onto her lips, and then turned to Bernice to take a bundle of cloth.

Black lace stockings and matching black gloves were the only articles of clothing Jane was allowed, and then her entire ensemble was covered by a flowing, silken black cloak.

"The finishing touch…" Marcine moved to stand behind Jane.

The next thing she knew, something dark and black went over her eyes and was tied tightly in the back. Just as Marcine finished, somewhere in the house a clock struck six.

"Perfect. You are just ready. Come now, girl…let us go to meet your master."

And Jane, blindfolded, enveloped in a sensuously silken cloak, was led from the chamber.

VIII

A S JANE WALKED ALONG, the innermost parts of her upper thighs rubbed against her sex. Because of the addition of the jewels there, Jane felt even more pressure than usual on her sensitive clit and swollen quim.

Every step was a little tease of potential pleasure, and with the silken cloak sliding over her tight nipples at the same time, she felt as if her body was slowly coming alive and aware.

She couldn't help a sense of trepidation as she was prodded along to meet Darkdale, for how well she remembered his threat of last evening: that she was to be punished tonight… with the help of his guests.

What sort of punishment could he have in mind? One of unbearable pleasure, or a tortuous one of frustration and humiliation? Or some combination of both?

After being directed for what seemed like an interminably long walk, Jane was pulled to a halt. Still blindfolded, she could see nothing—not even a crack of light from beneath her black sheath. There was silence for a long moment, and she wondered briefly if she had been left alone.

Then suddenly there was a soft clapping sound. "Brava, Marcine." She recognized Trevor's voice. "He will be well pleased."

"Naturally," was the woman's throaty reply. "Has he returned?"

Before Trevor could respond, there was the sound of a door opening, and a gentle waft of outside air followed. Now Jane recognized where she was: back in the octagonal room where she'd been left on her hands and knees for hours yesterday. The room one could see just beyond the main entrance of the house, where Darkdale sat in his chair and she sucked him dry.

"I see you've finished your task." Darkdale's voice was accompanied by brisk footsteps that drew near then stopped. Along with him came the scent of London—dampness and coal smoke—mixed with his own male essence.

Jane stood silently, feeling his presence as he circled around her. The edges of her cloak were pulled up and away, presumably by one twin on each side, as he examined her.

"You are well worth the extravagant expense, Marcine," he said. "She is even more lovely than before, and yet has adopted an appropriate air of mystery as well as passion."

Marcine gave a husky chuckle. "A feat that is captured in the amount of my bill, Kellan."

Darkdale laughed in return—a satisfied sound—and Jane felt him brush against her as the edges of the cloak fell back into place. As the silken covering settled over her once more, she sensed that the woman had led Darkdale a short distance away.

Marcine murmured something low and provocative, then he gave another laugh, this time of surprise. "What a splendid idea. Indeed, I shall arrange that with all haste. That will be a night I shan't forget."

"Very well, then, Kellan. If you have no further need for my...*services*"—this was said with that low timbre of invitation—"then I shall take my leave."

Jane heard Marcine and her two maids walk across the chamber, then the sound of Trevor bidding them farewell from the front door. She stood unmoving, trembling slightly as she waited to see what Darkdale intended to do with her.

"I must wash up and dress for tonight," he said. "Trevor, see that Jane is prepared to greet our guests."

Jane was shocked at the twinge of disappointment she felt at the announcement that Darkdale didn't intend to…well, to do anything to her at this time. Perhaps she'd expected him to want to enjoy Marcine's work.

But she had no chance to dwell on these shameful emotions, for Trevor approached her. She could tell it was him by the sound of his footsteps and the way he moved. Jane couldn't help but tense in expectation, but unlike every other man—or so it seemed—who'd been near her, Trevor didn't touch her in any intimate way.

Instead, he took her wrists and slipped them through armholes in the cloak. Then he brought them together in front of her, wrapping them with some sort of soft, velvety material in a figure-eight pattern, then bound them together at her belly. He released her, and Jane stood, still blindfolded and now bound, growing slightly more apprehensive due to his silence.

Moments later, she heard a soft noise above her, and then her arms began to rise of their own volition—pulled up by the bindings on her wrists. Her hands rose above her head until her arms were taut and she was standing on her tiptoes, and then, mercifully, the ascension ceased.

Jane licked her lips, her belly fluttering nervously and her heart pounding, waiting to see what would happen next.

But nothing did. Silence reigned. She wasn't even certain whether Trevor—who seemed to move soundlessly—was still in the chamber.

There she stood—very nearly hanging by her wrists. It was only the tips of her toes that touched the ground and kept her from spinning slowly in a circle. She was stretched, long and lean, still in darkness, with the silken cloak molded to her curves. She could tell it was open only slightly in the front, due to the brush of air on her belly and throat, but where it touched her body it felt heavy and cloying.

She waited, and waited—just as she had last night, in this very same chamber, on her hands and knees—wondering when or if someone would come, and when they did, what they would do to her.

At last Jane heard the distant sound of a door closing, and the soft pad of footsteps she recognized as Darkdale's. As they came closer, her heart leapt—and at the same time, she felt a shaft of lustful hope dart down to her sex…and then she immediately was ashamed, and attempted to banish that dark desire. *Zaren.* She should think of Zaren. He was the man she loved, the man who should cause her heart to skip a beat and her body to become warm and ready…

But when Darkdale drew near and she smelled his familiar male scent—a combination of the pomade he used on his hair, the herbal water he splashed on his face when bathing, and whatever essence clung to his clothing—Jane's breathing quickened.

Her skin prickled, and she felt herself warm and dampen… everywhere. She bit her lip, trying to ignore the feelings as he came closer, brushing against her cloak, sliding it over her sensitive skin…

"What a lovely sight," he murmured, and covered her lips with his.

His tongue thrust deep into her mouth, and heat and lust surged through Jane as he kissed her, long and sleek and hard. As she dangled there, stretched and long and helpless, as he devoured her, mauling her mouth with his tongue, sweeping inside it with strong, firm strokes, her body yearned to press against his… She needed his mouth and hands on her, his cock inside her. Jane gave a soft, desperate moan as he pulled away, arching and lunging awkwardly toward him.

Her lips throbbed and her breathing rasped as she waited, helpless, blind, and ready. Would he take her now? Would he touch her and tease her into a frenzy of need?

Half of her wanted it—wanted to beg him for his touch, wanted him to slide his fingers up inside her, to stroke her and then fill her with himself—and the other part of her despaired of her lusts, of her desires, and wanted to be left alone. Untouched.

She wanted to wait for Zaren. Tears stung her covered eyes and she was overwhelmed by grief and fear. Would she ever see him again?

Would she ever find pleasure from a man who wanted nothing from her but to give it to her?

And to love her?

Then Jane heard that sound again, and all at once, the tension on her wrists eased ever so slightly. She was able to lower her straining calves so her feet were on the ground, and her arms loosened so her elbows had only the slightest bend… and the noise stopped.

She felt Darkdale behind her, and she began to quiver with heat and nervousness…and hot expectation. His hands were on her hips, sliding over the silky cloak, causing erotic prickles to rise over her skin. His mouth burned against her bare neck, and his hands pulled her legs wider.

Jane moaned in expectation and hope, and when he lifted the cloak and she felt the brush of his cotton shirt against her lower back, she began to pant in anticipation. Her clit pulsed and her nipples tightened, and she shook, trembling, arching back into him as much as her bindings would allow. His fingers curled around the soft, sensitive skin of her thighs, and then he thrust up and inside her.

She cried out in delight and pleasure, immediately tightening herself around his cock as he withdrew and then slammed up inside her again. Heat and pleasure traveled through her, and it was only by sheer force of will—and more than a little fear—that she didn't explode

"Oh," she cried, biting her lip as he plunged in and out, faster and harder. "Please…oh, please…*Master*," she remembered to add in a sort of gasp. Her fingers curled desperately into each other as her weight jolted against her bonds as he fucked her and fucked her and fucked her.

"Ahh…" he grunted with one last savage pump, deep and high and sharp. He pulsed inside her, his hands tight at her hips, his weight heavy against her.

Jane couldn't stop herself: she quivered, and the lust overtook her. She came, her ecstatic shuddering mingled with pleasure and trepidation, her skin damp with heat, at the same time turning cold with fear.

"Jane," he said in her ear. His voice was cold and accusing. "Did you just break the fifth rule? So soon?"

"Nooo," she moaned, half sobbing with relief and terror. His hands cupped her breasts from behind, and she strained into them as he rubbed the silken cloak over her taut, sensitive nipples. "Oh, please, no…please…Master…"

"You are very disobedient, Jane," he said, tweaking one of her nipples sharply.

She gasped and jolted from the pain—which was laced with pleasure—but he tweaked the other nipple, and then the first one, and then each of them in turn, in rapid succession until she was sobbing harder, twisting and writhing in vain to escape the unique combination of pleasure and pain.

To make matters worse, that awful noise from above sounded again, and as Darkdale continued his torture, Jane's wrists began to rise once more. Soon, she dangled again by her arms, her toes barely touching the ground. She was completely helpless and unable to do anything but twitch slightly, her toes skittering lightly over the floor.

At last, Darkdale ceased his tweaking and twisting and stepped away from her. Her nipples pounded and pulsed, nut hard and flaming with heat. Surely they must be bright red and shiny from the abuse visited upon them. Jane hung there, feeling every throb as it ricocheted through her body. Sagging, her weight hanging from her sore arms, she sobbed softly, panting and trembling.

When the edges of her cloak were drawn away, exposing her tortured breasts to the air, she stiffened and stilled. Her sobs ebbed into soft little gasps, and suddenly a warm, wet mouth covered one of her angry, throbbing nipples.

Jane couldn't hold back a moan, and then she jolted, giving a soft scream when he sucked hard, drawing her poor red nipple deep into his hot, slick mouth. She began to pant with frustration and hope as he kissed and licked her, as if to offer a partial apology for the abuse…but it was no relief, and surely no apology. Of course she couldn't deny the resurgence of pleasure and desire, building deep in her belly and shooting down to her sex.

Darkdale held her still as he feasted on her breasts, sensually enough to make her even more tight and wet and hot, and roughly enough that there was a double edge to that slick, pleasurable sword of his attention.

By the time he finished his sensual onslaught, she was fog-minded with lust and pain, sore and overripe, desperate for one single, soft touch that would send her vaulting into relief.

Darkdale seemed to sense her peak was near, for he suddenly released her. The edges of the cloak fell back into place, adding the insult of their sensual sweep over raw nipples to the injury of her being left unsatisfied. Her quim was so full it seemed to be twice as thick and swollen as usual, and so wet her thighs slid against each other. Her little pip pulsed softly, insistently, hard and tight and needy.

Jane sniffled and shook, tears running down from beneath her blindfold. She trembled so hard beneath the smothering cloak her breasts jolted against its satiny fabric, adding more fuel to the erotic sensations she prayed would ease.

"Although one would hope you'd learned your lesson by now, I confess, I'm not confident that is the case," Darkdale said conversationally. "However, once my—er, our—guests have arrived, Jane darling, I give you leave to take any pleasure you desire. In fact, the more pleasure you take, the more satisfied I shall be."

She heard him walk away and wondered dully how long she would be left to hang here, throbbing, desperate, and needy.

And how soon she would have the offered pleasure of release.

After a stretch of silence and, Jane presumed, her isolation, a distant clock struck seven. She had no time to mull on the fact that she hadn't heard any timepieces last night when she was left in this same chamber (but on her hands and knees), for just then she heard a knock at the front door in the foyer.

She tensed, realizing whoever came in through the front door would see her almost immediately. She could only imagine the image that would confront the guests: herself, blindfolded, stretched long and lean beneath a black cloak, a hint of her pale skin showing in a long, slender vee. Perhaps the glint of the jewels circling her areolae, and at her quim…the black lace stockings from her feet to over her knees, and the long expanse of matching black gloves pulled taut above her head. Her red-gold hair, the only spot of color, in a thick braid over her shoulder…and beneath the black blindfold, her full, red lips, puffy and damp.

She drew in a deep breath and struggled to remain calm, even as she realized how erotic and titillating the vision of her would seem.

The more pleasure you take, the more satisfied I shall be.

She couldn't subdue a hot dart of fear and anticipation as voices from the front entrance reached her ears. There was Darkdale, greeting a man—two…no, *three* different men. They were speaking jovially. Trevor was being told to take their coats, their footsteps were coming closer; Jane dangled and trembled and her insides fluttered…

"My gad, Kellan," someone said, his voice falling into a near-whisper.

They'd seen her.

Anticipation and delight fairly crackled in the chamber, and the surge of lust and desire was so strong, Jane could feel it wrapping around her like a hot, heavy cloak.

"This is Jane." Darkdale's voice was cool, but she knew him well enough—such a shameful admission!—to hear the layer of pride in it.

Jane's skin prickled as she felt them circling around her like hungry dogs. She felt the weight of their eyes sliding over the enveloping silk, sliding down over her arms, her hair, her breasts, her arse. The breathing from her admirers changed subtly, growing dark and lustful, and perhaps her keen ears even heard the movement of cocks—shifting or being shifted— behind the plackets of their trousers. Shoes scuffed softly, cloth whispered against cloth, and she smelled a variety of scents: of men, of outdoors and cigars and smoke and brandy and others.

The quiet clink of glass against glass tinkled across the chamber, and then the familiar sound of something being poured…once, twice, four times. The soft slosh of liquid, the scent of whiskey now faint in the air…and still no one spoke. No one touched her.

She dangled. She pulsed and throbbed and struggled to keep her breathing even, to subdue the fluttering and anticipation and nervousness in her belly. The cloak smothered her, her toes strained to keep her from spinning slowly from the bonds, her arms felt as if they were growing longer and longer by the moment.

Someone drew near her, brushing near her throat…and all at once, the cloak was whisked away in a gust of refreshing air. There were snatches and intakes of breath from all sides, and she felt the scoring heat of want and desire as their eyes feasted on her.

Even when she was on display in Cold Eyes's village in the jungle, Jane hadn't felt this vulnerable. She had never experienced the weight of such lust, and in such a civilized— yet untamed—sense. There were no whistles or animal sounds, no grabbing and groping, no words. Simply admiration…

Or so she assumed.

Then…that noise from above. She nearly cried with relief when her feet were allowed to settle flat on the floor and her arms sagged slightly. Not very much, but just enough that she could almost touch the top of her head with her wrists.

Then someone touched her, lightly, brushing over a breast. Her nipple immediately shot to hardness, and Jane felt an answering twinge between her legs.

The man hefted the weight of one breast, then both of them. She felt him standing in front of her, sensed the heat of his body emanating from him, smelled his scent…it was Darkdale.

She couldn't help it—she arched toward him, for she had no control over her body. There came a soft chuckle accompanied by the faint scent of whiskey, then he stepped away and she was left to wait once more.

Someone murmured something in a low, masculine voice, and then glasses clinked together, as if in a toast. And then… everything changed.

A hot, wet mouth closed over one of her breasts, and Jane gasped in shock and delight as someone sucked and licked her sensitive tip. She shuddered, pleasure coursing through her as he drew her poor sore nipple deep into his mouth—tighter, harder, using his tongue to flicker wildly over its tip.

Jane gasped and jolted, trying to shift away as the sensation became unbearable, but she bumped into someone behind her. His hands covered her from the back, one hand sliding down over her pussy from the front, and the other covering a breast. She arched and writhed when his probing fingers found her arsehole, and one slid inside, deeper and deeper, as his other hand pinched her nipple.

Jane cried out and twisted so sharply she lost her balance. She would have fallen but for the bonds at her wrists, which yanked her upright as she stumbled into a solid figure. She had no chance to recover before his whiskey-scented mouth covered hers, thrusting between her lips with a strong, probing tongue. She could hardly breathe as he drew from her, mauling her and sleekly exploring her mouth as he held her chin with forceful fingers.

After that, her world became a dark blur; hands and mouths touched her everywhere. She tried to escape, but they stroked and licked and pinched, sucked, scratched, and bit wherever she went. As she stumbled, bucked, and twisted, insistent fingers probed, sliding inside her or curling into the soft flesh of her hips and arse while countless strong hands squeezed her flesh and still others held her immobile.

The men feasted on her, slurping and sucking hard, and Jane could hardly fight them off. They were soft and slow, sensual and tender, then turned more rapid and rough in turn, until the world behind her blindfold was red with painful, throbbing lust and her body shook with the intensity. Hands, mouths, fingers, tongues…everywhere she turned, everywhere she tried to free herself.

The more she fought, the more they became rougher and more frenzied, and her arms jerked in their sockets when she stumbled and twisted, trying blindly to free herself from the greedy mouths and hands. Half sobbing, she pulled away, then stumbled and fell into someone else, then was yanked away to be fed upon and nipped by still a different mouth…and then it happened over again and over again.

Then someone grabbed her by the thighs and forced her legs open wide. Jane cried out as a rough mouth suddenly settled over her quim, giving a long, sharp suck that was intense enough to make her scream. An orgasm blasted through her, colored with more pain than pleasure, as she undulated against the figure who'd moved behind her.

He fondled her breasts, holding them while different mouths closed over each nipple. His breath came rough and dark against her skin as his companions sucked and licked her, tongues moving around her sensitive flesh, kissing and nibbling in a riot of sensations. The combination of erotic tortures—at each breast, over her quim and teasing her little pip—had Jane bucking and twisting, helpless to free herself while trapped in a world of rough, intense lust. They were silent as they fed on her, and the only noises were her soft, gasping sobs and the sound of slippery suction, over and over… Lost in a world that was hard and slick and wet and hot, Jane at last gave herself up.

Then she came and came, and the peaks undulated into each other…or else they were one long, interminable orgasm; she didn't know. By now, Jane was barely conscious, hardly aware of anything but the erotic torture being visited upon her body.

Suddenly, they released her and she stumbled away, once again nearly falling. She remained upright, trembling and swaying, only because of the ties at her wrists. Panting, tears trickling down from beneath her blindfold, she sagged against her bonds, dizzy, confused, and weak.

"That was quite lovely," said a voice she didn't recognize. "A wonderful way to begin the evening."

"Most delectable—for a start," agreed a second man. "Now, shall we get down to the real business, Darkdale?"

Her master chuckled softly. He was standing very close to her, and Jane felt his hand linger over the thick length of her braid. "If you thought she was delightful thus far, you shall be very pleased with the rest of the evening. The night has hardly begun, hasn't it, my darling Jane?"

Z AREN HAD NEVER IMAGINED anything like London.
He felt as if his eyes were going to pop out of his head, they were moving so rapidly, taking in so many things: buildings, carriages, horses, shops, churches…and people. So many people! He couldn't believe there were so many of them in the world.

Though he'd been king of his own habitat, utterly at home in the dangerous, lush, complicated environs of the jungle, Zaren wasn't certain he could ever become comfortable here in this loud, busy, dirty, dark, and smelly city. There was just so…*much*.

The smells alone were almost too intense for him to bear, and the lurching motion of the carriage was even more uncomfortable than the ship had been during the one stormy night they'd experienced. Yet the tall buildings fascinated him. The cacophony of sounds—so different from those in the jungle, most of which he could identify as easily as his own fingers—made him strain to understand and differentiate them.

He gawked at the variety of vehicles and carts where men or women stood and shouted at passersby, trying to give them flowers or other items unfamiliar to Zaren. He thought it strange that most of the people simply walked past when a girl thrust a bunch of flowers at them, or a man shoved a steaming item that looked like something to eat toward a group of three men.

Though he thought Everett and Effie had prepared him for the city, Zaren found he had infinite questions about what he saw…and there were so many he couldn't even begin to organize his thoughts and ask them. Instead, he merely watched out the window, half listening to the conversation of his companions and understanding very little of what he heard.

"The house won't be open when we get there because the staff isn't expecting us, but I'll soon set things to rights," Effie was saying. "Those lazy girls will be shocked right out of their stockings, they will."

"And I'll send word to my lawyer immediately," responded Jane's father. He sounded unconcerned and almost jovial.

"Best to keep your return quiet. If them Scotland Yard boys hear you're back, you'll be thrown into Newgate faster'n a soiled dove pickpocket," said the woman. "Can you trust your lawyer to keep it quiet?"

"Utterly. He should be able to sort this out with very little delay, as I have a solid alibi for the time of the crime. I cannot even begin to imagine how they meant to convict me—and in my absence! What is England's legal system coming to?"

As he, Everett, and Effie trundled through the crowded streets (he had to remind himself several times of the word "street") in a taxi (another strange experience and even odder word), Zaren felt a sudden sharp pang of grief and loneliness. Oh, how he missed Jane! He needed her—not just to touch and kiss and hold, but to be with him as he entered this new world. He wanted to see it through her eyes, he wanted her to share her world with him just as he had done—albeit ever so briefly—with his.

My beloved Jane. Where are you? He stared out the window, the once-fascinating sights fading into a blur of gray and black shadows when his eyes grew damp.

His heart hurt so much, and though he would hardly admit it to himself, he was terrified he'd never find her in this maze of people and streets and vehicles. How would it be possible? How could anyone even find their own way, let alone search out someone else?

Zaren was in a strange place and had no information except the name Darkdale—the man who was with her on the ship— and of course the beauty and personality of Jane herself (surely anyone who saw her wouldn't be able to forget a woman such as she!). He'd also remembered most of the letters on the ship that had taken her away, and Everett and Effie had helped him make sense of them so he now knew the name of the vessel was *The Fighting Hawk.*

And then, settling back into the amazingly soft cushions of his seat, Zaren suddenly became calm. His nostrils flared with determination as the realization struck him: when it came down to it, this task was no different than hunting in the jungle. He would track them. He would learn his adversary's strengths and weaknesses. He would investigate and scent his quarry, and with the help of Effie and Everett, he would follow the trail through this strange and different sort of jungle.

Zaren was an excellent hunter.

⌒⌢⌒

"Do you remember anything more?" Everett asked. "Are any of your memories coming back, now that you've returned?"

"Don't force the boy," Effie said. They were sitting in a chamber that was called the "study" that night after dinner. "You'll sure as shootin' get him to forget whatever's in there! Whatever he knows'll slip through his mind like water through a sieve."

Zaren's head hurt when he tried to remember—but only a little. It pounded less than it had in the past when he'd tried to remember anything of life before his childhood in the jungle.

Recently, it had become easier. And since he'd been traveling on the ship with Jane's father, more images seemed to have erupted in his mind. Perhaps because now he had the words to describe them.

And then there'd been that vague dream when he was lying injured in the jungle village while in Cold Eyes's captivity, restless and feverish. He remembered his mother. He saw her face.

It had been his offhand comment about this during dinner that caused Everett and Effie to seize upon the possibility that Zaren might be able to recall how he came to be alone in the jungle, and perhaps even learn his identity.

Identity was an odd concept for him. He was who he was—Zaren, a name he'd given himself after hearing the way his wolf mother crooned over him, combined with the sounds made by a human mother he once saw bathing her child.

He was Zaren. Who else would he be? And what did it mean to "be" someone else?

"I have something to show you," he said quietly. Both Effie and Everett stopped their energetic discussion and looked at him, for he rarely offered comment of his own volition.

Zaren rose from the table, vaguely remembering there was something he should know about manners and polite society and how one should act when one meant to leave a meal—but he didn't care about that. When one was finished eating, one hid away whatever was left of one's food and went about one's business.

Since he had no belongings to speak of—definitely not the many trunks Professor Clemons, Jane, and Effie had brought with them—Zaren had kept the small bundle of objects on his person at all times during the voyage. The large, attached sacks in his loose pants were the best part about wearing English clothes (if he ever returned to the jungle he would incorporate that convenience in the pieces of animal skin he normally wore to protect himself). He reached into one of the pockets and withdrew the tattered piece of fabric.

"I found many things in an abandoned nest—treehouse," he corrected himself. "I was always drawn to the place, perhaps because I recognized it belonged to people like me. There were many things there, but there were some things that…" It was still difficult for him to express complicated thoughts, especially the way these items made him feel.

His throat always hurt when he looked at them, and oftentimes his head did as well. But he kept them, treasured them, protected them, and now he unbundled the small packet and spread the items on the table.

He hadn't looked at them since he met Jane. He'd intended to show them to her, but the time had never seemed right. Perhaps he'd been afraid of what they meant, or what she would think of them.

Effie and Everett were silent as Zaren laid the items out on the table among the shiny forks and spoons he'd so recently learned to use. There was the small silver disk on a chain, and Zaren realized with a start that he'd seen that very item around his mother's throat during his fevered dream. He hadn't remembered that until now. And there was a stiff piece of leather with letters on it in gold, long faded and hardly legible. Finally, there was a circle of metal that Zaren often slipped onto his finger, although he wasn't certain why.

"I'll be damned," murmured Everett. He picked up his eyeglasses and reached for the piece of leather. "This looks like the cover of a book—I can't quite make out the letters. Wait… ah. Here we go." He set his spectacles in place and Zaren watched as the older man's eyebrows knitted together. "Hmm. *Manifest of the Wind*—blast it, Effie, what is that word?"

"Wind…stead. Windstead," she repeated crisply.

"It appears to be the cover from a ship's manifest," Everett was saying, but Zaren hardly heard him. "No other pages attached. Just the cover."

"Windstead?" That word was familiar. He'd heard it before…but when? When?

Then he remembered. Something cold moved over him and his lungs felt restricted. Cold Eyes…he'd been taunting him, speaking to him, talking in circles about things he didn't understand as he gave Zaren something to drink that made him ill. What had he said?

The ship was called the *Windstead*. It carried a well-known family from England…

His heart was pounding, and not simply because he remembered Cold Eyes's words. No…that word, that name Windstead…

"Why, it's a locket," Effie was saying.

Hazily, Zaren looked over and saw that she'd opened the silver disk that his mother had been wearing around her neck. Inside were tiny, very tiny pictures of…

"Father," Zaren breathed. All at once he was hot, swimming with perspiration and his head was pounding. "F…father." He pointed at the pictures, images flooding back like a huge rush of water surging over him.

"*Windstead*. Wasn't that the ship that went missing? With …oh bloody hell, who was it—ah! Hampstead!" Everett said triumphantly, snapping his fingers. He was turning the gold circle around in his fingers, his voice filled with wonder. "Effie, I think it's very possible this young man is the missing Hampstead son." He looked at Zaren, his eyes magnified behind the round spectacles. "If that's the case, then you, my boy, are John Berkeley, Viscount Hampstead…who is a very wealthy young man."

"THE NIGHT HAS HARDLY BEGUN…"

When Jane heard those words from Darkdale, she could hardly contain a cry of frustration and anxiety.

How much more could she bear?

But she had no time to think about it, for suddenly her blindfold was yanked away—taking some of her hair with it. Jane blinked rapidly, trying to focus her eyes from behind the fabric and tears that had crusted them shut. The ropes that had been attached to her wrists and used to raise and lower them were removed, and the next thing she knew, Jane was being prodded down the corridor.

She had difficulty seeing as well as feeling any sensation in her long-raised arms. They prickled painfully as the blood rushed back into them. Her legs were awkward and her knees weak, and if it hadn't been for Darkdale taking her by the arm, Jane surely would have fallen flat on her face.

The other three men seemed to hardly notice her as they made their way down an unfamiliar hall. They were all neatly dressed in shirts, neckcloths, and coats, and hardly looked as if they'd just manhandled her into the most draining bout of pleasure she'd ever experienced.

The chamber into which she was led looked like nothing more than a man's study. There were four large leather chairs arranged in a loose circle, a fireplace with a roaring blaze, a wheeled table boasting a variety of liquor, carafes, and glasses, and a longer sideboard on which an extensive repast was displayed. The only element that seemed out of place in the chamber, however, was a large bed with four thigh-thick posts.

But Jane hardly had time to notice the details, for she was shoved into the center of the circle of chairs. She landed on her knees. Fortunately, the floor was covered by a thick, shaggy carpet that protected her from the fall. As the other men went to refill their drinks or fill small plates, Darkdale came to stand by Jane. Looming over her—for she'd remained on her knees— he lifted her chin so she could look him in the eyes.

"Behave yourself, darling Jane. Make me proud and pleased, and you will reap great rewards. Disobey me and you shall find your punishments even more severe." His words were low, meant only for her ears.

Before she could respond, he bent and kissed her tenderly, and very thoroughly. His tongue swiped deep and slow, and he nibbled gently at the corners of her mouth. When he withdrew, she was panting and warm, and that familiar lick of pleasure had begun to build once again. She nearly moaned at the sudden absence of him, and he patted her on the head.

"That's my dear Jane." He gave a pleased laugh as he turned to take a seat.

Jane waited uncertainly as the others did the same, but they weren't even settled when Darkdale snapped his fingers. She looked to him and a bolt of heat shot through her when she saw he'd unleashed his cock. It rose like a lusty red rod from the dark expanse of his trousers, and a dot of something pearl-like glistened at its tip.

She drew in a deep breath, and when he nodded, she couldn't move fast enough to slide between his legs. She took him into her mouth without hesitation, filling herself to the throat with his thick rod as she began to slide up and down over him. Her hands closed over his width as she worked, sucking and licking and tasting him in the same way he'd done to her… the way they'd all done to her.

Suddenly, she felt something behind her: warmth against her arse, then hands on her hips—and a cock. Jane gasped around Darkdale as something thick and hard and bold plunged inside her. She jolted, gagging a little as Darkdale's rod jammed deeper in her throat, but the sensation of being filled in her swollen, dripping channel was delicious. The man moved, sliding back out and then filling her just as abruptly once again.

Jane's eyes widened as pleasure slid over her, hot and wet and strong, building into something even more intense as the man behind her pumped and stroked faster and harder.

"Jane," Darkdale said sharply. "Finish me before he finishes, or you will be very sorry. And if you finish first…by gad, I will whip you until you scream."

His words penetrated her lust-fogged mind, and, suddenly nervous, Jane began to move faster and more purposefully over his cock. He was thick and hot and tasty, but the lovely sensation building inside her would not be denied. The man fucking her from behind held on more firmly and his rhythm became more frenzied. He was getting close…but Darkdale had to go first.

She closed her mouth tighter, sucked as hard as she could over his velvety, round head, and pumped faster and faster. Her fingers gripped tight around his cock until she used her saliva to help slip one up inside his arse. Darkdale arched and shuddered when she fingered him, and to her surprise and delight he immediately erupted in her mouth, shooting his thick wad into the back of her throat.

Relieved and delighted, Jane reached for her own release, crying out around the massive cock in her mouth. She arched and trembled as the other cock plunged in and out of her swollen, wet quim and the man behind her gave his own cry of release.

When the man withdrew from her, Jane sagged against Darkdale. Her head rested in his lap as she panted softly, waiting for her body to settle. He stroked her hair as his softening cock lay next to her cheek, glistening from her saliva…but she was given no further opportunity to rest.

"Get up," her master said, and made a sharp gesture behind her. "Ride him."

Jane staggered to her feet and turned to the man opposite Darkdale, who'd unleashed his own purple-red erection. He lay sprawled in his chair, a glass of whiskey in hand, completely dressed except for his raging cock. His eyes were dark and they glittered with the familiar light of lust as they swept over her. He made no move to assist as she climbed onto his lap, awkward due to her weak legs and sore arms.

She was so slick and wet it was nothing to impale herself upon him. Despite the pleasure she'd already received, Jane felt that familiar rush of lust as she slid down on his ready penis. Her legs trembled as she began to rise up and down over him, braced by placed her hands on the arms of his chair.

Jane had pumped only two or three times when the fourth man came up behind her. He covered her breasts with his hands, sliding his hot, firm cock down her arse crack. She shivered as he skimmed his palms over her sore nipples, and then gave a soft, shocked gasp when he slid a finger inside her.

Holding her with an arm across her chest, pinching and fondling the opposite breast, he fucked her slowly in the arse with his finger as she struggled to keep her own rhythm steady and sure over the third man's cock.

"Faster," cried the man she rode, and Jane tried to make her legs move, but she was clumsy with weakness and she could hardly ignore the hot, dark sensations rising in her own body.

She panted and struggled, half sobbing with frustration and exhaustion.

Suddenly the man beneath her grabbed her by the shoulders and pulled her to him. She flew forward, her hands landing on his chest as he jammed his tongue deep in her mouth, devouring her lips. His cock shifted forward, somehow still buried deep inside her, and then Jane felt something else at her exposed arse—something thick and hot and hard.

Her shocked cry was muffled by lips and tongue, and she froze as the hard cock probed her from behind.

"Fuck me," growled the man against her mouth. "I didn't tell you to stop."

Jane tried to obey, but the other cock—slick and wet with her juices or some other lubricant—was pushing its way inside her and she could hardly move in the necessary direction. Then all at once, she was filled from both ends, her mouth covered by a rough, biting one.

Half sprawled in his lap, her breasts crushed into the palms of the man fucking her from behind, Jane no longer had control of her own movements. Instead, she could only feel... the sensation of being very full, of very intense, dark pleasure building in an unfamiliar way. She struggled to keep moving her hips, to breathe, to cease from falling into a vortex of hot, red lust.

Hands and mouths were everywhere...she was filled, probed, pinched, pumped, faster and faster and harder until finally her world exploded; a cock rammed the back of her throat, another buried itself deep inside her tiny hole, and she felt the waves of dark, hot pleasure convulsing over her...on and on and on.

When she finally came back to herself, Jane was on the floor, weak, breathless, sore, and damp everywhere. Her lips pounded, her nipples throbbed, her clit and quim pulsed and raged from the intensity of the last hours.

She was dimly aware of conversation going on around her—something about poker—and that all of the men had returned to their chairs, still fully clothed.

"On your hands and knees, Jane," said Darkdale. "We are in need of a table."

She obeyed quickly for fear of what would happen if she didn't. After she drew herself up onto her hands and knees facing Darkdale, the man behind her stood and wedged his foot between her knees, kicking them apart.

"Much better," he muttered, sliding a finger down over her red and swollen clit. It was all she could do to keep from moaning or pulsing around him. "Excellent view, Kellan."

"Of course," her master replied. "Jane, I need not tell you what will happen if you disrupt our game or otherwise confuse our cards or bids."

She bowed her head in acceptance, privately wondering how long she would be able to hold herself up on her shaky arms. At least this was a reprieve from being teased and probed and fucked.

The cards were dealt, the bets distributed onto her back, and Jane had nothing to do but hold herself still as the hand was played. The chill metal of coins and the tickle of bills brushed her skin as they bid and drew and discarded.

She was nearly as relaxed as she'd ever been in Darkdale's home, head bowed, shoulders at ease, hair sagging to the floor, when the hand ended.

"Excellent bluff, there, Bruce," said her master. "You won. Take your winnings."

"It will be my pleasure."

The rest of the men chuckled softly and Jane saw one of them rise to his feet. But instead of scooping the coins and bills from off her, he came around to the rear. She stiffened, but she already knew what was to occur, and when he knelt and grasped her by the hips, she was ready.

"For every coin or bill that falls to the floor," he said as he positioned his cock at her wet and ready opening, "you will receive one lash from the whip."

Jane froze and gave a soft whimper as he slid inside her. Any pleasure she might have felt was eclipsed by fear as the coins shifted and slid on her back. She felt them moving, clinking together and jouncing as he withdrew and then thrust himself inside her again.

She bit her lip and fought with every ounce of strength to remain utterly still; to keep even the slightest bit of rocking from her hips, knees, and shoulders…but it was impossible to remain still, and impossible not to feel desire rising in her once again, to want to move to take him in deeper.

He pumped and slammed, taking no care to be gentle, and despite her apprehension, Jane couldn't keep her well-trained body from responding to the familiar, delicious friction against her overripe clit. A haze of pleasure settled over her even as she was horribly aware of the threatening movement of his winnings in the dip of her spine and on the angular slide of her shoulder blades.

Jane was lost in the fog of pleasure when one coin slipped off and bounced to the floor, jolting her back to the moment and the punishment that now seemed inevitable. Someone made a soft sound of satisfaction, but she dared not look up to see whom. Instead, she bit her lip and fought desperately to remain rigid and unmoving, but he was going faster and faster, and she could hardly keep her hips from moving to meet his.

Another coin slipped over, and then another, and a pair of bills fluttered to the ground, and Jane couldn't hold back the sobs of fear mixed with pleasure as more of the winnings cascaded down over her shoulders, hips, and even over the back of her arse.

He finished with one last, sharp thrust and Jane couldn't help but meet his orgasm with her own—there was no sense in denying herself any longer, for she was already about to be well punished. Not one coin or bill remained on her skin, and she trembled with fear and apprehension as the last vestiges of pleasure left her.

"Well, now. That didn't go well, did it, my dear?" said Bruce with great satisfaction in his tones. "You must learn to obey if you're to please your master."

He pulled Jane to her feet, and she looked at Darkdale, pleading mutely for him to intervene. But her master merely looked at her over the rim of his glass as he sipped, then turned to speak with the companion on his left.

Jane stifled a sob of desperation when Bruce brought her to a wall in the chamber. It was terrifying in its stark, blank whiteness. There was nothing on the entire wall, nor in front of it, except for a set of manacles that hung down from near the top.

She thought about kicking and screaming, but knew that would only bring her more punishments. Instead, she forced herself to move as directed and do as she was told as her wrists were spread wide and fastened to the wall just above the height of her shoulders. She rested her cheek against the wall, waiting for the torture to begin.

Bruce opened a cabinet and she stiffened when she saw the array of whips and crops within, and when his hand hovered over the thickest, most wicked-looking one of all, she nearly began to cry. Its handle was thick as three fingers, and even from her awkward position, she could see that the tip was a cat-o'-nine-tails, with a variety of tiny knobs that formed an octopus-like end.

But to her intense relief, he selected a much less frightening-looking whip. When he brought it from the cabinet, he cracked it sharply in the air and she felt the breeze, wincing at the snap sound. Jane braced herself, wondering how many coins and bills he'd won in the game, wondering if she'd even be conscious at the end of this torture.

For one wild moment, she almost begged, cried for Darkdale and for mercy—but she knew that was what they wanted, and it would only be an excuse for her to be punished again.

And that was when she realized she didn't have to stay here.

She could leave. Escape. And find some other way to save Papa…somehow. Now that she was back in London, she could—

Crack!

Jane muffled a shriek as the slender leather snake bit into the soft, fleshy part of her arse. Her reaction was more from surprise than pain, for though it stung, the lash hadn't cut deeply.

Crack! Crack! Crack!

She jolted and winced with each new lash, her fingers curling into her palms as she was bounced against the wall. The stinging continued, on and on until she was no longer able to control her sobs.

Then, to her surprise, it stopped. She heard him put the whip down, and when he came up behind her, she relaxed, expecting him to release her from the manacles.

But instead, he spread her arse cheeks and shoved himself inside her wet and ready quim. Jane gasped, and suddenly, she was undulating with pleasure as he pumped and thrust against her rosy red cheeks, pushing her against the wall as he fucked her.

He gave a groan of completion before she reached hers, and withdrew then stepped away. She'd hardly recovered from the surprise when *crack!*

This time, Jane screamed; the sensation was so unexpected, she was taken by surprise. He whipped her again and again, the strokes coming faster and harder, and her buttocks were stinging and hot.

But this time, she was writhing against the wall, for what Bruce had started by fucking her was only exacerbated by the lashing she was receiving. Somehow, she became more and more aroused as he continued to whip her. She gasped and begged now, begging not for him to stop, but for anything… anything to relieve the tension and growing pleasure.

This time when he put the whip aside, Jane was ready…but it was Darkdale who came up behind her. "There, there, my love," he whispered into her ear as he filled her. He pushed her against the wall, reaching around to touch her hard, shiny clit as he stroked long and slow inside her. "It will soon be over, my darling Jane. And you will be much better for it."

He gave a grunt and came inside her just as her own body exploded—this time, in a shocking blast of hard, rippling heat. She sagged against the wall, still undulating with the pleasure when the whipping began again.

And so it went until all four of them had taken their turn with her, fucking her in between the whippings until she no longer could differentiate between pleasure and pain.

When they were finished, and she was released, she fell to the floor. There was no blood, surprisingly, for Bruce had wielded the whip with such expertise that her arse cheeks had merely become hot and swollen and red…but he did not cut her skin.

"Of course not," he replied when Darkdale commented on that. "I couldn't bear to see such beauty marred. Now…shall we play another hand?"

JANE AWOKE THE NEXT MORNING in Darkdale's bed. She hardly remembered coming here—perhaps he had carried her there once the card party ended. She was naked, of course, and even her stockings and gloves had been removed during the course of the evening.

Jane had lost count of how many hands of poker were played, and how many punishments she received. The only thing she knew was that even taking a breath was painful…and that she must have pleased Darkdale enough that he allowed her to sleep in his bed.

She could hardly move; her limbs were sore, her buttocks battered, and her sex still throbbed gently in a reminder of all its pleasurable activity in the last days.

Jane realized she had been wrong. Nothing that happened in Cold Eyes's village had prepared her for being Kellan Darkdale's submissive mistress.

As if her thoughts had wakened him, Darkdale moved next to her. He reached out and closed his hand over her breast.

"You were magnificent last night, Jane darling," he said, fondling her with his strong fingers even as his eyes remained hooded. "You made me very proud. Hence your sleeping accommodations." He opened his eyes and looked at her. "I don't apologize for the severity of your punishment, however, and until you learn complete obedience, you will experience similar sorts of consequences. But for now…" His fingers found her sex and stroked her only twice before her traitorous body began to quiver, to heat and dampen and respond.

He smiled, then parted her legs as he rolled over on top of her.

"It could be like this every day," he said as he filled her with long, slow, almost tender strokes. "And I would like that, Jane. I would very much like that." He bent to kiss her breast and tongued its nipple lazily. Jane shivered and closed her eyes as pleasure washed over her easily this time—like a soft wave on the beach.

Then, all at once, she was struck by grief and pain. Zaren. It was Zaren she wanted—Zaren being tender with her, touching her with awe and kissing her gently. She wanted to wake next to him and begin the day at his side.

She felt so much more when she was with her jungle man—there was a depth that went far beyond her body's physical reaction, and at that moment, Jane felt ashamed. Utterly ashamed at the unwilling, almost addictive response to the man who'd brought her here.

Yet, try as she might, she couldn't turn her body off. As Darkdale fucked her, she shifted and panted and arched and took pleasure from the action as one might take pleasure from a belch or a piss…but in the end, it was only Zaren she truly wanted.

Only Zaren she loved. Only Zaren with whom she could completely give of herself…to whom she wanted to give herself.

The difference between lust and love had never been so clear to her.

When Darkdale finished, he withdrew and yanked on a bell pull. "You may stay here for a time," he said, rising from the bed. "Because I am well pleased with you." He cast her a soft, affectionate smile as he reached for the chamberpot. "I suggest you rest well, darling Jane, for I have a little surprise for you tonight. Marcine will be visiting…and she is looking forward to seeing you again."

Jane couldn't control a sharp little quiver of apprehension and something else. Anticipation? Desire?

Either way, she wanted nothing more than to do what Darkdale suggested: rest before what was certain to be another active evening.

Unless she could find a way to escape before then.

The day went by very quickly for Jane. She slept until well into the afternoon—waking only to be served luncheon by a dour-faced Trevor, who seemed irritated that she should be ensconced in Darkdale's bed—and then luxuriated on the mattress for several more hours before she was taken to the same room where Marcine had prepared her only yesterday.

Bernice and Belinda were there, but their blond mistress was not. Still, the twins seemed perfectly capable of whatever task they'd been set to—which included bathing Jane, washing her hair, and removing the few stubborn gems that survived the poker party and its related activities.

After her bath, the maids massaged her body from shoulder to foot with a musky, delicious oil that made Jane's skin soft and wildly sensitive to the touch. Her hair was left to hang long and loose, and she wore no other adornment but a slender gold chain around her throat from which draped a diaphanous cloak of shimmery gold.

A clock struck seven in the distance, which seemed to spur Belinda and Bernice into more speedy action. No sooner had the last of the seven strokes echoed into silence than the door to the chamber opened to reveal Trevor.

"She is here." He spoke in a sharp, low tone to the twin maids—certainly not to Jane.

Before either of them could respond, Marcine walked through the doors. As yesterday, her blond hair was pulled back in a rather severe bundle, and she was dressed in an austere but extremely expensive gown of slate gray. Her hands were covered by startling red gloves, and her lips had been stained a matching scarlet.

Marcine's eyes went immediately to Jane, scoring over her as if to ascertain whether the maids had completed their work to her standards. "Excellent," she said when her examination was complete.

The maids and Trevor seemed to take this as a dismissal, for they bowed to Marcine and vacated the room. Jane was aware of a sense of foreboding as she waited for the other woman to command her.

"I have been looking forward to this evening ever since yesterday," Marcine said with a small smile.

She might have intended to speak further, but the door opened once more and Trevor stood there. "He is waiting."

Marcine glanced at Jane. "On your knees."

Jane dropped immediately, gathering up her translucent cloak so it wouldn't be trapped beneath her as she scurried out of the chamber in Marcine's wake.

She wasn't surprised when the other woman led her to the same chamber in which Darkdale had entertained his guests last evening. The sight of the large, bare white wall against which she'd been whipped made Jane's belly drop and her insides flutter with a strange combination of apprehension and anticipation.

Darkdale was waiting for them, whiskey in hand. When they entered, he went to Marcine and kissed her on the cheek, then handed her a glass of the golden liquid. "Make yourself comfortable, my dear. At least for now." His voice was heavy with anticipation, though he hardly spared Jane a glance.

"Oh, there's no need to delay things on my account," Marcine replied with a Cheshire Cat smile, which made her scarlet lips appear even more startling. "I've been anticipating this evening all day. The sooner we begin, the more pleased I shall be." Her husky chuckle sent a little shiver down Jane's spine.

"Very well, then. Far be it from me to dissuade you." Darkdale sounded particularly pleased, and he went to adjust one of the massive leather armchairs so it faced the large bed in the corner of the chamber.

Marcine went to one of the cabinets on the far side of the room and opened the top drawer. "Perfect," she purred, and pulled out a strange-looking item with leather straps and buckles. She glanced at Jane, and then smiled. "Let's wait for this, shall we? There are other things to be done first. Kellan, my dear, did you hear about Hampstead?"

"Hampstead? What do you mean?"

Marcine crooked her finger at Jane. "Come. And take off that ridiculous cloak. I want to see you unhindered." As Jane obeyed, her mistress turned to Darkdale. "Apparently the son of the missing heir has returned. So there is a new viscount, and poor George Lumley is now merely Mr. Lumley and has reverted to being the uninteresting—and poor—Hampstead cousin once more."

"That must be quite the disappointment for the bastard, after having availed himself of the pleasures of the Hampstead estate—not to mention the funds—for two decades. Pity the poor fellow." Darkdale didn't sound the least bit sympathetic.

"At least you are a self-made man," said Marcine, drawing Jane to her feet. "Absolutely delicious, if I do say so. You have exquisite taste, Kellan."

"I cannot argue with that either, my dear. Shall I suggest Bentley invite the new viscount to our masquerade? If Lumley is to be replaced by the true heir, we should also replace him in our social gatherings as well. After all, he won't have the funds to continue anyway. I'm certain if the new viscount is anything like Lumley, he'll find our forms of entertainment quite…*satisfying*."

Marcine seemed to be paying more attention to Jane than to Darkdale. Her eyes had changed from cool and anticipatory to warm and feral.

Jane couldn't control a shiver as the other woman reached out to brush a fingertip over her upthrust nipple. Marcine smiled, her eyes narrowing with delight. "So incredibly responsive. Was she always like this?" She slipped her hand down to cup Jane's quim as she had done yesterday.

"Always. According to Wheeling, anyway."

"Incidentally, do we know whatever happened to dear Jonathan Wheeling?" Marcine slipped one finger inside Jane's warm, wet vagina, and gave her own delicate shiver. "Very nice. Tight and ready." She pulled away and then, as Jane watched, sniffed her glistening finger, then slipped her tongue out to swirl around it.

Jane's breath clogged at the unexpected eroticism, and before she could look away, her gaze was caught by Marcine's. There was heat, delight, and determination there—as if she were about to embark on some delightful but exhausting task.

"From what I've heard, our old friend Jonathan Wheeling has met a very bloody end at the hands—or should I say claws—of an angry lioness. His greed finally caused the death of him, as I had so often predicted."

The fact that Darkdale and Marcine were speaking of Jane's former fiancé in such blithe terms had little effect on her. She'd long come to realize that Jonathan had never truly loved her— for it was due to him that she'd been given to Cold Eyes and his villagers in payment for a map to a diamond mine.

"I have my own desires," Darkdale continued in his mellow voice, "but they are more for flesh and blood than cold, hard stones."

"But wasn't Jonathan feared lost in the jungle? Isn't that why you went to Madagascar with—oh." Marcine's laugh was one of admiring comprehension. "It was never the diamond mine you were after, was it, Kellan? It was our darling, luscious, delectable Jane here, wasn't it?"

"Indubitably." Darkdale sipped from his drink. "You understand me so very well, Marcine."

"Of course. We are two of a kind." She turned to Jane. "Bend over that stool there, arse up, knees wide. I want to see your hot, wet cunt showing while I undress."

Jane's flutter of anticipation was immediately eclipsed by a stab of apprehension as she went to obey. The stool was rather large, and cushioned with purple velvet. She bent over, lying on the padding on her belly with her breasts tumbling just over one side, bracing herself with her hands and knees.

She arranged her legs as directed and felt the edge of the stool pressing lightly against her suddenly ripening clit. When she heard movement behind her—she recognized Darkdale— Jane couldn't help but tense. His trousers brushed one of her calves, and suddenly she felt the familiar, gentle slide of something hard and slender down her spine.

The riding crop.

"Shall I warm her up a bit for you, Marce?" he asked, slipping the flexible little rod down between her arse cheeks.

Jane closed her eyes as the two little nubs on the Y-shaped end of the crop slid down over her moist folds, then bumped their way across and over and around with slow, sensual movements. She quivered as he found her sweet spot, the hard little nub where all her pleasure was centered, and gently stroked it with the tip of the crop, and then *thwack!*

She gave a soft shriek and reared up a little, one leg bumping into his foot. Her buttocks stung on one side, particularly tender after last night's abuse. Panting, she focused on the carpet just below her nose and waited for the next blow to fall.

But it didn't come. Instead, she heard more shifting and then suddenly, "Stand up, Jane, and come here."

Wary, she pulled to her feet, very aware of the fullness of her quim and the slide of her juices between her legs. When she turned, she found Marcine standing in front of her, completely naked and with her long blond hair unbound.

She still wore the red gloves, which covered her from fingertip to past the elbow, and her scarlet lips blazed with the same color. Jane couldn't help but notice her small, tight breasts with hard nipples, her pale white skin, and the thatch of blond hair between her legs that had been trimmed and plucked to nearly nothing. She also wore laced-up boots like nothing Jane had ever seen, also in the same bright red color. They had long, slender heels that looked like ice picks.

Jane swallowed hard, aware that her lungs felt constricted and her head felt light. She couldn't suppress a sharp twinge of attraction and interest as she looked at the high, rose-tipped breasts and the interesting apex at her thighs.

On trembling legs, Jane walked over to Marcine as she'd been commanded, aware that Darkdale had resumed his seat in the chair and appeared ready to watch.

When she got close enough, Marcine stepped up to her, slid her arm around her waist, and pulled her against her own bare torso. Before Jane could react, she wrapped her other hand tightly in Jane's hair, then covered her mouth with hers.

Jane had never been kissed by a woman before, and her first reaction was a stab of revulsion and horror. Instinctively, she tried to pull away, but Marcine was stronger than she looked, and she easily held her in place. Her tongue thrust, strong and bold, swiping inside Jane's mouth, deep and wet and rough.

It was the oddest sensation—both erotic and disconcerting—to have her breasts pressing up against another pair of hard-nippled tits. She felt Marcine's bush and the press of her mound rubbing against her hipbone as the other woman kissed her, nearly mauling her mouth as if wanting to inhale her.

At last, Marcine pulled away and stepped back a little. She released Jane's waist but kept a good grip on the fistful of hair she had, and yanked back so Jane's chin jerked up sharply. Hardly able to swallow, barely breathing, she couldn't move as Marcine trailed a finger down over her breast to circle a nipple. Then, without warning, she dipped her head and began to suck on it.

Jane squirmed and shuddered, but she couldn't shift away as the sensation grew stronger and more intense. Heat rolled down through her body, centering at her throbbing, wet sex as she remained helpless under Marcine's onslaught.

Then, just as suddenly, she was released—so abruptly that she staggered back a step.

"Over there," Marcine said, gesturing to the bed as she wiped the smeared lip stain from around her mouth. For the first time, Jane noticed a set of manacles hanging from one of the canopy rods that stretched between the tops of the bedposts, and she felt a flutter of nerves as she made her way to the bed.

To her relief, Marcine ignored the manacles. Instead, she pushed Jane onto her back, shoving her roughly onto the bed. Then she climbed up over her like a feral cat, bracketing Jane's body on the mattress with hands on either side of her shoulders and knees over her hips.

Her eyes were a glittering, intense blue as she bent to kiss Jane once more, rubbing her own hot cunt against her shivering belly. She ground down into Jane's mound with her own, making hard little circles that shifted and stretched her own sex deliciously. By now, Jane was panting and unsure what to do, and when Marcine shifted so her breast was over her lips, Jane had no choice but to take that hard, thrusting nipple into her mouth.

She sucked and licked the warm, nubbly flesh as Marcine arched and ground against her. And when Marcine took her fingers and forced them inside that moist, wet quim, Jane nearly stopped breathing. The sensation was utterly unfamiliar and strange, and whilst revulsion teased at the corners of her mind, she couldn't ignore the hot, slick fullness of the other woman's cunt. It was deep and warm and wet, and as Marcine forced her to fuck her deep and fast, Jane realized her own body was responding in a similar fashion.

She was hot and throbbing, tight and ready, and the smell of female musk was strong in the air, filling her nostrils and adding a layer of eroticism to her world. Soft, smooth flesh slid against hers, so different from the hirsute, muscular body of a man, and Jane felt herself falling into the depths of blazing-red heat.

Marcine cried out, arching up and pulling away from Jane's mouth as she contracted around her fingers, tight and undulating. She released Jane's hand and settled on her belly, breathing hard and leaving a pool of musky wet over her navel.

"A wonderful beginning," she said in a voice that had become even huskier. "Now let us see if you taste as good as you fuck, lovely Jane."

She made a quick spin and switched so her dripping red quim was over Jane's face and her own mouth hovered over Jane's ready mound. She spread her legs wide, placing firm, red-gloved hands on each knee to position them as broadly as possible, and dove.

Jane shrieked and bucked as Marcine's wicked mouth began to lick and suck and slurp in and around her swollen sex. She came almost immediately, arching up and exploding under the intense, strong ministrations of a woman's tongue.

Before she could even catch her breath, even as the shivers continued to wrack her body, Marcine lowered herself onto Jane's lips. Musk, heat, wet…that was the sensation, and when Marcine pressed herself down, hard, grinding and sliding over Jane's swollen lips, she found herself licking and sucking in a manner she'd never expected.

As she was forced to devour and taste her, Jane felt Marcine swoop back down to her own sex and together they licked and swiped and thrust the other into another blossoming orgasm.

Marcine pulled away and turned around, coming back up to Jane's face. "You are a very fast learner," she said, her lips close to Jane's. "I could become quite enamored myself." And she kissed Jane again, this time mixing Marcine's own juices and dark, musky scent with that of Jane's.

She climbed off the bed then, leaving Jane breathless, panting, and still throbbing…and more than a little disbelieving over what had just occurred.

"Jane."

Darkdale's velvety voice drew her attention and she looked over to see that he and his cock were waiting for her attention. She didn't remember ever seeing it so large and purple and ready for attention.

Despite her recent bout of pleasure, Jane still felt a rush of anticipation at taking him in her mouth. She scooted off the bed and made her way over to him, on her knees, as quickly as possible.

He was very warm, and very hard, and when she took him into her mouth, Jane almost immediately felt him gather up to spew his seed. She managed three deep strokes before he gave his cry of release and shot up hard into the back of her throat.

When she finished licking him clean and sat back on her haunches, she found Marcine standing behind her. She was holding that unusual object she'd earlier taken from the drawer.

Now that Jane could see it better, she realized it was formed in the shape of a phallus…with two ends. A hot shudder rushed through her as she watched Marcine unbuckle the straps. The other woman looked contemplatively at Jane, then at the bed, and finally at Darkdale.

Then her red lips curled into that satisfied smirk.

"This way, lovely Jane." Then, over her shoulder, she said, "You might wish a front-row seat, Kellan."

He chuckled and pulled up a chair nearer the edge of the bed on the side where the manacles hung. "Your wish is my command."

Marcine manacled Jane so she was facing Darkdale, with her wrists bound and fastened above her. Her knees were on the very edge of the bed, and spread wide.

He'd taken a position in a chair directly in front of her, and he sat with a decanter of whiskey and a glass on the table next to him. His shirt was open, his neckcloth loose, his cock tucked away into his dark trousers. He looked rich and dark and very attractive, and Jane wanted nothing more than to sit her sleek, ready quim on his lap and ride him.

But she heard the soft clink of metal and the swish of leather and looked over to see Marcine. As Jane watched in horrified fascination, the other woman slipped one end of the double phallus inside her, then strapped it on so the other end stuck out proudly.

She walked over to Darkdale to show him, and he grabbed the end of the protruding cock and began to jimmy it roughly. Those movements soon turned into long, fast strokes. Marcine gave a soft laugh that turned into a husky sigh, and Jane saw heat light her eyes.

The next thing she knew, Marcine took off the phallus and flung it aside, then came to straddle Darkdale, right in front of Jane. She opened his shirt—something Jane had never dared to do—and made him lift so she could drag his trousers away from muscular, hirsute thighs.

The image seared in her mind: the blond Marcine, with her hair long and flowing over her bare back and shoulders, riding Darkdale—who, with his dark hair and strong hands, looked utterly masculine and powerful. Their sighs and gasps filled her ears, and the scent of musk and coitus hung in the air.

Though she didn't want to see it, didn't want to know what was happening, Jane couldn't look away. It was a combination of fascination, arousal, and unwilling jealousy that kept her attention riveted on the couple. When Darkdale rose and roughly turned Marcine around so he could fuck her from behind, her hands clinging to the arm of his chair, Jane became even more aroused and frustrated.

The sight of his bare, muscular arse and broad shoulders had her mouth watering and her insides clenching with desire. If only she could be the one beneath him, the one crying out with pleasure and need…

Jane forced herself to close her eyes, ashamed and confused by her thoughts, desires—and most of all, the jealousy. *I must get away from him…from this. This isn't how I truly feel; this is some sort of hypnosis or lessoning that's caused me to want him so.*

Then, instead of the image of Darkdale and Marcine, it was Zaren's beautiful face and deep blue eyes that settled in her mind—like a talisman. It was his powerful shoulders and lean, muscular arms that filled her thoughts; the way he always looked at her in wonder and with reverence and respect—not as if she were his pet. The way he interacted with the animals and other wildlife in the jungle, with the same care and honor. Even the odd jokes he made, so utterly unexpected from a man who'd been living without human companionship for nearly two decades.

Zaren. I will return to you.

∞ XII ∞

JANE OPENED HER EYES as the bed shifted behind her. She tensed when she felt Marcine moving onto the mattress, and looked over to see Darkdale back in his chair. He looked at her with eyes weighted by satisfaction; they gleamed beneath their heavy lids with the heat of anticipation.

She didn't know how long the two had left her alone, how long they'd been fucking…but it seemed as if a significant bit of time had elapsed.

It didn't matter anyway, for Jane had had her reprieve—and now, it seemed, she would be drawn back into their activities of hot, slick pleasure.

Something bumped her from behind. It was hard and yet pliable at the same time. Jane didn't need to look over her shoulder to know that Marcine had strapped on the phallus once again, and now it was prodding her sleek, swollen quim from below.

No sooner did the tool begin stroking Jane than she was submerged in that familiar world of heat and eroticism. A stab of lust shot down to her sex, for she was still frustratingly aroused. She needed the stroking and licking and thrusting.

"Open your eyes, lovely Jane," said a voice in her ear. Marcine's breasts pressed into her from behind, her nipples hard, warm little points just above Jane's shoulder blades.

"Kellan likes to watch the way you fight against the pleasure you know you desire."

Her long blond hair fell over Jane's shoulder as Marcine nuzzled her neck. The phallus slid between Jane's thighs, rubbing gently along her wet folds…enough to tease, but not enough to take her where she suddenly needed to go.

Jane obeyed Marcine's command and found her gaze trapped by Darkdale's. He watched her steadily, heat and lust blazing in his eyes as Marcine's hands came around from behind to play with her breasts. Their long red and blond hair mingled and tangled over her skin, and the phallus continued to slip and slide slowly and teasingly.

Jane realized she was breathing heavily already, that her hips were twitching and she wanted more. Marcine seemed to realize this, for she tweaked a nipple with one hard pinch, then slid her hand down to cover Jane's mound.

She gasped, biting her lip when those clever fingers found her tiny, hard nub and began to play with it. She closed her eyes and shuddered, allowing the pleasure to wash over her as her arousal built and billowed.

"You do not have my permission to take pleasure, Jane."

Darkdale's voice was cold and soft, and cut sharply into the fog of her lust. Her eyes flew open to find his trained on her.

Jane shuddered, suddenly trying to fight the inevitable, the rush of orgasm that had begun to gather between her legs.

Marcine gave a soft laugh near her ear and slid her fingers around and over Jane's taut, overripe pip, pinching it between them and sliding back and forth, up and down, as Jane trembled and shivered against her.

Please… she thought, and wondered if it would make sense to beg. Would he allow it?

She was nearly there, nearly over the edge—where there would be ecstatic pleasure and punishment waiting for her— when Marcine slid her hand away, up over Jane's belly. She slipped her wet fingers over her breast, painting it with her musky juices and using the lubricant to tease a nipple into a hard, painful point.

Then, without warning, she bucked her hips and used her other hand to shove the phallus deep inside Jane. Both women cried out in pleasure and relief, but Jane fought to stifle her lust and passion as the phallus began to move inside her.

"Open your eyes, lovely Jane," said Marcine. "I won't tell you again."

She forced her eyes open, knowing Darkdale could read the fear and struggle—and the desperate need for pleasure—in them. He was focused on her, watching comfortably from his chair as Marcine fucked her from behind, her hands and fingers playing with her breasts and nipples as the phallus stroked both of them simultaneously.

Trapped by his gaze, stroked and probed and fingered from behind, Jane felt as if she had been stripped bare—down to her soul. She had no choice but to allow him to see her twisted desires, the struggle to control her body even as it was coaxed and teased into a frantic need for pleasure and release.

Marcine was moving faster now, her own sighs and gasps matching Jane's as the phallus impaled each of them in turn. She'd ceased playing with Jane and now merely held on to her hips as she pumped and thrust, harder and faster, on and on and on…

Jane tried to fight it, but she couldn't hold back. The hot red wave of lust had her, and she saw the challenge and triumph in Darkdale's eyes as the orgasm came upon her.

It rocked her, and she screamed in frustration and release as she was bowed forward by Marcine's own last thrust. Her arms stretched and her body arched awkwardly as the other woman shuddered against her.

Jane hung there, half sobbing as she panted, knowing she was about to be punished. She felt movement and opened her eyes to find Darkdale standing in front of her. Marcine was still impaled upon her from behind, and all at once, Jane was trapped between them.

Darkdale grabbed her by a hank of hair and covered her lips with his, rough and strong. He thrust into her mouth, devouring and taking as he reached beyond to touch Marcine behind her. The phallus slipped free and Jane felt Marcine undulating behind her, writhing against her spine, her hands everywhere as Darkdale punished her with a deep, breath-stealing kiss.

When he released her, Jane gasped for air, terrified as to what was going to happen next. He pulled Marcine off the bed and she came to stand in front of Jane as Darkdale climbed up behind her. She had no time to prepare before he shoved himself inside her, impaling her on his massive cock.

Three strokes and he was finished, arching into her and shuddering against her in the same position Marcine had been only moments before.

She had taken his place in the chair and watched with glowing blue cat eyes, licking her lips with pleasure and anticipation.

"There is a punishment to be meted out," he said as he climbed off the bed. He was speaking to Marcine, but Jane trembled in fear when his attention went to the cabinet where Bruce had withdrawn the whip the night before.

She remembered seeing the cat-o'-nine-tails there, and all the other weapons that would surely peel the skin from her buttocks.

"I look forward to assisting you," Marcine said. "May I choose?"

"Be my guest."

Jane closed her eyes and allowed herself to sag from her wrists. She fought back tears, somehow knowing whatever the woman intended to inflict upon her would be worse than anything she'd thus far experienced.

When Marcine turned, she was holding a riding crop. It was longer, and, as she demonstrated by bending it threateningly as she approached Jane, it was harder and firmer than the one Darkdale had used on her.

Jane couldn't control a whimper as the woman drew near, a hot gleam in her eyes. Marcine made certain Jane saw the single tip on the end—a slender, flat rectangle Jane suspected would be sharp and hard against her flesh.

"Turn around," Marcine ordered, smacking the crop against her palm.

At first Jane didn't understand, but then she realized what was required. It was difficult—nearly impossible—for her to obey, but she managed to shift herself so that her back was to Darkdale. She was still on her knees, of course, and her legs hung slightly off the bed.

She'd hardly finished her adjustments when the crop struck. *Smack! Thwack! Smack! Crack!*

There was no hesitation, no rhythm, no more than the briefest of reprieves between lashes. Jane cried and shook, fighting her bonds, jolting with every strike. Her buttocks burned and swelled, and her well-trained body also responded by growing hot and wet and swollen.

Thwack! Crack! Crack! Smack!

It went on and on…until finally, just as quickly as it had begun, it stopped.

She hung there, sobbing, her body pulsing and pounding with pain and frustration. Her feet had slid off the bed during the onslaught, and now she stood, leaning against the edge of the mattress.

Suddenly, someone kicked her legs apart and she lost her balance, swaying backward helplessly. She was caught by her bound arms and a pair of hands, which grasped her by the waist.

Jane cried out again, this time with relief and desperation, as Darkdale impaled her from behind. He pounded into her, his hands reaching around to play with her clit from the front, and Jane needed nothing more…she came, with a hard, deep shudder and the fear of even more punishments.

Before Jane had recovered from her release, Marcine was there in front of her, mercifully untying her hands. Jane fell forward as soon as she was released, and Marcine took her onto the bed over her.

Darkdale followed, and Jane found herself sandwiched between the two as he fucked her until she cried again… and then pulled himself out and shoved inside Marcine. She was trapped between them, a victim of hands and mouths everywhere, of slick strokes, and pinching, biting, sucking… and a rhythm that went on and on and on…

Finally, Darkdale gave a last heave and he and Marcine groaned their release. Jane lay gasping between them, suddenly fearful of what would happen next.

They rolled away, all sticky and hot and flushed.

"She came again," Marcine said.

"She is quite disobedient. Frankly, I don't know what to do with her. She doesn't seem to learn." Darkdale seemed to relish this about Jane, a fact that made her even more terrified.

"I believe she might be a hopeless case. However, there is the masquerade tomorrow night. DuVal will be there. He is a master at such problems."

Jane felt their eyes score over her, but she remained in a heap on the bed, silent and sniffling, still pulsing and needy.

"What a brilliant idea. If I turn her over to DuVal, he'll have the bitch trained in no time. Have I mentioned lately how much I adore you, Marcine?"

"Indeed you have. Now, Kellan, I do believe it's time you gave me some pleasure."

XIII

THE NEW VISCOUNT HAMPSTEAD couldn't help but feel slightly foolish.

Why on earth were people suddenly bowing to him all the time, calling him by the name of a place where—apparently—he now owned a large plot of land and a huge home, and acting as if he had the power to do something for them?

His name was Zaren, or if not that, then at least John, which had sounded familiar as soon as Everett began to explain things to him. If his mother had given him the name John, he would use it, but being called Hampstead felt very odd.

What was even more odd and unsettling was the number of people who'd begun sending little white cards with their names printed on them, or other information, called "invitations." Apparently, he was an important person—and in a world he hardly knew how to navigate.

Zaren missed his jungle. He missed his home: the blue sky, the lush greenery, the variety of creatures, the colors. London was drab and cold and dark.

But he thought that perhaps he could accept even London if he only had Jane with him—and that was why, feeling even more foolish than he'd ever felt in his life, he was climbing out of a carriage and striding up the path to a large house…while wearing a mask.

Apparently that was what it was called, this strange covering over his head and the top of his face. It left his eyes unshielded so he could see (although Zaren had extremely acute hearing and knew how to move through the jungle in utter darkness), and his mouth and the top of his nose unencumbered.

What, he wondered, was the purpose of such a thing? He understood animals using their surroundings to blend in, but why would a man wish to do this when attending a…party. That was the word. A party.

A masquerade party.

Effie had tried to explain it, but Zaren still thought the entire concept was ridiculous. However, when he learned that Kellan Darkdale meant to attend this party, Zaren decided nothing would keep him away—including not having the foggiest notion what one did at a party, and how to comport himself.

All he needed to do was find Kellan Darkdale. Once he had the man, he would find Jane.

His nostrils flared a bit as he stepped into the house, the door having been opened by a man called a butler. A number of smells assaulted him—some familiar, some not, some pleasant, and others not at all.

But an underlying scent that immediately penetrated Zaren's consciousness was that of mating. Of intimacy and bodies and mating.

It was odd that the smell was so strong in a location where he'd learned something called Polite Society would be attending. The realization made him even more acutely aware of his surroundings, and had his instincts sharpening.

This entree into a party—to which he'd nevertheless been invited—was just as dangerous as hunting a mad lion. Or attempting to free oneself from the attention of one of the massive snakes that could crush one to death. Despite the fact that he was unfamiliar with this sort of environment, Zaren was fearless.

He would find Darkdale.

He would find Jane.

They would leave.

He pushed his way past a cluster of people, finally glad for the mask that hid his features—and the fact that he was a stranger. The scent of mating and coitus was stronger now, and over the constant buzz of conversation, laughter, and music, he could hear different sounds…ones that didn't seem to belong.

Following his animal instincts, Zaren made his way through the house. There was another scent, something familiar, that led him through a chamber and then into a corridor, and to a closed door. His heart was pounding, for that scent was stronger—and it was a scent he recognized.

A man stood in front of the door, clearly meant to keep unwanted visitors out. "Private party inside," he said. "There is no admittance without a special invitation."

Zaren didn't hesitate. "I am Hampstead." He wasn't about to let this puny man keep him from finding out what was beyond that door.

"You are Hampstead? By God, how fortunate can we be?" A woman's voice behind had him turning.

She was tall and had pale hair. She wore a mask, of course, but her lips were unnaturally red and she also wore scarlet gloves and boots.

Zaren bowed. "My pleasure. I wish to go in there."

Her red lips curved. "Mistress Marcine," she said, extending her hand, which he had learned meant he should take it and press his lips to the top of her glove.

He did so, but his attention was already at the door. If they didn't let him in, he would force his way in.

"Kellan will be pleased you chose to attend tonight. But I must say, his pleasure won't be even near what mine is, walking in on your arm. Come with me."

The man stepped aside and Marcine led him through the doorway.

Zaren took two steps inside and was assaulted by her scent. There was no mistaking it.

Jane.

Jane is here.

He froze, his nostrils quivering, and every muscle in his body went taut and tense.

"What is it, my lord?" his companion asked, but he had pulled his arm from her grip and was stalking across the chamber.

***

Jane could hardly see from behind her mask. She was hot and flushed, and her eyeholes had been knocked askew during one of the "sessions," as Darkdale called them.

She and other "submissives"—as they'd been called in fond, affectionate tones—had been commanded to act out certain erotic scenes for the pleasure of their masters and, apparently, some mistresses. The latest one had involved them managing a threesome on a table.

She was exhausted and nervous about what might happen next, but at the same time, she knew this was her best opportunity to escape. It was the first time she'd left Darkdale's home since arriving there, and although he'd introduced her to an odious man named DuVal, he had been distracted by a game that included betting on how long a man could hold off from orgasm when he was being sucked by a woman. There were three men in contention, and they'd been going for more than twenty minutes.

Jane knew it was only a matter of time before she was dragged into such an activity—or worse—and she thought this would be her single chance to escape. She looked around, beginning to ease through the crowd, much of which had descended into an orgy-like atmosphere. People were fucking everywhere she looked—some with whips and some without.

Just then, she saw Marcine walk into the chamber. She was on the arm of a tall, broad-shouldered man who immediately drew Jane's attention. Her insides shifted and her mouth went dry, and she turned away as a sharp, agonizing pain stabbed her belly.

Now she was imagining Zaren everywhere. Desperation was causing her to hallucinate…or, at least, to wish for the impossible.

Still, her attention went back to the man and she saw him scanning the chamber from behind his mask. He was so like Zaren, she couldn't hold back the tears. They welled in her eyes as she imagined what he must be doing, far away in Madagascar, wondering if she would ever return.

Suddenly there was a shout, and heads turned. Jane looked over to see that the cock-sucking competition had ended, and Darkdale was the winner. No surprise there.

But that meant he'd be looking for her. She turned, trying to duck behind a pillar, and all at once she slammed into a tall, muscular body.

Muffling an excuse—for she was a submissive, and shouldn't even be on her feet, let alone doing anything she wasn't commanded to do—Jane started to turn away.

But then she looked up, and when she saw the blue eyes behind the mask, she clapped her hand to her mouth. *No. Impossible.* She started to cry as she turned away, shaking and trembling with grief and confusion.

"Jane."

Her heart stopped as a hand reached to touch her tentatively. She slowly turned, her heart now pounding as if it were about to burst from her ribcage. "Zaren?" she whispered.

"Jane." His mask was gone, and there, impossibly—*completely,* utterly *impossibly*—he stood there. In front of her. Dressed like any other man in the room. His hair cut shorter, but not too short, and clubbed at the nape. His eyes…oh, God, his eyes…

"Zaren." She could only stand there, suddenly, utterly aware of her nakedness, of the decadent lasciviousness that surrounded them, that had been part of her—that likely clung to her in scent as well as aura.

"Will you come with me?" he said, question and determination blazing in his eyes.

"Yes," she whispered. "Yes, God, yes, Zaren—"

"Hampstead! I see you've met my darling Ja—"

But Darkdale never got the words out, for Zaren had him by the throat and pinned against the wall in a trice.

Jane's throat convulsed, for she'd never seen Zaren look this way—this fierce, this dark, this utterly wild and uncontrolled. "She goes with me."

Darkdale kicked weakly, but Jane saw his face turning purple. And at the same time, she noticed his trousers sagging from his hips, as if he hadn't even taken the time to close himself up after winning the cock-sucking competition.

No one else in the chamber seemed to notice—which was no surprise, considering the other violent and sexual activities occurring in every corner.

"Jane goes with me," Zaren said again. He abruptly released Darkdale, who slid to the floor. He looked down at him for a moment, then, as if there was absolutely nothing wrong with her being garbed in nothing but a mask, he took her arm. "Jane. We are going home now."

They had taken two steps when Jane felt Zaren tense. He spun before she could even draw in a breath, and the next thing she knew, Darkdale was airborne.

He landed in a heap on the top of the table where Jane had just been laid out and fucked from two ends, then Darkdale crashed to the ground. The pistol he'd been holding…well, it was in Zaren's hand now, and he showed it to the chamber at large.

"We are leaving." He said the words clearly and distinctly, looking around to make certain they all understood.

As they walked out of the chamber, Jane heard someone behind her saying, "The new Hampstead is a beast. It's a bloody shame he doesn't like to share." The female voice carried, and was dripping with salaciousness.

Jane glanced back. Marcine was watching them leave, regret stamped on her pretty face. As their eyes met across the chamber, the woman gave her a heavy-lidded, knowing smile, then turned to help Darkdale up off the ground.

❦

Moments later, Jane climbed into a carriage with the Hampstead crest, and she and Zaren were alone. Blessedly alone.

Although she wanted more than anything to drag him into her arms, to rest her head against his solid chest and taste him, she did not.

"What is it, Jane?"

"I…I don't know what to say, Zaren. I have…I left you."

"Did you want to leave me?"

"Of course not!"

"Are you glad you did?"

"No, Zaren. He lied to me. He tricked—"

He was nodding, and it was so odd for Jane to look at this man who was dressed so normally, who looked so civilized and proper and gentlemanly, and know that he was Zaren, her jungle man. He was also, apparently, Viscount Hampstead—however that had come to be—and what did that mean for her?

"I know. He tricked you, he brought you away—and he made certain your father was convicted of murder."

"What?" Jane sat up. She was wrapped in his coat, but her breasts moved beneath it.

"It didn't take long for Everett to learn that the—what did he call it? The nail in the coffin?—of his conviction was a witness who claimed he saw your papa near the site of the murder, shortly after. The witness turned out to be Kellan Darkdale's manservant Trevor, and he was lying. Your papa has set things right, and he is no longer in danger."

She burst into tears. It was all too much.

The next thing she knew, Zaren was next to her, gathering her into his arms. She breathed in his scent as she felt his chest expand while he did so with hers, and she sagged against him.

She'd just spent the last week caught up in a decadent whirl of sensuality and pleasure, and all she wanted now was a long, slow caress from the man she loved. She wanted to erase all of the memories of Darkdale and what he'd taken from her, and Marcine's salaciousness, and the dark and lustful things she'd done.

But could Zaren forgive her? Did he still want her?

"I love you, Jane." He seemed to read her mind. "I don't know what happened with Darkdale and you, but it does not matter to me. I love you. I want you. And…if you want me, I would like to make you Lady Hampstead." His words sounded extremely stiff and formal, as if he were taking great care to say the correct thing.

"Oh, Zaren. There is nothing that would please me more." She looked up at him and felt as if she would drown in his eyes. "Let us never be separated again."

"Never."

Two weeks later

THE MOMENT ZAREN CLIMBED into the carriage after Jane, he bundled her into his arms.

"Hello, my darling Lady Hampstead," he said, for they had just been married in a small, unassuming church. No one had been in attendance except for Effie, Everett, and some close friends of the Clemonses. "Now you are officially my mate, and you cannot find any excuse to leave me."

"As if I would need one." She giggled when he slid a hand over her breast, and then began to try and free it from its confines.

When he found it too complicated, he gave up in disgust. "I suppose we shall have to wait until we get home."

But Jane would have none of it. She gathered up the wild mass of her skirts and petticoats, opened the slit in her drawers, and freed him from his very correct—and now very tight—trousers.

"See, my darling husband? There is always a way." She slid down over his hard, ready cock and closed her eyes in bliss.

There was nothing, absolutely nothing like having the man she loved inside her. He shifted, his pupils dilating with pleasure, and he leaned forward to give her a soft, long and tender kiss.

"I love you, Jane Berkeley."

"I love you." She rose up then slid down. His eyes crinkled at the corners, and he covered her breasts with his palms. "And I love more than anything to see the pleasure in your face."

It was so unlike her experiences with Darkdale. There was no lasciviousness, no hardness and violence in Zaren's face when he made love to her. It was bliss and openness—just the same way she felt when they lay together.

He moved his hips too, and looked longingly at her breasts, which were, of course, still covered beneath layers of fabric and lace and buttons. She moved, he moved, and suddenly they were jouncing up and down in a definite anti-rhythm to that of the carriage.

When her orgasm came, it was long and sweet and intense. And tears gathered in her eyes; tears not from fear or apprehension, not from the desperation of relief and release, not from pain—but tears from the pure beauty of it. The joy of her man.

She sighed and leaned against him, still joined, still jouncing along gently against his spent cock.

"I cannot wait to return to the jungle with you. But we can remain in London as long as you wish. There is much for you to do here, my lord viscount," she added cheekily.

But he didn't seem to comprehend her jest. "And if I wished not to remain at all? To live simply again in the wilds of Madagascar, Jane? Would you come with me? Would you leave this behind—the beds and carriages and shops and parties?"

"Without hesitation. Zaren...John," she added with a bashful smile as she pulled away to look at him. "It seems so odd to call you by that name, for you will always be Zaren to me. And I will always want to be with you, wherever you want to be—whether here or in the jungle, or anywhere else."

He kissed her forehead, then slid his hand down over her shoulders as he pulled her into a close embrace. Her voluminous skirts were still bunched up between them, and her breasts crushed against his powerful chest. "There are many things I may come to appreciate about living in the city, but there is one thing I do not believe I shall ever count as a convenience."

She looked up at him, and for a moment she felt as if she were drowning in his sea-blue eyes. "And what would that be?"

"The fact that you must wear so bloody damn many clothes."

❦

Several months later

"Goodbye, Papa," Jane said, pressing a kiss onto her father's round cheek. She straightened his spectacles then brushed a wisp of windborne hair down over his pink scalp. But as soon as she removed her hand, the gray-white lock blew up again. "Take care of Effie for me."

"Who's gonna be takin' care of who, I ask you!" Effremina snatched Jane into a big, rough bear hug and squeezed her tight. "You two be safe and you'd best promise you'll send word back with Captain Morris once you get settled…and whenever you can."

"We will, of course. We'll be back next May," Jane said. "And I expect you to have your treatise on the triple-spiked indigo not only completed, but published as well, Papa."

"Well then, I'd best be back to work," he replied—and Jane could already see his mind drifting back to his studies.

"Shall we, my lady?" Zaren was there, tall and muscular and strong. Jane's heart skipped a sharp beat whenever she saw him, but today, he appeared particularly handsome and confident. Perhaps it was because he knew he was returning home—albeit only temporarily, but he would soon be back in his beloved jungle.

The wild man had been temporarily subdued into trousers and boots and a neckcloth, but Jane suspected that persona of the gentleman would be easily shed as soon as the ship left the Thames for the open sea.

They walked on the gangplank, boarding Captain Morris's ship, and waved to Papa and Effie one last time.

***

As the striking couple of Lady and Lord Hampstead strolled across the deck to speak with the captain, a set of eyes watched them from the crow's nest above. Dark, angry, and vengeful eyes peered down upon them as the anchor was raised and the gangplank drawn up…and then the eyes crinkled at the corners.

For they were smiling.

Smiling with malice and determination.

Lady and Lord Hampstead would never make it back to London.

They wouldn't even make it to Madagascar.

Colette Gale

ONEY...MOON? HOW can that be...to put honey on the moon?" Zaren looked down at Jane with such a quizzical expression she couldn't keep from laughing. "I do like honey—on bread, the way Effie showed me, but I don't understand all this honey-moon talk from you."

He lay next to her on the unusually wide and comfortable bed in their cabin aboard *The Racing Gull*. They'd been at sea for more than two weeks already, and had spent very little time of it dressed.

"No, darling, it's what we call an 'expression.' It doesn't mean what it sounds like—to make the moon honeyed or to put honey on it or anything like that. It just means...we're married now, and very often a husband and wife take a trip together to celebrate being married." She smiled and swiftly rose to slide her leg up, then straddled his naked body. Her soft, lush quim settled over his warm belly, teased by the rough hair that grew above his magnificent jutting cock. She slipped a bit when she settled into place from the damp gathered there, and smiled at the lick of pleasure that rolled through her.

Zaren—for despite the fact that her husband was the wealthy and powerful John Berkeley, Viscount Hampstead, he would always be Zaren to her—looked up at her with delight in his intense blue eyes. "Again, my love?" he murmured, reaching to cup her generous breasts as they swayed above him.

"As often as you wish," she replied saucily. "And then another hundred times over, my lord viscount." She sighed when his hot, slick mouth closed over one very ready nipple, sucking and sliding his tongue around and over the throbbing tip. A little shooting pleasure from nipple to her tiny, tight pip turned into a full-strength orgasm that rippled through her like a long, hot wave. "For that…" she sighed, closing her eyes, "is what a honeymoon is about."

When the pleasure eased, Jane lifted herself up and slipped his thick, ready cock into position. As she lowered down over him, Zaren's brilliant blue eyes widened with pleasure…then sank half closed as he grasped her hips to help her with the slow, steady rising and falling as she rode him at a leisurely pace. He filled her with his thick, swollen cock. Every tiny movement, every long, deep stroke, brought with it a blooming of desire.

Jane was a lusty woman—one whose body craved pleasure and was rarely satisfied for long. She was passionate, responsive, and easily aroused; quite different from the other strait-laced, corseted, and repressed women of London society. At least, as far as she knew.

But one thing Jane had discovered over the last months— since she'd met and fallen in deep love with Zaren—was that having sex with her husband was the most arousing, satisfying, and shattering experience of all. It was because of the way he looked at her—with purity, love, and respect—every time. Even when it was rough. Even when it was fast, and hard, and urgent.

Even when she begged for release, when he teased her and taunted her and licked her until she was ready to scream…it was so very different from the other experiences she'd had.

He loved her. She loved him. And fucking someone you loved…well, it was simply heaven. And then some.

Her long red-gold hair tumbled around them like a silken curtain as she rode him, teasing and stroking his length with her tight pussy. This time, she refused to allow him to come, as she had so recently done, loving the expressions that filtered over his face…loving that she had control of him and his pleasure as so many had done to her over the last months.

She loved the way his cock filled her to stretching, the way its purplish head bumped against her clit and slid deeply inside her. She loved the way her labia swelled and grew slick and wet, and the soft sucking sounds her quim made as she moved up and down, back and forward, and in little circles around the jutting rod she rode.

Zaren's handsome face wavered between tension, wonder, and delight as she alternated her rhythm: fast, slow, *verrry slooowwww*, and then fast and faster and *faster*, until they were both gasping and crazy-eyed and ready to explode.

But just as she was gathering up to tip into the glorious white heat of release, he yanked her down flat against him, wrapping a length of hair around his wrist to bind her in place, crushing her breasts against his chest. Before she could react, he trapped one of her legs with his powerful thigh, and curled a strong arm around her waist so she could no longer move and tease him. Jane sighed and moaned, bucking gently against his muscular torso as he held her close…and then forced her to be still. Her face was buried in his loose, silky hair, and she drew in a long breath of him: his arousing, delicious essence.

Each heart thudded against the chest of the other, and Jane's tiny little pip quivered and throbbed, pressed between his cock and torso. She wanted more…she wanted movement! Pressure! Stroking…*release*.

She shifted impatiently and was rewarded with nothing but a little bit of friction before Zaren tightened his arm and chuckled deep and low in her ear. "So very eager, my Lady Hampstead," he murmured, then snaked his tongue deep and quick into her ear as he slipped his other hand down along the cleft of her arse.

Jane jolted and shivered as his tongue invaded the sensitive, ticklish depths of her ear even as his fingers slipped around and below the curve of her bottom to find the hot wetness there, around his cock and slicking the lush folds of her pussy. She shivered and bit her lip as he did something to twitch his cock deep inside her, sending pleasure jolting through her while using a wet finger to tease the tiny pleats of her arsehole. She shuddered at the sensation, heard the soft, slick sounds, felt the low moan of lust gather deep in her throat…her orgasm was so close, and yet still out of reach. But it was a beautiful anticipation…a welcome one.

Yet she was impatient. She wanted *more*.

"Zaren, don't tease," she whispered, then nipped sharply at his ear. He was salty and warm and tasted of male and sex and fresh air, and she sucked while twitching and shifting as much as she could though still imprisoned beneath him. It was a convivial battle of wills, an amusing contest that would finish with the contentment of both as she struggled to find movement, and he kept her tightly imprisoned. Every so often, he would twitch deep inside her…or give the slightest movement of his hips, allowing her to settle even more deeply onto him. His fingers were busy, slipping around where they were joined, around her tiny pleated hole, and then…to her utter delight and frustration…around between the fronts of them to find the tiny core of her pleasure.

Jane shivered and sank down close, tasting the salt of his skin, and then shifted softly, slowly…hardly noticeably, but enough that her pleasure began to rise and rise—

"I don't think so, my lovely lady," he muttered, shifting a little. But then she managed a few sharp, desperate movements that caused his breath to catch, and with a little laugh, he held her even tighter. This kept her hips from teasing him but forced her ready clit to be pressed even more tightly between them. "Let us just remain here…soft and easy…and enjoy this honeymoon of which you speak."

"I don't *wish* to be soft and easy," she argued, nipping at his ear again, and, when he jolted in surprise, giving a good, hard, noticeable thrust of her hips down onto him. *Gad, he was so big and hard and full…* She shifted hard again, faster, and reached around to find his ballocks, stroking and teasing the crisp hair growing there, tugging gently, and then grinding her hips down, down, down onto him…

"Uhhh…" he groaned, and Jane grinned with delight and triumph. *That* was the sound of her man, giving in…giving up.

With a sharp, quick movement, he had her on her back and her hips in his hands as he thrust and pumped inside her with breathless speed. Smiling at her win, Jane arched up and gave a little cry as they reached their peak at the same time, coming with a hard, undulating release that left them still panting and gasping moments later.

"By all that is good," Zaren said, his damp body pressed against hers, one hand stroking what he called her fire-hair, "I do not know what I would do without you, Jane, my love."

"And I you," she replied, and couldn't help but remember those dark days when they had been separated, and when she thought he was dead, or lost in the jungle of Madagascar. "It will be so different to see the jungle with you now," she added. "Captain Morris says we should reach Madagascar in one week."

"Only one week left of this?" he asked, his sensual mouth quirking as he gestured to the luxury of the large, soft bed. "Then we must be certain to enjoy every moment we have left, Lady Hampstead. For very soon, we shall be sharing our nest with monkeys and butterflies and the other many-legged creatures of my home." His voice dropped low on the word *home*, and she reached to touch his dear, handsome face. She knew how much he missed Madagascar—the freedom, the wildness, the beauty.

And what an amazing transformation he'd made in the last nine months—from his appearance, to his speech, to his understanding of the world in which she lived and he now belonged.

When she first encountered him in the jungle, his nut-brown hair had hung well past his shoulder blades, and had formed long, soft coils from lack of combing and cutting. He'd been naked except for an animal skin he wore around his waist, and the long, sleek, tanned muscles of his arms, torso, and legs had been enough to make her mouth go dry. Never—even when she'd visited Michelangelo's *David* in Rome—had she encountered a more breathtaking image. Certainly not when she thought of the pale, stringy fops back in London, with their padded-shoulder jackets and breeches.

She'd found Zaren's initial appearance both unique and attractive, but now that he'd had his hair cut and combed and wore it tied back into a short tail at the base of his neck, she thought him just as handsome. And she was the only one in London who knew precisely how broad and muscular his shoulders were beneath the tailored coats and crisp white shirts he wore in public. Her Zaren was the perfect combination of wild jungle man and proper, well-dressed gentleman.

"I love you," she said, pressing a soft kiss to his sensual lips. "More than you can imagine."

Before he could reply, there was a sudden odd lurch, as if the ship had come to a sudden stop. The telescope that Zaren had found so fascinating tipped over and rolled off the dresser. The sound of shouting, alarmed and urgent, reached their ears.

Jane looked at her husband, whose expression had changed from that of a tender, intimate lover to a sharp and prepared hunter. In the jungle, he'd been able to best any beast with hand, speed, or weapon…and though he looked civilized in his gentleman's dress, he was still the wild man of the jungle.

"I know you won't stay here," he said, yanking on a pair of trousers with less grace than a man who'd been wearing them for decades would do. "But I will ask nonetheless."

"I cannot agree more," she replied, pulling on a loose shift that required no corset. "I shan't stay here. But I shall take care and stay close to you. Is it a storm coming? Or perhaps we've struck something? Or a sail has torn. Or…"

She dared not say the word *pirate*. Surely not. Surely not in this day and age…

"Be still and safe and do as I say," Zaren ordered as he took her hand. "I do wish you would remain here, but if you won't do that, then at least promise to listen to me."

"Yes, of course," she said, bumping into the wall of the narrow corridor as the ship gave another sharp lurch. Had they run aground? Struck some land or rocks somehow?

But Captain Morris was a seasoned sailor. Surely he wouldn't make such a mistake…

The shouting had ceased by the time Jane and Zaren were making their way up the short set of steps that would take them to the main deck. The door that led to the outside loomed just above them when he paused, listening and, as was his way, sniffing at the myriad of scents in the air. All was strangely silent, and then suddenly there was the sound of thudding footsteps just above them, followed by the definite noise of altercation.

When it became quiet again, Zaren began to ease open the door that led to the deck.

"Where is she?" demanded a voice.

Zaren reacted instantly, spinning Jane around and shoving her behind him—for she was the only *she* on the ship. She felt his muscles quiver with tension as he looked about, and could read his mind as he searched for a way to protect her, hide her—

Someone shouted on the deck above, and then there was a sound…a sound that made the hair on Jane's neck stand on end. It was…violent and wet and…

Zaren stiffened against her, his nostrils flaring as he drew in whatever new smell was on the air. She felt rage and fear shuttle through him—fear, she knew, not for himself or for anyone else on the ship but her.

For Jane smelled it now too: blood.

"Bring her to me, or this man is the next to die," proclaimed the voice. "You have until I reach the count of three. One…!"

She contained the gasp, barely covering her mouth in time to smother it. Eyes wide, she pushed at Zaren, trying to free herself from his powerful grip. "No," she said, "no, I can't let them—"

"Two!"

"Jane, don't be a fool," he hissed. "Don't even *think* I will let them—"

"Three!"

There was another dull thud, this time directly above her head. She heard the sound of something heavy falling, and then rolling across the deck. Nausea surged in her belly, and Jane stared at Zaren in horror. "No," she said. "There's no other choice. Let us see…let us see what it is they want."

His eyes blazed down at her. "I know what they want. They want *you*. I won't let them have you, Jane, I cannot."

"But there is nowhere for us to go, nowhere for me to hide…they'll find me—and after how many others? How many others will die? What about *you*?"

"Jane, *no*," he began, but it was too late.

"I'm *here*," she shouted, trying to push her way out of his arms.

"Jane, *no*," he roared. "No!"

But the door was open and figures stormed down the stairs, filling them with their shadowy bulk. One of them lunged for her, and Zaren roared, blocking him with a powerful upthrust of his forearm.

"Don't touch me," she snapped as the man slammed against the wall, then tumbled to the floor. "I shall come up, and you do not need to lay one finger on me." She gripped Zaren's arm, felt the muscles trembling beneath his skin as he fought to control himself.

His face was a black mask of fury as they climbed the steps. Jane's heart thudded, and she reminded herself to hold her head high and proud. Zaren would allow nothing to happen to her.

On the deck, a terrible sight greeted them, and for the first time, her confidence was shaken. The crew of *The Racing Gull* had been taken captive by a group of men who could only be described as pirates. A second ship, close and dark and threatening, loomed next to the *Gull*, and Jane was quick enough to spy the gangplanks that had been dropped as two narrow bridges from vessel to vessel.

Two distinct pools of blood, along with the heads and headless bodies from which they sprang, decorated the wooden deck in a grisly fashion. Captain Morris stood to the side, his arms bound behind him, and a man Jane vaguely recognized as one of the *Gull*'s mates had a gun shoved into his chin.

"Take him!" cried a voice as soon as Jane and Zaren came into view. "Quickly, for he is a beast!"

Zaren had only a moment to give Jane a desperate look followed by a wild cry before three men launched themselves from above, landing on top of him with a heavy black net, just as a fourth man grabbed her by the arm and yanked her out of reach.

She shrieked and began to fight, kicking and clawing as she watched the three men and their heavy black net imprison Zaren. He roared like a feral cat, the sound so lifelike and fierce that several of their attackers looked around as if to see a four-legged feline ready to pounce. And though her husband was magnificently strong and fast, the three subdued him with the help of the tangling net and the heavy wooden clubs they brandished. They slammed and thudded into him over and over, even as he roared and lunged while hampered by the heavy covering.

"Stop!" she shrieked, whirling in the grip of the man who'd grabbed her. "Stop it! Whatever it is you want, you shall have… only cease beating him!"

"Of course I shall have what I want," said the man…who looked vaguely familiar to her. "And you are indeed the prize I was promised. I have no doubt you will easily snare Zenovia's attention, and put me in a most welcome position."

Jane felt the blood leech from her face. "You! I know you… You were…you are a friend of Darkdale." Her head was light, and the world spun a little as she remembered the faces and—more worrisomely—the cocks and hands and tongues employed by those who called Kellan Darkdale friend. He had no name, but she remembered him well.

"Indeed. And you, my lovely, delicious darling, will be coming with me."

Zaren roared and lunged again, this time dragging the heavy weight of the net. He slammed into her captor, knocking both of them heavily to the ground. She pulled away, running, stumbling, dashing *somewhere*, looking for a weapon, something, *anything* to use to save herself, to save her husband and the good captain, but when she spun back around, she stopped as if slamming into a brick wall.

"No!" she screamed. "*No!*"

But she was too late. As she watched, the kicking, bucking, black-wrapped bundle of her beloved husband was lifted by no fewer than six men and heaved over the side of the ship…

The resulting splash acted like punctuation to the sentence of her life: a short, sharp period. An end. *The* end.

Jane ran to the side of the deck, slipping through spilled blood and evading the hands that grabbed for her. "Zaren! *Zaren!*" she screamed.

The empty black net fluttered against the side of the ship, hooked on something that had caused it to unfurl as Zaren was pitched overboard.

Even as strong hands dragged her away from the edge, Jane searched for something, for a shadowy head to emerge or a hand…

And just as a heavy black cloak enveloped her, Jane saw him.

Zaren. Erupting from the sea like furious beast.

Relief and hope surged in her, and then everything went black.

JANE ARCHED IN A LONG, LAZY STRETCH and reached languidly for her husband.

The bed next to her was cool and empty. She opened her eyes, expecting to see him sitting in the chair, looking out the porthole with his spyglass.

That was when she realized it *wasn't her bed.*

And she wasn't in their small chamber.

She bolted upright, suddenly assaulted by the memories and terror of the attack on *The Racing Gull.*

"Zaren," she whispered, pressing a hand to her mouth. "Oh my God, Zaren…" Her heart thudded harshly and her stomach roiled. "What have I done?"

Then Jane shook her head. No. She'd saved the lives of any number of sailors who would have been beheaded—or worse— if she hadn't stepped forward. But had her stubbornness caused the death of the man she loved more than anything?

Jane bit her lip, drawing in a long, deep breath. She had seen his head bobbing in the ocean. She *had.*

If anyone could have survived that fall, that attack, it was Zaren.

And if he were alive, he would stop at nothing to find her… wherever she was. And so she must do everything possible to stay safe and alive until he did.

She sat up and looked around the chamber. It was smaller than the one she'd shared with Zaren, but the gentle rolling of her environment told her she was on another ship. She was still dressed in the shift she'd pulled on before leaving her room with Zaren…and it boded well for her virtue, such as it was, that she was still clothed.

Just then, the door opened.

"Ah, then. You're awake, lovely Jane." The man who'd taken her—the man she recognized as a friend of the controlling and masterful Kellan Darkdale—stood in the doorway. "I'm very glad to see that, for you've been sleeping for three days and we are very nearly at our destination."

Three days? She vaguely remembered a pinprick in her arm and realized she must have been drugged.

"I am Lady Hampstead to you, you disgusting cur," she said haughtily. "And I need not tell you what fate awaits you when I return to London and inform the Met that you've abducted a lady of the peerage and attempted to murder my husband. However, your immediate cooperation may possibly lighten your sentence."

When his eyes raked over her, she made a move to cover herself with the flimsy blanket. He laughed, stepping inside the chamber. The door closed sharply behind him. "You need not bother, my dear Lady Hampstead. I have no interest in you in that way—at least at the moment. However, it's the rest of the crew about which you should worry. And that is what I've come here to tell you."

She drew herself up, aware of the picture she must make: disheveled, half dressed, and with her reams of fiery hair tumbling over her shoulders and the blanket. This nameless man was probably the first one she'd ever encountered who did *not* wish to touch, probe, stroke, taste, or otherwise enjoy her body. But she shivered at the reminder of the rest of the sex-starved crew, and what might happen if she were given over to them. Jane pulled her courage and every bit of strength about her. "Return me to London immediately, whoever you are. If you are lucky, my husband survived being thrown off the ship and you will only be charged with *attempted* murder and kidnapping—"

"I beg your pardon, my lady. I am remiss in not introducing myself. Captain Bradley Holt, at your service. And unfortunately, my lady, your request must be denied. You see, I do have plans for you, but they do not involve returning to London." He smiled and gestured to the sea beyond the walls of the chamber. "We are headed for the Lost City of Amazonia, which is on an island in the Atlantic not far from the coast of Nigeria, but well off the normal trade routes. It is a place with which I've been desperate to do some trading—for they grow the most valuable of all hallucinogenic substances there, called *blinkalo lobia*—known more commonly in the opium dens as heather-hash. It can only be found in their gated city, and the Amazonians are very shrewd trading partners. You are going to be the key to my new arrangement with them, for I am certain they will find you quite fascinating."

A knock came at the door. "And there is your bath, my lady. I will need to you to wash and dress, for the last three days have left you rather…pungent." He wrinkled his nose. "You smell of coitus and other unpleasantries. And unless you require assistance, which I'm certain any number of the gentlemen on this ship would be happy to provide, you will refresh yourself quickly and without help. For we will be approaching the city within the hour." His eyes danced with excitement.

Before Jane could respond, he opened the door and three men came in, carrying a large tub half filled with steaming water. As she watched in astonishment—and lust, for it had been some time since she'd bathed—more of the crew came in bearing buckets of warm water.

Each of them looked at her with hot, lascivious eyes, clearly more than ready to assist with any sort of lady's maid task in order to be alone in the chamber with her. But her captor stood guard at the door until the tub was filled and an elegant emerald and sapphire gown was laid upon the bed.

When she sat mutely on the edge of the bed, her arms crossed over her chest, Holt's face darkened. "You will be ready in three-quarters of an hour…or I will allow the entire crew to take their turns—er—assisting you to prepare. And then, whatever is left of you, I will leave to bake in the sun for two days on the deck where all can see you."

With that, he left the chamber.

Jane fumed, but she wasn't a fool. Whoever the Amazonians were, she would at least have a chance to plead her case to them. Once she explained she was a lady of the peerage, surely they would help her return to England. Perhaps they'd even assist her to find Zaren, and *The Racing Gull*.

Amazonians… Hm. The Amazons were legendary female warriors. Could these be descendants of the storied women? If they were, surely if it was a matriarchal society, they'd be even more willing to help someone of their own gender. Especially when they learned she'd been abducted and brought there against her will.

Jane sank into the bath, unable to completely muffle a sigh of pleasure as she submerged in the steaming water. She was feeling slightly more optimistic at what lay ahead. At least she was to remain untouched and kept safe from Holt's crew, and even he had no designs on her.

All that would be left was to convince the Amazonians to help her return to London…and to pray Zaren had made it safely aboard a ship or to land.

She was nearly ready at the appointed time, garbed in the emerald and sapphire froth—but not without difficulty, for the evening gown was heavy with many layers of crinolines and skirts.

"Allow me, my lady," said Holt when he opened the door to find her struggling with the buttons. He made quick work of them, then stepped back to examine her appearance.

Jane had no mirror, but she'd braided part of her long hair into a slender plait, and then pinned up the rest of the curls in a loose knot at the back of her head. She could not deny the gown was stunning and highly fashionable. With her green eyes and fire-gold hair, she knew it looked good on her, and her fine appearance would likely give credence to her story of abduction. The bodice cut straight across her chest, leaving arms and shoulders bare, then molded to her breasts and waist like a pair of greedy hands. Lace and flounces decorated the skirt in tiers, and dragged across the floor in a short train when she took Holt's arm to follow him out of the chamber. He had also seen fit to provide flimsy silk slippers and a lacy green wrap to cover her bare shoulders. However, she was given no jewels.

"Perfect," Holt said, looking at her with a cool, objective eye. Not a hint of lust or desire in his face, but something more like satisfaction. He made no other comment as he escorted her from the ship's hold up and out onto the deck, where his crew watched avidly. Jane shuddered, glad she'd escaped the fate of their dirty hands and lascivious mouths on her…and held her head high as they disembarked the ship.

The City of the Amazonians was white, and it sparkled in the sunlight as if coated by silver. Jane saw many domed roofs of various heights, most of which were decorated by white and blue flags. In the center was the largest and most ornate building—presumably where the ruler lived—and it was a beautifully symmetrical collection of tall, slender domes. The entire city was barricaded by a seemingly impenetrable wall made of white marble, and as she and Holt approached, along with a contingent of his own men, they were met by four tall, powerful guards at a massive gate.

"Identify yourself and your purpose," demanded one of the helmeted guards, holding—but not brandishing—a long, curved sword. It wasn't until the guard spoke that Jane realized it was a woman…a tall, muscular woman who stood larger than most men. Like her companions, she was wearing black leather breeches and a matching vest over muscled arms and legs. Long boots reached over her knees, and her armor was of hammered silver. Her shoulders were broader than that of Jane's captor.

Holt released Jane's arm and stepped forward. "I am Captain Bradley Holt, at your service. I've come to discuss a trade agreement with High Chief Zenovia." For a moment, Jane considered the option of bolting forward right then and asking for the guards to give her sanctuary from her abductor.

"And what makes you believe the high chief would deign to see you?"

"We bring gifts, of course," replied Holt, gesturing to the chest two of his men carried between them. "Gems and jewels… as well as a special adornment from my native England…all carefully chosen to appeal to the high chief. Please be assured, I offer a most lucrative proposal in return for an audience."

The guards conferred, then it appeared as if some sort of messenger was sent off into the depths of the city walls. Jane thought once again about asking for help, but Holt returned to her side and took her arm firmly.

"Remember my promise, dear lady," he murmured. "Behave yourself and act appropriately, or you will be a welcome feast for my crew. And then for the sun and wind and rain." He smiled down at her with something like affection.

She lifted her chin haughtily and turned away. Bastard. The moment she had an opportunity to speak to the high chief, she would explain the situation. It was obvious the Amazonians were not particularly welcome to strangers. Surely that would be a point in her favor.

"The high chief will see you."

Holt's excitement was palpable as he took Jane's arm firmly. They followed the messenger into the city, walking on a white stone pathway. Everything inside the walls was just as clean and white and sparkling as it had appeared from her view on the ship.

The only color was that of green grass and leaves, along with the occasional brown trunk of a tree—and even those hues seemed subdued. All other vegetation was white flowers or silvery leaves. The bricks were white. The lampposts were white. Even the clothing of the few people (all women) they passed—which seemed to be a sort of livery—was spotless white, down to the shoes.

Jane didn't realize until this moment that Holt and his men were dressed all in black and white, and she was the only spot of color in their entourage.

Indeed, as they made their way toward another gate that led into the palace, she felt countless pairs of eyes watching them…watching her. And when they crossed over a small moat that surrounded the castle, she caught a glimpse of herself in the company of all the black and white: a beacon of sapphire, emerald, and fire. Intense and bold.

Her palms became damp as they were led into the palace. Double doors, guarded by more female sentries (these not quite as large and hulking as the others, but still taller and more muscular by far than Jane), were flung open…and there in front of them spread a circular room.

Holt strode forward, leaving Jane to follow behind the two men carrying the chest of jewels. She hesitated, but was prodded forward by Holt's other men, who were positioned behind. The female guards looked at her with cold interest as she stepped into the chamber.

Vast. Tall, open, and opulent. The décor was silver and white with an occasional—very occasional—glittering aquamarine accent. Light poured in from windows set around the base of a domed ceiling that rose high above a dais, on which there sat a silver throne.

Next to the throne was a much smaller chair—unoccupied—and arranged on the circular stairs leading to the dais were several guards, ladies in waiting, and other servants. As far as Jane could tell, every one was female. They stood such that they could see both the throne and the chamber at large. Silvery trees and palm fronds ruffled lightly from some unknown breeze. An unfamiliar scent hung in the air—something sweet and lush and heady. It seemed to be wafting from a trio of shallow bowls on three-legged stands.

On the throne sat a woman.

She was tall and solid, and her toned, muscular arms were bared by a black, toga-like gown. She wore a silver band around her upper arm, and another silver one across her forehead like a low-riding tiara. The band was a crown, and it kept her thick, moonbeam hair from tumbling into her face. Instead, waves of it fell over her shoulders. Even from across the chamber, Jane could see intelligence in the woman's dark eyes. Yet the expression in her attractive face was one of boredom and distaste as Holt came forward and made a very low, obeisant bow.

"Captain Holt. You again. Why on earth would you believe I will consider a trade agreement with you when I have already indicated my disinterest in such an arrangement?" The woman—presumably the high chief—had a voice that filled the room with its volume and confidence. In fact, every element of the woman exuded power.

Jane's sliver of hope grew into something larger. This was someone who was no victim, no subservient female.

Holt rose from his bow. "But this time, your grace, madame High Chief Zenovia, I have brought you gifts. I was remiss in not doing so during my last visit—"

"Gifts? What on *earth* would I have need of from you, you puny, weak Englishman? I have all I would ever need here in my beloved city. I have no interest in anything from you, and the only reason I allowed you audience was to make *certain* you would not darken my court ever again." She turned and gestured languidly to a group of six female guards who stood at the ready. "Take him. And all of his *men* and put them to work until we determine which of them might be put to other use."

This was Jane's opportunity. She rushed forward far enough to be seen, then fell into a deep curtsy in front of the throne as several guards lunged toward her, pikes and swords at the ready. She did not cower, nor did she rise from her curtsy. "Madame. Your grace. I beg sanctuary and assistance from you and your people," she announced loudly enough to be heard from her near-prostrate pose.

There was silence for a moment, and at last, "Rise, then, woman, and explain yourself."

Jane did as she was bid, and the guards fell away, ordered by some unseen command. After a brief glance at the woman on the throne, she kept her eyes slightly averted—neither too bold nor too subservient—and said, "Thank you, your grace, Madam Zenovia. I—"

"Gifts! Do you now see what I have brought you?" Holt cried out, struggling in the grip of the guards. "You cannot imprison me when I bring you such jewels! Such a treasure! How dare—"

His voice was choked off, and though the brutal sound of it made the hair at the back of Jane's neck lift, she did not deign to turn and see just what had been done to Holt. Instead, she looked up again at Zenovia, only to find the woman's attention fixed on her.

"Speak, then, woman."

"Of course. I request safety and assistance from you, for that man seized me from the ship on which I was traveling and made me his prisoner. He brought me here against my will, and I beg of you to assist me in returning to my country of England…and to find my husband, who was thrown overboard during the attack. My husband is the Viscount Hampstead, a very wealthy man in England, and he will compensate you handsomely for any assistance you provide me." Jane sank into a curtsy once more.

"Rise, then, Lady Hampstead." Zenovia drummed her fingertips on the arm of her throne. Her dark eyes glittered with interest. "Your husband—he is very wealthy, you say? And a peer of England? Not like that silly, puny fop of a man who thought to *bargain* with me or tempt me with the likes of jewels and gems? Indeed." She nodded regally. "I shall accept you as my guest for the time being, Lady Hampstead. You shall join me for dinner this evening, at which time we will discuss your predicament and determine the best way to proceed. Alena! See to it that my lady here is made comfortable until we dine."

A gust of relief swept over Jane as she turned to follow the dark-eyed Alena from the chamber. She released her pent-up breath in a long, slow whoosh.

Everything will be all right. Zaren is alive. He is. *And you are one step closer to finding him again.*

JANE HAD THE OPPORTUNITY FOR A NAP in the chamber that had been assigned to her, with Alena promising to return to help her freshen up before dinner. She found no fault with the chamber, and her optimism grew—for the room was clearly meant for a guest and not a prisoner. It was large, open, and airy, with windows shielded by translucent shades of paper (white, of course), and, amazingly enough, a small square tub with warm *running water* set in the floor of the room.

She was delighted when the promised "freshening up" turned out to be a full bath in the sunken tub. Alena and another maid assisted her, soaping her body and then plastering her face and neck with a mud-like substance. While Jane lay there, allowing the heavy, aromatic mud to dry (such a curious experience), the two women used impersonal hands to spread a very warm goo over her legs, under her arms, and, strangely, around the apex of her thighs. Jane peeked when something firm was pressed into the warm, sticky substance, and saw that it was a strip of fabric. She shrieked, bolting half off the table, when Alena yanked the fabric away, and then the other maid did the same…and they did this over and over until her body was denuded of hair in those areas.

At first, Jane attempted to protest and to push their hands off, but they ignored her and guided her back onto the table. She considered ordering them away, but in the end decided it was more prudent to cooperate with these customs of the Amazonians, since she was hoping for assistance and cooperation from them. Nevertheless, the stripping left her skin achy and pink and stinging. What little of the fiery red hair left between her legs was trimmed very short and neat. Alena massaged a soothing lotion—again, with impersonal hands that did not linger—into Jane's abused skin, then washed the mud from her face with steaming cloths. Finally, Jane's long, thick hair was plaited into an impossibly intricate mass of braids intertwined with flowers and gemstones.

Like Zenovia and the other women who were not acting as guards, Jane was garbed in a toga-like gown that fastened over one shoulder with a sapphire brooch and was gathered at the opposite side of her waist by another. One shoulder was bare, and the gown fell in neat pleats from shoulder to waist, and then waist to floor. To her surprise—for all the other clothing she'd seen was white, except for the high chief's black toga—the gown provided for her was a brilliant sea green, embroidered with blue designs. The fabric was so light and airy she felt as if she were wearing nothing at all—and in fact, since no undergarments had been provided, her breasts were left to hang and jounce freely beneath the gathers of the toga. Her nipples thrust out like two hard points jutting through the otherwise smooth and neat folds of the fabric, and with her every movement, the material slid sensuously over them. The gown fell to the floor in an elegant cascade, and her newly smooth thighs brushed against each other as, barefooted, she followed Alena down a high, arched corridor.

"Madame," said Alena when they came to a set of relatively unassuming double doors. Two expressionless guards, female, of course, stood at the outside and opened the doors in tandem to reveal a beautiful chamber that was more cozy and sedate than the ostentatious, high-ceilinged throne room.

"Lady Hampstead. Please, come in." Zenovia stood at a desk, but she looked over as Jane appeared in the doorway. "That will be all, Alena."

As the door closed behind, leaving the two of them alone—at least as far as Jane could tell; there might be some servants waiting in one of the silk-draped corners—Jane stepped into the chamber and looked around. A low, square table set for two also held a large decanter of red wine and several silver-domed dishes. Low, sofa-like benches lined two sides of the table, meeting at one corner in an ell. There was a large, curtained area in one part of the room, and Jane suspected a bed might be hidden therein, for the rest of the chamber seemed like a very large private sitting room.

A soft gurgle of water drew her attention, and Jane glanced over to see a rectangular pool set into the floor. It ran along the length of one wall, and was three times the size of the one in her guest chamber. Everything gleamed white and silver with occasional pale blue accents.

"What brings you from England?" asked Zenovia as she gestured for Jane to take a seat at the table.

Jane sat and accepted the glass of wine poured by the high chief. She couldn't help but feel a combination of surprise, delight, and apprehension that this powerful and strict leader of Amazonia would choose to dine alone with her.

But perhaps she merely missed female companionship—someone to whom she wasn't a ruler or mistress.

"My husband and I were on our way to Madagascar," Jane explained. "We've been married only four months, but since we both spent quite a bit of time there previously, we decided to go for our honeymoon."

"A fascinating choice for a honeymoon," Zenovia replied with a genuine smile. She'd taken a seat as well, and instead of being positioned across the table from each other, they were seated at perpendicular sides…which gave their conversation a more intimate feel.

Jane noticed again how tall and solid and strong her hostess was. Although definitely very feminine, with proportionately sized breasts and sleek, defined hips, Zenovia possessed toned, muscular arms and broad shoulders. She had regular, attractive features, with a full, wide mouth and almond-shaped eyes. Her skin was smooth and fair, even lighter than Jane's English peaches-and-cream coloring.

The high chieftain's bare feet, though very wide and long, were adorned with silver rings on the toes and a single cuff around an ankle that gave them a particularly female appearance. Her blond hair was plaited into a single braid that fell down her back, and the silver band that she had worn around the front of her forehead was gone. As before, she wore black.

"Are you not hungry?" she asked, gesturing to the table. She removed the silver domes covering a variety of food—some unfamiliar to Jane, but it all looked and smelled delicious.

She said so, and, following her hostess's lead, began to fill her plate and eat. As she did so, they continued to converse, with Zenovia leading the choice of topic.

She wanted to know all about what had happened on *The Racing Gull*—where they had been, what the name of Holt's ship was (*Chromium*), and why Jane believed Zaren hadn't perished when he was thrown over the ship.

"Because," Jane said, reaching for her glass of wine—which had been refilled yet again, "he is the strongest, fiercest man I've ever known. I saw him surface in the water, and I know of what he is capable. Nothing would keep him from me. *Nothing*."

Zenovia nodded, her eyes lingering on Jane. "I am not surprised you should attract such devotion from a man. With your coloring—that incredible, bright hair and your emerald eyes—you are like a beacon that draws the eye. And it isn't only your appearance that demands appreciation."

Jane paused with the glass halfway to her mouth, and felt her heart do a little trip. Zenovia was looking at her with such an expression of…consideration? Contemplation? Fascination?

"Do you play chess, Lady Hampstead? Or may I call you Jane?"

"Please…of course I am Jane to you. I'm very appreciative of your hospitality, and your willingness to help me."

Zenovia gave an enigmatic smile and rang an unseen bell. And sure enough, they weren't alone: two servants appeared immediately from a discreet corner and cleared away the food and serving wares, leaving only the wine and some water. Then one of them brought a large chess set—one of the most beautiful Jane had ever seen—and arranged it on the table between them.

Unable to resist, she reached for the queen to examine it. The piece was made from colorless glass shot with cracks and imperfections. It was beautiful. The other half of the set was made from translucent white glass.

"Now," said Zenovia. "In a moment, we shall play. But first…"

Her eyes glittered as she moved toward Jane.

The next thing Jane knew, Zenovia had pushed her back into the cushions and covered her mouth with hers.

Jane was so stunned at the sudden, completely shocking onslaught that at first she didn't react…but when Zenovia deepened the kiss with determination and greed, she tried to twist away and free her mouth.

But her hostess was too strong, and had positioned herself expertly, holding Jane firmly in place. The kiss went deeper, and Jane could no longer keep from responding. Zenovia's lips were firm and warm, and she licked and kissed and sucked at Jane's plump ones. Her tongue thrust boldly into her mouth, strong and sleek and demanding, tangling and taking from Jane as she panted beneath her, familiar pleasure vibrating through her belly and down. Jane found herself taking Zenovia's bold, thick tongue, caressing it with her own, and then discovering the heat and wetness and lushness of Zenovia's mouth as lust began to rise within her.

By now, Jane was caught beneath Zenovia, pressed well down into the soft cushions of the sofa on which she'd sat. The sharp plane of Zenovia's hip dug into Jane's belly, and one solid leg straddled her as the chieftain pulled away from the kiss. Then, her hands strong and quick, Zenovia caught hold of Jane's wrists and moved them out of the way, positioning them firmly at her waist.

Her lips were full and glistening, her eyes dark and glittery. Unlike Jane, who was panting with surprise and shock, Zenovia was only slightly out of breath. But there was no mistaking the lust burning in her expression. "You taste as delicious as I'd hoped. But…" Her face tightened and her eyes narrowed in anticipation as she transferred both of Jane's wrists to one hand. That left the other one free to slide down along Jane's gown.

"What…" Jane said, still out of breath from a kiss that had left her more hot and aroused than she'd like. Her lips throbbed, and her nipples had sharpened into tight little spikes, jutting up through the sensuous silk of her gown. They shuddered and shivered as she tried to catch her breath and subdue the sudden, unexpected onslaught of lust that had overtaken her.

Zenovia was looking at them, her own breasts showing tight and aroused through the folds of her own gown… hovering near Jane in large, heavy teardrops, but not touching. Jane could not take her gaze from the sight of them, so close, quivering and tempting and lush.

The chieftain made no response to Jane's attempt at speaking. Instead, she kept her eyes trained on her guest as the free hand slid beneath the folds of Jane's toga and found the juncture of her thighs. Before Jane could press her legs together, those large, bold fingers found her: soft and full and wet.

"What…" Jane tried again, a little more stridently this time. "I don't—"

Two fingers thrust inside her, deep and fast, and Jane arched in surprise. "Oh!" A rush of heat flushed over her, sudden and strong, and she looked at her hostess in shock, trying to pull out of the hot haze. "This…isn't…what…"

But those fingers remained inside her, and they moved slowly and with expertise, sliding in and out, then spreading wide and curving up inside her to stroke a point of pleasure she hadn't even realized was there…and then a third finger joined them and Jane couldn't hold back a gasp as the rhythm became faster and more regular, faster…faster…She gasped, panted, moaned, tried to pull away, tried to keep her hips from moving and meeting those strokes, but she was trapped—both by her hostess and by the desires of her own body.

Zenovia watched her without blinking, almost impersonally, as she fucked Jane with her fingers, stroking, exploring, caressing…teasing and coaxing and then becoming demanding and rough. Lust overtook Jane, and her body became tight and hot, her quim dripping with juices that made soft, wet sounds that seemed to punctuate her arousal. Jane bit her lip, writhing and lost in the moment and unable—unwilling—to claw her way out of the dark well of desire.

She closed her eyes, unable to bear seeing the satisfaction in her seducer's face as she gave herself over to the sensation she could no longer fight. Something pressed against Jane's little pearl, the tiny throbbing center of her being, stroking it oh so gently as the fingers pumped faster and faster. She could no longer remain silent. Her moans and sighs filled her own ears as she shivered and shifted and pumped, meeting the deep, pressing thrusts with her hips, climbing to the heights of release.

When the climax came, it was sharp and hard and fast, shooting through her body like a whip crack that left her stunned and shaken and a little ashamed. The fingers withdrew; Zenovia moved away, and, still panting, collapsed into the sofa cushions. Jane at last opened her eyes.

Shaky, confused, and yet incredibly sated, she pulled herself up into a sitting position. Zenovia had returned to her seat and was arranging the chess pieces as if…as if nothing had happened. As if that interlude had never occurred, and they were preparing to play a game of chess after dinner.

Still trembling, Jane looked down at herself and discovered that, though her breasts were tighter and more aroused than ever—completely outlined by the clinging toga—and her thighs slipped together at their apex, her netherlips wet and full and still throbbing with little licks of delight, she was still completely clothed.

It was as if nothing had happened.

"I…" She tried to speak, but didn't know what to say.

Then Zenovia looked up at her, and Jane was nearly felled by the intense heat and lust in her eyes. "You are even more than I had hoped for." She smiled with pure delight and lifted her glistening fingers to her nostrils, smelling deeply. "Delicious. Incredible. And so very so passionate. So easily aroused. And all without any artificial enhancements. I couldn't be more pleased, Lady Hampstead. *Jane.*"

Jane reached for a goblet of wine and gulped half of it. It was very light and watered down—very nearly just grape juice—and it was true. She'd felt no effects from the several glasses she'd already imbibed.

"And now, if you are as interesting and intelligent as you seem to be…why, that combined with your beauty and your passion…will make you the perfect woman." Zenovia sipped her own wine, looking at Jane from over the rim. Her eyes were still filled with lust and heat, but other than that, she gave no other indication of her thoughts.

"I don't understand," Jane managed to say, collecting all of her thoughts. She started to stand. "I mean to say, I appreciate the compliment, but—"

Zenovia pulled her back down with a firm grip. "We shall play chess, Jane. And we will make a wager on the outcome of the game."

Jane had no choice but to sit. "What sort of wager?"

Zenovia looked at her, wickedness flashing in her eyes. "I mean to keep you, Lady Hampstead. *Jane*."

"*Keep* me?" She couldn't control the fury in her voice. "What do you mean *keep* me? You cannot *keep* me. I am a free woman, an English citizen, a member of—"

"And your *fire*! By the gods, Jane, you continue to enthrall me. And this is only the beginning." Zenovia swept a hand over the chess game. "We shall play and we will have a wager on the outcome of the game. If you win, I will release you… tomorrow. After we spend what will, I'm certain, be a most pleasurable night. And if I win…you shall become my most favored concubine."

IV

ANE'S HAND TREMBLED AS SHE set the rook in place. "Check."

She kept her expression of triumph subdued, looking down at the board while Zenovia considered her next move.

The most stressful, important game of chess she'd ever played. It had taken all the clarity she possessed to play carefully, to take her time with her moves, and to think ahead with strategy. Jane was an excellent chess player thanks to Effie, who'd spent many an evening playing with her while her father worked in his study.

But considering that her body still hummed, and she was utterly aware of the woman sitting across from her—and the predicament in which she found herself—Jane had had a difficult time concentrating.

But now, she'd just played what she hoped would be the third-to-last move in a game she would win…and then…

Jane swallowed hard. Though she despised the situation in which she found herself, she also could not keep from looking at Zenovia…noticing the thrust of heavy raindrop breasts that shivered behind her toga, and the full sweep of her lips…and the *hand*. The hand, the fingers that had so easily and ruthlessly drawn pleasure from her.

The scent of Jane's own musk still hung in the air.

Zenovia reached with that very hand to move her king's bishop into place, and Jane's heart nearly stopped. *That was not the move I expected.*

"Check…mate." Zenovia looked up at her with a most satisfied expression, her hot, dark eyes pinning Jane in place.

A rush of cold shock followed by a wave of heat flooded her as she stared at the board. *No,* she thought. *No!*

But there was no way out. No escape. The game was over.

"You were much more skilled than I anticipated, but in the end, lovely, lovely Jane, you've succumbed." Zenovia's voice dropped into a caress. "Nevertheless, I'm not at all disappointed. You were more of a challenge than most men I've played. And because of that, you will take on a most powerful, important position."

"No," Jane said, standing abruptly, moving out of reach of Zenovia. "You cannot keep me here. You cannot force me to stay and be your…"

"Concubine." Zenovia smiled and rose easily from her seat. "You have no idea of the honor which I would bestow on you."

"It's no honor to me. I'm a married woman, I love my husband, and I have no desire to be your concubine or to even stay here in Amazonia. I want only to return to London." Jane started toward the door, unsure of what she would do if she even made it through, but determined to try.

To her surprise, Zenovia didn't attempt to stop her. And when she reached the exit and flung the doors open, Jane realized why: the guards were there. And they were not about to allow her to pass. Long pikes came down and blocked the way, and one of them prodded at her, leaving Jane no choice but to back into the chamber.

The doors closed again and she turned, her heart pounding, her breathing fast and shallow, and her body tingling with unwelcome anticipation.

Zenovia appeared to have waited patiently for Jane to realize she would not be going free, and in the mean time she'd walked over to the large sunken pool. Through the roaring in her ears, the thudding of her pulse, Jane heard the splash of water as it tumbled enthusiastically into the large pool. A soft floral scent filled the air.

"Come, Jane. You won't be leaving…and you might just as well relax." Zenovia turned away, and when she pivoted back around, she pulled the silky black toga from her body and let it fall in a crumpled, dark cloud on the tile floor. "And enjoy."

Jane could not pull her eyes away, for Zenovia was pale and beautiful. Strong, tall, powerful, with lean muscles in her arms and legs, a firm, ridged belly with a flat navel. Not a soft curve anywhere but at her breasts. They were the size of grapefruits, hanging in gentle teardrops that swayed enticingly with each movement. She had dark areolae and eager red nipples, and the patch of closely trimmed hair at the apex of her thighs was the same corn-silk color as that of her braid.

"I…" Jane's mouth went dry even as that subtle tingle in her belly darted again, deep and strong. She knew what was going to happen. She knew those hands, that mouth, that body would be on hers…against hers.

And already her own desire grew. Already, she felt herself swell and dampen and begin to throb.

"I have been patient thus far, but I warn you, Jane, it is not boundless. Clearly you are a passionate, experienced woman who enjoys pleasure. Allow me to give you some."

"I am married. I love my husband," Jane said again, desperation in her voice. "I…" She moistened her lips. She really had no choice. "One night. One night, and then you will release me."

Zenovia held out her hand, the cords of her muscles long and taut. "Come to me, Jane. Let me give you pleasure."

"Please…" Jane said, her heart thudding. "Promise me you will allow me to leave. Tomorrow."

Zenovia's eyes darkened, and Jane's heart lurched at the fury suddenly blazing therein. She remembered suddenly, acutely, that she was at the mercy of this queenlike woman, that there were guards everywhere, and that she had nowhere to go and no one to help her should she be released or find escape. "You try my patience. Take that off." Zenovia's voice cracked out like a whip, and a surge of apprehension overtook Jane.

With trembling fingers, she unfastened the brooch at her waist and then the one at her shoulder. Once released, the fabric slithered down over her breasts, belly, and thighs like a silky hand and puddled in a soft pile at her feet.

"Magnificent," Zenovia purred, but the burn of desire in her eyes was not nearly as controlled…and its intensity frightened Jane. "Come to me."

Jane sensed she must obey or risk truly infuriating the woman, and so she walked steadily toward her. Her heart beat faster and her palms became damp. Sensation sparked through her at every jounce of her breasts, and the delicate swipe of pressure against her tiny pearl with each step. Her hair, which had come loose during Zenovia's gentle attack, brushed against her skin like a trickle of fingers.

Jane expected to be dragged close, and kissed and fondled… but when she reached Zenovia, the other woman merely held out a hand. When she took it, strong fingers closed around her smaller ones and the chieftain took her toward the pool. The water steamed and bubbled with some delicate white froth, and the gentle floral scent was stronger now, filling Jane's nostrils.

Zenovia led the way into the water, stepping down several steps until she was submerged to just beneath her breasts in the pool. She tugged Jane after her, gripping her firmly as if to ensure she didn't pull away. The hot water closed around her, lifting the tips of her hair, relaxing her muscles and releasing an even stronger flowery essence.

She hadn't stepped all the way into the water when Zenovia turned and met her at the end of the stairs. Here, Jane was taller than normal, and her hostess didn't tower over her quite as much, so they were nearly eye to eye.

"Surely this is not the first time you have been with a woman," murmured Zenovia, wrapping an arm around Jane's waist. She pulled her close so their bellies plastered together and the water surged around them, then reached up to brush a lock of hair from Jane's face. Their breasts touched, and Jane couldn't help but shiver at the unexpected, unfamiliar sensation of soft globes of flesh brushing against her.

"It is," she whispered, trying not to look at the way their nipples *nearly* touched, nearly kissed…quivering so close to each other. Hers seemed to strain toward the other, larger, darker pair…

"Someone with your passion…your responsiveness? I can hardly believe it," Zenovia said. "There has been no woman to touch you and taste you…to give you pleasure the way only a female can?"

Images flashed through Jane's mind. There had been Marcine, of course, and the women in the jungle village…but that was different. She hadn't *been* with them. Not in the way she suspected was about to happen now.

"No," she managed to say. Her mouth was dry, yet her pulse pounded and her belly was filled with the flutter of wings.

Zenovia smiled at this—a smile that was hot and triumphant and possessive. Then she pulled Jane close and began to kiss her thoroughly, easing her into the steaming pool as she did so.

The sensation of warm, scented water lapping gently against her sensitive skin and the damp mist, combined with the hot, slick kiss and Zenovia's bold hands as they covered Jane's arse, washed away the last bit of her reticence. The next thing she knew, Jane was kissing her back, their tongues thrusting strong and deep, teeth nipping gently and yet fiercely on lips, jaw, the soft part of her ear. Breasts crushed together, bodies hot and damp, hair tangled, the alluring smell of flowers and cinnamon and Zenovia…

Still holding Jane close, Zenovia sank lower into the pool until their long hair floated around them like fiery red and corn-silk seaweed. Their bodies slipped and slid against the other, one all soft curves and the other an erotic mix of firm muscle, generous hips, and sleek, heavy globes.

Jane realized she'd slid her legs around Zenovia's waist, supported by the water as well as her lover's hands. Her quim was hot and full against the taut belly beneath her, and Jane found herself unable to keep from pressing against her, jolting and nudging against the smooth skin.

"So eager." Zenovia laughed when she realized what Jane was doing. She released her into the pool, and Jane discovered it was deeper than she'd realized, for her feet didn't touch the ground and she was forced to tread water to keep from slipping under.

Holding her eyes, Zenovia sank beneath the water, and the next thing Jane knew, she was being dragged down too. She had barely enough time to snatch in a breath before the water closed around her…and so did Zenovia.

Jane arched and nearly gasped in a mouthful of water when the other woman's hot mouth covered one of her nipples. Hands, strong and sure, slid down along her torso, holding her at the hips as Zenovia kissed her, teasing the taut flesh with her tongue as their waterlogged bodies tangled like two mermaids.

Jane struggled to hold her breath as Zenovia kept her below the water, feasting on her as though she were a mermaid and could breathe beneath the surface. She battled between the necessity of holding her breath while desperately *needing* to gasp and moan and somehow relieve the delicious lust building inside her, and Jane's world became nothing but the pleasure of strong, delicious tugging at her nipple…incessant and demanding.

Lights flashed behind her closed eyes, and she knew she would have to breathe soon…but the pleasure was so beautiful, so hot and strong, and her netherlips throbbed and swelled, left unattended and ignored.

At last, just when she knew she could hold her breath no longer, Zenovia gathered her up and they shot up out of the water. Gasping and panting, Jane clung to the other woman, slipping along her curves and muscles, the world spinning and her body cool from the change of temperature.

Before she fully came to herself, Jane felt herself lifted completely out of the water. Zenovia set her on the edge of the pool in front of her. As Jane collapsed back onto the cold tile, still panting, aroused, and lightheaded, Zenovia spread her legs, holding them wide apart by the knees.

Jane felt as if she had burst free from some sort of chastity belt, for now, exposed and open, her quim seemed to expand and swell more fully. Her little pearl throbbed and ached for attention, and Jane felt the chill of the air against her hot, wet self.

Zenovia made a desperate, erotic sound that shot a stab of lust through Jane, and her fingers tightened on Jane's thighs as she began to kiss all along the inside of one of them.

"So thick and red and wet," she muttered as Jane shivered at the gentle, ticklish feel of her mouth on shivering skin. "Full and ready. I cannot wait to taste you, Jane, my darling."

"Please," Jane whispered, feeling herself grow even larger and more aroused as Zenovia made her way up and along her thigh. She arched and shifted, lifting her hips in anticipation, and then sighed with frustration as those full, sensual lips ignored her most needy parts and went on to the other thigh.

The tile was hard and cold against the back of her head, but the air was warm from the steamy pool. She tried to sit up, but Zenovia pushed her back with a strong hand over her belly, and then used those fingers to pull the skin from her mons taut, lifting it up and away from her swollen lips.

Jane felt herself lift and open even more, exposed, stretched, tight and hot and ready. Zenovia groaned something she didn't understand, and then her mouth was there: on Jane, sucking and kissing and licking.

Bold and strong, Zenovia's tongue slid around like a cock-tease, in and out of the wet, swollen folds of Jane's pussy. Fingers spread her wider, tighter, and more open, and then Zenovia's mouth was pressed against her: hot and sweet, sucking and tonguing, slurping and licking. She nibbled and nuzzled, blew softly over the raw, aching folds, and then licked again, slowly…long and slowly, like a cat stroking its fur.

Jane was breathless, her head rolling from side to side as she rode the hot wave of lust as it ebbed and flowed. Her feet still dangled in the pool, her legs spread wide, and her body was a hot, tight coil ready to explode…ready, but unable to get there.

When Zenovia's smooth tongue slid slowly over her aching pip, petting it, stroking it, lifting and jiggling it, Jane could no longer keep from crying out. She dug her fingers into the tile and tried to keep from begging even as she writhed and shivered, trying to push herself closer, trying to shove herself deeper into the unyielding rhythmic mouth and tongue.

Yet Zenovia would not allow her to climb the peak. She seemed to know when Jane was about to reach the point of no return, and she eased off, gentled her onslaught…and became slower, more tender, more teasing. But she continued to taste and kiss Jane's swollen pussy, now lapping and sucking audibly at the hot juices mingling with saliva and scented water.

Through her haze of desire, Jane heard her lover panting, heard the soft sounds of delight as Zenovia feasted as if she had all night…as if Jane wasn't ready to scream with frustration and beg for relief.

"Please," she moaned. "Please let me come." Jane reached down blindly, and her hands fell on Zenovia's warm, wet hair. With a sigh of desperation, she curled her fingers into the damp skull and pushed Zenovia's face deeper into her ready, wet quim.

Yesss… She arched deeper into the lush lips, pressing and grinding herself against the teeth and tongue and hot skin there. Zenovia cooperated, her soft groan vibrating sharply against Jane as she used the tip of her tongue to slide and slither over the needy clit pulsing against her.

Jane came, loud and hard and with deep, undulating tremors and a surge of her juices. She cried out, tears seeping from the corners of her eyes as she came, and came, and *came…* for Zenovia did not release her. She held her tight, her mouth suctioned against her pussy, and ate and licked and sucked, stroked and vibrated, over and over until Jane was sobbing from the magnificent, painful, elongated orgasm.

"Please, no," she managed to say as another orgasm ratcheted through her body, leaving her gasping and sore and bucking uncontrollably on the hard tile. "Please…no more… no…more…"

T LAST, OH, AT LAST! ZENOVIA'S MOUTH moved away, and before Jane could open her eyes, she was pulled off the edge of the pool. She sighed with another form of delight when her pounding nib and swollen quim met the steaming water, soothed and calmed as her body slid against Zenovia's.

Just as she opened her eyes, Zenovia covered her mouth with hers, smothering anything she might have said with full, wet, musk-scented lips. Jane felt the wall of the pool behind her, and her toes skittered around, automatically reaching for the bottom as Zenovia took one of her hands and brought it to the apex of her own thighs.

Jane's eyes flew open when she felt the soft, swollen folds of her lover—the thick, hot, slick juices that were so different from that water in which they floated. Zenovia moaned with relief and something like pain when she positioned Jane's fingers over her swollen pip, then sighed as she turned away from the kiss, panting in Jane's ear.

At first Jane wasn't certain what to do…and when she merely settled over her lover's pussy without moving, Zenovia fit her hand over Jane's and showed her. How to move over the tiny little knot that pulsed and leapt beneath her fingers, how to stroke and jiggle and slip through the juices faster and faster…

She held her hand tightly, as if afraid Jane would move away at the wrong moment, guiding the movements with strong fingers and determination as her breathing rose faster and harder in soft, panting grunts.

When Zenovia came, Jane felt the sudden surge over her fingers, the rush of wetness and muscle contraction and the same, deep shuddering she felt. Her lover cried out as she sagged against Jane, trapping her between her warm, wet body and the hard edge of the pool, trembling so hard that Jane felt it too.

Zenovia lost her grip on Jane, and she slipped down beneath the water—partly because it was too deep for her to stand, and partly because she needed *space*. She needed to get away…to put distance between her and this woman who'd somehow brought her to a state of desire and lust she'd never before experienced.

When Jane surfaced, she was halfway across the pool and her hair was plastered to her skull and over her shoulders. The tips floated in the water, and when she turned back it was to see Zenovia climbing out of the pool.

Her arse was strong and tight, its sides sculpted with gentle indentations. She hadn't a bit of fat on her body, and her back was just as lean and muscled as the front of her torso. Jane's heart skipped a little beat, and she immediately pushed away the ping of desire.

I love Zaren. I might enjoy this—heaven help me!—but it's Zaren I love. Zaren whom I'll find and return to, so help me God.

But when Zenovia came to the edge of the pool where she floated and looked down at her, legs spread, hands on hips, Jane couldn't completely subdue another shiver of lust. Even now, the chieftain's cunt showed red and full between her legs, glistening and ready. Jane swallowed, remembering the soft, pulsing sensation, the sleekness of those folds, the tiny, hard erection of the engorged pearl hidden beneath them…and her own little pip tightened at the thought.

"Come out," said Zenovia, and turned to walk away.

Jane hesitated for only a moment, then found a set of steps and slogged out of the pool. By the time she was standing on the tile, dripping, her lover had returned. She was wrapped in some fluffy white cloth, and she held a second one for Jane. It felt as if she were being enveloped in a cloud—it was soft and warm and seemed to draw every bit of moisture from her skin.

No sooner had Jane wrapped herself in the towel than Zenovia took her by the hand and brought her to the curtained side of the chamber—the area where, as Jane had suspected, there was a bed.

A large bed, half the size of the pool, piled with pillows and cushions, furs, and blankets, and enclosed by a filmy curtain. Zenovia pulled her down onto the surface, tossing the towels aside.

More? was all Jane could think, desperation and apprehension sizzling through her. She was exhausted, sore, and, beneath it all, distraught.

"You are everything I'd hoped for," said Zenovia, reaching to fondle Jane's breast. Her nipple tightened, hardening into a sensitive point, ready to be kissed and sucked and licked once more. When Zenovia saw the instant response, she chuckled softly and used her finger to brush lightly over the tip. "Magnificent."

Jane shivered as the wide, sensual mouth lowered to her quivering breast. She couldn't keep from arching in to the sleek tongue as it danced around the jutting point, and the familiar sweetness began to tingle in her belly, sweeping lower to her core. Zenovia fondled her breasts, holding them, weighing them in her palms as she kissed and licked each one in turn.

Then, when Jane was utterly aroused, her pip throbbing with readiness, her quim dripping with need, her lover pulled her down next to her on the bed…then rolled her beneath her. Rearing over her, Zenovia straddled Jane's trembling belly, pressing her hot, wet pussy down over her mons and grinding herself deeply onto the hardness.

She groaned, grasping Jane's breasts with two greedy hands, and rode on her, pushing and circling her soft, swollen cunt own and around as Jane shivered beneath her. The smell of musk filled the air, penetrating her senses and arousing her more deeply. Zenovia pinched her nipples, teasing them roughly between her fingers as she shifted back and forth faster and faster, pressing harder and harder, slipping over the cropped hair covering her pubis, drenching Jane with her juices.

"*Uh!*" she cried at last, shuddering to a climax on top of her. Jane felt the sharp pulsing against her skin, and when Zenovia reached behind to touch her angry little pip, it took only one stroke to make her come again—hard and sharp and quick.

Then, before either of them had recovered from the ride, Zenovia bent forward, bringing her breasts to Jane's face. "Kiss me. Lick me. Taste me."

Shocked and disturbed at the leap of lust jutting through her, Jane turned her face away…but Zenovia would have none of it. She took Jane by the chin and brought her back. "Kiss me, Jane. Do it. Taste me. I know you will like it."

Jane shuddered, aware of the warm, soft, wet quim positioned on her belly…the musky scent from it…and she suddenly wanted to taste her *there*. Instead, she closed her eyes and tentatively kissed the thrusting nipple in her face. Soft, hard, pebbly…larger, thicker, more prominent than the one she'd licked and sucked on Zaren's chest…

Zenovia trembled when Jane took her into her mouth, licking around the tip of her nipple as the woman had done to her. She tasted silky, salty flesh and felt a stab of arousal when her lover shuddered against her. Jane sucked harder, the heavy globe pushing into her face, and then nearly lost her grip, crying out when she felt Zenovia's fingers slide up inside her pussy. The fingers worked as she sucked and licked, drawing the slender nipple deeply into her mouth…sucking hard, harder, sliding her tongue around and flickering it over the tip. Zenovia sighed, arching deeper into her face while pushing her cunt down hard on Jane's belly. And then all at once, Zenovia turned around in a swift movement, straddling Jane from the opposite direction.

Her glistening labia rose over Jane's face, and just as she lowered to her panting lips, Zenovia buried her face roughly in Jane's pussy.

Jane couldn't breathe, could hardly think as her world became heat and wet and musk, pleasure and salt and unique female essence. The mouth that ate at her made her writhe and cry into the lush red folds pressing down into her face, rubbing against her.

She tentatively flicked out her tongue, tasting salt and heat, and Zenovia cried out. She surged her hips sharply toward Jane's mouth, wet and thick and musky, smothering her with her essence, grinding down into her lips and teeth. Jane couldn't breathe, and didn't understand the conflicting feelings erupting in her—arousal, delight, shame, confusion—and as Zenovia shuddered into a strong, wet climax, Jane twisted her face away, sobbing with confusion, desire, and exhaustion.

Her lover rolled off, leaving Jane pulsing and throbbing, with juices glistening on her face and quim, and in the place on her belly where Zenovia had sat.

"Gorgeous," said the chieftain, surging down to capture Jane's mouth with hers, cutting off her panting sobs. Musk against musk, their scents and tastes mingled in a heady, arousing essence as Zenovia kissed and licked the last bit of herself from Jane's lips and face.

Then, as Jane lay there, panting and shaking, aroused and yet horrified, the chieftain kissed each breast softly, swirling her tongue around each angry red nipple until Jane was shivering and shifting with pleasure…then made a trail down Jane's soft, trembling belly, pausing to lick up the last bits of her own dampness there…and then she went between Jane's legs.

"Ohhhh…" Jane moaned, tears streaming from her eyes. "Please…" She arched a little, ready for the onslaught, the teasing, the furious stroking…but Zenovia settled in softly. She kissed, licked, coaxed…lapping and teasing almost lovingly until Jane slipped up and over the edge in a long, easy, beautiful climax.

And as Jane rode the wave, Zenovia licked and thrust and sucked gently, prolonging the pleasure until the last bit of orgasm slipped away.

Jane closed her eyes. She was hot and sticky and oh so sated. Sore. Gently throbbing with a reminder of everything that had happened. Strong hands pulled her close, and Zenovia gathered her up against her, arse to belly. She settled a hand over one of Jane's breasts, just as Zaren would do when they slept together, and held her close. She stroked her hand along a hip, down over her belly, and found Jane's pussy once more.

Jane stiffened and closed her eyes. *Again?* Surely not again…

But yes…it was as if those fingers couldn't get enough of her. And, shamefully, Jane's body could not be denied its pleasure. Zenovia lazily traced her fingers over the topmost part of Jane's swollen labia, making a vee with two of them to slide down over the little hood that protected her pip, and Jane shivered when the familiar stab of lust arrowed down from her belly and centered there, where Zenovia touched her. Up and down, up and down, over and around the sensitive hood with the little pearl swelling beneath it. She heard her own wetness, slick and hot, lubricating the movement…the steady, even breathing of her lover…her own pulse thudding in her ears.

Struggling to keep from sobbing with pleasure and pleas to cease, Jane lay there on her side with the other woman's strong, warm body gathered around her: breasts pressing into her shoulder blades, one strong thigh positioned over one of hers, a face buried in the nape of her neck.

Jane found herself immobile, captured, as those fingers stroked…teased…feathering over her. The heat blazed in her again as Zenovia kissed her neck, using her tongue to trace along the tendon of Jane's throat, nibbling sharply at her shoulder…all the while stroking ever so gently, yet constantly.

"Come now, lovely Jane," Zenovia whispered hotly into her ear. "Come with me…I love to hear you beg for it. I love the sound you make when you come, the expression on your face…come now and let me smell your juices again. I want to *drink* you dry."

A tear leaked from Jane's eye as she fought to end the torture, fought to find the orgasm and have it done with…but the fingers that teased her seemed to linger, to slow, to draw out the moment. And then she stopped…those fingers stopped and settled right over her pussy. Flat and wide and still.

Jane made a soft sound of desperation and desire, and bucked against her hand. Zenovia's powerful arms and legs tightened around her, holding her still. Her mons pressed hard into the small of Jane's back, and she held herself there, rubbing in small, quick circles. "Ask me, Jane, and I will give it to you. Ask me." She was a little breathless herself, and the rhythm from Zenovia's own body only added to Jane's frustration.

She bit her lip, utterly controlled by the demanding pulsing of her little pearl, the itchy, unfinished sensation of dissatisfaction, and the rhythmic jolting from behind. Jane drew in a deep breath. "Please," she whispered. "Yes, please."

She felt Zenovia smile into her hair. "Very good. Oh, yes…very…good…" she murmured, moving faster and harder against her. Then she slid her fingers up and inside Jane in a smooth, slick movement. Her thumb positioned over the top of the raging little kernel, pushing down with *just* the right amount of pressure, holding Jane still as she ground into her from behind…and she stroked deeply once, twice, and—

"*Oh!*" Jane cried out, more loudly than she intended…which resulted in a pair of teeth clamping down on her shoulder as Zenovia shuddered behind her. The orgasm ripped through Jane, leaving her legs weak and her entire body shaking. Lights flashed before her eyes, and her face was wet from tears of frustration and desire.

"Oh, yes. I shall most definitely keep you, Jane," murmured Zenovia after several minutes, and she pressed a tender kiss beneath the hair at Jane's temple.

Startled, Jane pulled out of her loosened grip. "No." She submerged her fear and apprehension and scrambled from the other woman's embrace, sitting up on the bed, and met Zenovia's eyes directly. "You cannot *keep* me. I am a free woman, a peer of England, and I am married. I will not be your concubine."

"No?" Zenovia looked at her, lifting an eyebrow. She sat up and reached to touch Jane's hair, leaving the scent of her own quim there upon the curl. The earthy, feminine scent teased her with the memories of the last hours. "You do not wish to be my concubine? The most respected and honored woman in this court, besides myself, of course, and even then…I do believe *I* would adore you, Jane. I do believe I could be completely enraptured by you. You could *own* me if you wished."

"No," Jane said again. "Please understand. I have no dislike for you—"

"Well, that has certainly been most evident this night." Zenovia gave a low, husky laugh. Her eyes glinted with heat. "By the gods, I can still smell you as if my face were buried in your cunt." Her face narrowed and she reached for Jane yet again. "I'll have you, my darling Jane. And you'll enjoy it. Again and again…just as you have tonight."

Jane moved out of reach, shaking her head. "*No.* I don't want to stay here. I want to find my husband. I want to leave this place and return to England and find the man I love." Tears threatened, making her voice shake. She steadied it. "I refuse to be your concubine."

Zenovia's expression turned cold. She sat up straight, and all the lust drained from her eyes. "Indeed. You refuse my offer—made with all respect and honor? Very well, then. If you will not be my concubine, you will then become my *slave*."

VI

LINK.

Clink.

Clink.

Jane stood passively, fighting to keep her expression calm and her demeanor queenlike as the heavy brass cuffs were locked around her wrists and one ankle. Each cuff had a small hook on the outside, and they clicked into place with elegant, complicated latches.

Alena and another servant named Obelia worked silently with both efficiency and blank expressions as Zenovia watched from a large chair in her chamber. Jane refused to look at her, despite the fact that the woman's heavy gaze had not left her naked body during the entire event. Instead, she held her head high as she had done when paraded through the jungle village by Cold Eyes.

I will find a way to escape. And Zaren is looking for me. It's only a matter of time until he finds me.

Until then, Jane could hardly imagine any experience worse than what she'd encountered at the hands of Kellan Darkdale and his orgiastic cronies back in London. If she could live through that, she could live through anything.

Alena moved behind her, lifting the heavy hair from neck and shoulders as Obelia brought a wider, larger cuff forward.

Jane stared straight ahead as they snapped it in place snugly around her neck. She swallowed hard and felt the chill of the metal, the weight of the necklet and its embrace against her skin.

"It becomes you, Jane darling," said Zenovia. She rose from her chair, holding a large, dripping handful of golden jewelry. The servants stepped back, bowing their heads in obeisance as she approached Jane. Zenovia hesitated, then snapped her fingers.

Immediately, Alena and Obelia left the chamber.

Zenovia and Jane were alone. "Look at yourself." Zenovia gestured to a tall mirror leaning against the wall. "Look at us… mistress and slave. The sun, being eclipsed by the moon."

Jane did as she was bid, and was startled at the picture she made—the picture the two of them made together. It was as Zenovia said: the sun and moon, with the moon raging larger and more powerful than the sun for once.

Her hair fell in tangled, red-gold curls, tousled and full, tumbling over her shoulders and brushing her hips. Her soft skin glowed like dusky honey next to Zenovia's sleek white flesh. Mistress loomed above and beyond slave, broad shoulders as wide as a man's, her chin brushing the top of Jane's fiery head. Zenovia's blond hair had been caught up in a loose bundle, woven with colorless jewels that glittered like moonbeams. Silver cuffs studded with diamonds glinted at wrists and throat in cool contrast to the warm golden ones that imprisoned Jane. Her dark eyes held Jane's in the mirror as she slid a pale hand down and around to cup a breast. Her thumb teased the nipple until it became hard and taut, a dark pink temptation in the midst of golden curves and fire.

Jane thought she felt a little shudder in the woman next to her, a soft sigh of regret…but Zenovia's expression remained cool and remote.

Then she stepped around in front of her, lifting Jane's chin with too-tight fingers. "It's a shame it has to be this way, but at least you wear it well. And this…" She opened her hand to display a complicated mass of delicate chains and a curved, triangular metal piece. "This will ensure you remain firmly in your position as *slave* rather than lover. There is no pleasure for slaves, Jane." Her smile was taut and cold, and gone was the light of humor and affection that had been there only hours earlier. "Only service."

The chains rattled quietly, somehow ominous in the delicate sound, as Zenovia lifted them and separated out the strands. Jane's heart thudded as the other woman began to fasten them around her hips, three on each side. The curious metal piece hung from the smaller chains, and when Zenovia fit it tightly over Jane's quim, threading two more chains from the bottom of the piece between her legs, she realized exactly what it was.

A sort of chastity belt. A shield. A cage.

The chains were drawn tightly, and the triangular metal shield settled snugly over her netherlips in a little cuplike shape. There was a narrow slit in the center—large enough for her to urinate through, but without enough space for a finger or anything else to penetrate. Zenovia fastened all of the chains at the base of Jane's spine, ensuring they were tight enough that she had no ability to slip a finger behind the shield. They bit gently into her hips and rode up through the crack of her arse. The metal triangle curved away from her swollen folds and pip, so even putting pressure on the shield itself would give no relief to a swollen, needy pearl. There was no way to touch herself… or for anyone else to do so.

For some reason, this terrified Jane more than anything else.

When she finished, Zenovia came back around to look at her. Her wide, sensual mouth was set in an odd smile as she reached for the cuff around Jane's throat, and there was another delicate jingle and a soft *snick*. Now, a sturdy golden chain hung from the collar. The end was wrapped around the chieftain's hand.

"Now," said Zenovia, shoving Jane to her knees, "pleasure me, slave."

Jane hit the ground hard and nearly lost her balance, but she caught herself in time. Zenovia's flat navel was directly in front of her eyes, and just below was the neatly trimmed blond hair growing in a triangle over her mons and down beneath, along the lips of her pussy. Her muscular legs spread wide, and Jane realized her mistress had settled herself onto the edge of a chair.

Her cunt was red and full and wet. Ready. The familiar scent of her sex was strong and alluring, and Jane's clit gave an instant, impudent pulse. Heart thudding, knees shaking, Jane put a hand on each of Zenovia's thighs, closed her eyes, and moved into the apex of her mistress's legs. Her mouth watered at the smell as it enveloped her, and with a deep breath—not such a good idea, for the musky scent aroused her even more— she plunged in.

Zenovia jolted and sighed the moment Jane's mouth touched her. Her thighs tightened then relaxed as Jane got to work, using her tongue to trace each soft fold of her labia, the tiny kernel of pleasure hooded above, and then tentatively slid into the hot, wet cavern below. She ate and sucked and licked, burrowing her face into the warm, sweet juncture of Zenovia's thighs.

Jane was filled with a combination of guilt and horror as her body tightened, heated, dampened, pulsed as she licked wildly at the tiny little nub. She couldn't ignore the sounds, the smells, the feel of Zenovia's arousal, and it lit Jane with lust as well. By the time Zenovia surged up into her mouth, crying out in triumph and convulsing against Jane's lips and tongue, her own quim was hot and full and dripping, and her breasts ached to be touched.

As her mistress's pleasure eased, Jane settled back on her heels and waited nervously for her next order. She firmly ignored the indignant throb of her little pip and tried not to think about the heat coiling in her belly.

"Very good, slave." Zenovia stood, the golden chain attached to Jane's collar still wrapped around her fist. "Now, you will dress me, Jane."

With trembling knees and a pulsing, needy body, Jane did as she was bid. She draped the toga-like black gown over her mistress, fastening the brooch at one shoulder. As she reached up to do so, Zenovia slid one hand under her breast and began to stroke her thumb over the raging nipple. Jane couldn't control a shiver, and she bit her lips to hold back a soft groan as that insistent thumb circled and teased.

"If you were my concubine," murmured Zenovia, "and not my slave, I would lay you on the bed there and eat your pussy until you screamed. And I would lick you and suck on you and make you come and come and come." She tweaked the nipple hard, and her hand fell away. "But you've made your decision."

Jane avoided looking at her mistress, and, miserable in her state of arousal that seemed to have no chance of being sated, bowed her head and waited for her next order.

"Come. You will walk politely just so behind me." Zenovia pointed to a general area just behind and to the right of her foot.

Her knees still trembling, her nipples thrusting desperately, Jane obeyed, and Zenovia led her out of the chamber as if she were a pet on a leash.

Jane was wearing nothing but the chains and her collar, and the delicate ones that held her chastity belt in place shifted and swung against the insides of her thighs. Her unfettered breasts bobbed and swayed as they made their way down a corridor, past servants and guards until they reached the same vast chamber in which Jane had first set her eyes on Zenovia.

The chieftain walked through the doorway, leading Jane, greeting some of her guards and others—all women, of course—who appeared to be advisors or members of whatever sort of peerage was in place in Amazonia. Jane felt countless eyes on her, stroking over her bare skin, lingering on her high, generous breasts, and settling at the gold-plated contraption that covered her labia.

Once on the dais, Zenovia seated herself on the massive throne and directed Jane to remain next to her, kneeling upright so that her shoulders were about the same height as the arms of her chair. Jane was able to rest on her haunches as long as she kept her back straight. This position left her with her breasts quite boldly on display, thrusting out and up. Zenovia arranged the golden leash so it hung down between them, then curved beneath one breast toward the throne, where she kept the leash in her hand.

And then commenced Zenovia's day of governing. Jane remained silent and immobile while the chieftain met with her advisors, made judgments, and settled disputes. During this time, Jane could neither move nor speak or slump. Her legs and buttocks ached from holding the same position for so long.

And to make matters worse, Zenovia often stroked her hair absently, as if she were a dog sitting at attention next to its master. Her hands would filter down over the long curls, petting and stroking as she asked questions and listened to the answers given by her subjects. Jane felt every touch like a burning brand, heavy and hot, and knew it was meant to display her subservience to everyone.

At last, there was a moment when no one waited to see the chieftain. A double row of guards stood at attention on either side of the chamber, and several pages awaited their orders. Zenovia turned to Jane, and, gathering up the leash, began to draw it around toward the front of her chair. Jane followed, scooting along on her knees, until she was close to the throne.

"Come here," Zenovia said, and gave a sharp yank on the chain, directing Jane toward her lap.

Mortified, for she felt every eye in the room fixated on her, Jane obeyed and climbed onto Zenovia's sturdy thighs. Her mistress settled her in place as if she were a small cat or child… but when her palm closed around her breast and she began to idly stroke Jane's nipples, her position became much less innocent.

Jane tried to control a shiver of lust as the light, teasing fingers played with her. But her body, which had been full and tight, ready to explode only a short time ago, eagerly surged back to arousal. She felt the telltale insistent throbbing of her tiny clit tucked safely behind its golden cup, and tried very hard not to think about it.

But she couldn't keep from squirming a little, trying to find some sort of relief. Zenovia chuckled softly and kissed her ear, then bit her lobe gently, sliding her tongue around and inside her ear. Jane shuddered and stifled a soft moan as spikes of arousal stabbed her at every touch. Knowing she had no chance of easing it made things even worse.

"You are so delicious," Zenovia murmured into her ear. "I can feel you quivering with lust…and it's so unfortunate you made the choice you did. For there is *no pleasure* for slaves. You shall simply have to stew in your own lovely juices." With that, she gave one last nip at Jane's earlobe. Then she clapped her hands together sharply, drawing the attention of everyone in the chamber. "Bring in the possible studs."

The double doors opened a moment later, and in marched two tall, broad, and muscular female guards. Behind them were two columns of men, lined up side by side, and linked by manacles on their wrists and ankles.

They were naked.

Jane's breath caught as she recognized Captain Holt and one of his men from the ship. The others—of which there were fewer than a dozen—were unknown to her.

But each of them was a fine specimen of masculinity. All were muscular and handsome, with clear eyes, thick hair, and powerful legs and arms. They carried themselves well, though most of them sported bruises or wounds of some nature. It was clear they'd each been physically subdued, but only after fighting back.

She caught Holt looking at her, and she gave him a cold, lethal look that clearly denoted her disgust with him. He appeared miserable—but surely not as miserable as she. This mess was of his making, not hers—and yet here she was, imprisoned and enslaved with no release in sight…and aroused beyond belief. As if to punctuate this thought, her little pearl gave an insistent pulse that made Jane bite her lip in frustration.

As she watched, the men were paraded past the dais, pausing so Zenovia could take a close look at each one.

"It's such a difficult decision," said the chieftain. "They all seem as if they could perform accordingly, but *I* have no desire to determine their capabilities." She gave a little shudder that appeared to be completely genuine. "Only five are needed to add to our breeding crew, and they must be excellent specimens of the male sex. We want only the best to continue our race. What do you think, slave?" She tugged on Jane's leash. "How does one choose a man for breeding?"

Pulled out of her frustrated, aroused haze, Jane blinked and discovered Zenovia was truly curious and seemed to want her response. Then, in the next instant, the full realization of the situation dawned on her.

"Do you mean…you use the men to father children? On— with whom?"

Zenovia laughed. "I see you are horrified, my little slave. But for what other reason do we require the male species here in Amazonia? We certainly are far from wanting or needing any males to tell us what to do, how to act, or what we can own—as is the case in your England, is it not? We are fully capable of doing everything necessary—including giving and receiving pleasure—except continuing our race. The breeding process is an undignified and unpleasant necessity, but a necessity nevertheless."

Jane pursed her lips, struck just for an instant about the truth of that matter—except, of course, for the part about the breeding process being unpleasant. But Zenovia was right—even in a queen ruled England, men had all the power. Yet she knew firsthand how delightful pleasure could be with a man… and the depth of emotion and physical connection there could be when "breeding."

"And so, my little slave who has a mind of her own, I would very much like your opinions on the matter. How would you pick the five studs we will add to our breeding program for the next several years?"

"But what happens to them after that? And surely…well, you must have more than five men, or there would be quite a lot of inbreeding." Even as Jane spoke the words, she was aware of the utter absurdity of the situation—that she was actually discussing using free men as brood mares (or, more accurately, stallions), and that she was having the conversation with her mistress.

"We have only room for five more studs in our stables at this time. Every year we retire some of them of them, or they become ill or injured or otherwise unacceptable breeding partners, and we replace them as needed."

"And what happens to the ones you—er—put out to pasture?" Jane couldn't quite keep the horror from her voice.

Zenovia shrugged. "They are put to work in the heather-hash fields and gold mines, as well as doing other menial labor."

Her eyes glinted as she saw the shock in Jane's eyes. "The same will happen to the ones not chosen to be the five."

"I see."

"Now, I have asked for your opinion—something I do not do lightly, especially with a slave, and my patience begins to end."

Duly chastised, Jane turned her attention to the columns of men. Had they heard the conversation? Did they know what was to befall them? Was there any way to help them?

But if she could not help herself, how could she help them?

She drew in a deep breath. Perhaps the best option was to look at the situation from the Amazonian perspective and be honest. What other choice did she have?

But perhaps she could delay the process…

"One would want to select a breeding partner for his physical appearance and strength, as well as for his intelligence and mind. Both are important elements in continuing your race. I don't suppose you…er…interview any of them?"

Zenovia's eyes lit with admiration and delight. "Interesting."

"And perhaps you'd want to interview them not only to discover whether they have intelligence, but also to find out whether his parents and family were weak and sickly, or strong and lived long."

"Quite excellent thoughts, my darling slave. You are a treasure." Zenovia's regard turned warmer, and she stroked Jane's head. "And I am pleased to inform you that such interviews, as you call them, have already been carried out and these men have been culled from many candidates. All that remains is to determine whether they can perform their duties." Her eyes darkened and her lips curled in what could only be called a mischievous smile. "And in that regard, I do believe you might be of further assistance, my pet."

Zenovia stood abruptly, sending Jane tumbling to the ground, bare breasts bouncing and legs splayed crudely. The gold chains and metal cup over her labia jingled and shifted alarmingly, digging into the soft hollows of flesh at the insides of her thighs. But before she recovered from the ignominious fall, she was yanked up by the leash and led off the dais.

The male captives stood silently, their manacled wrists covering the juncture of their thighs. Most of them had downcast eyes, though there were a few bold ones who peeked up at the female ruler and her slave.

"Jane, you will demonstrate the virility of each of our candidates. You may begin with him." Zenovia placed her in front of the first man, unhooked the leash from Jane's collar, then turned and climbed back up onto the dais. When she realized Jane hadn't moved, she made an impatient gesture. "Use those lush lips of yours, and that talented tongue, to bring him to orgasm. Now."

Jane heard a sort of roaring in her ears that dulled everything around her as she positioned herself in front of the first candidate. He obligingly moved his manacled wrists from where they'd settled over his genitals, though he wore an expression of shock and suspicion.

But his cock was already becoming interested, presented as it was by the naked Jane, who, most likely, smelled of her own arousal, and that of Zenovia's as well. She swallowed hard and, cupping the man's ballocks, took his half-flaccid cock in her mouth.

He gave a soft grunt as her lips settled around his member, which began to thicken and lengthen readily. Jane closed her eyes, trying to block out the sensation of the rod surging suggestively in her mouth. But it was a familiar experience, an arousing one, and she found it nearly impossible to keep from reacting to his enthusiastic response: the groans and shivers and the turgid cock filling her mouth.

Nevertheless, she focused on her movements: up and down, nearer and farther away, using her hands to keep his rock-hard member in her mouth. She sucked hard on the knob of his rod, pumping faster and faster, praying this would end quickly and easily, all the while trying to ignore the stabs of lust shooting from her belly down to her protected quim.

Mercifully, it was a very short time before he arched and grunted and shot his seed into the back of her throat. Jane swallowed the salty wad and backed away quickly, settling on her haunches as she tried to cool down her own body's demands. She happened to glance up at the man, and he had a loopy, sated smile on his face that made her even more frustrated.

"What are you waiting for, slave? There are fifteen other men waiting for you."

She obeyed, moving to the man next to the one whom she'd just sucked off. He was already hard, and his cock, though not as long, was thick and ready for her lips. She slid down over him, tasting the saltiness of the little droplet at the tip of his rod, and used her tongue to lick it away. He shivered and shifted himself deeper into her mouth.

Jane held his hips and began to work her puffy, swollen lips over him, over and over. He was ready and shot hard and fast into the back of her throat, nearly choking her.

This time, she didn't wait. She finished, swallowed, and moved on to the second row of men. By now each of them had erections of some sort—from anticipation as well as from watching and hearing her pleasure the others. She took them each deep and hard into her mouth, pumping and sucking until she thought her jaw would never close again.

Each one was new torture—the scent, taste, feel of hard cock in her mouth, the noises each man made: groans and grunts and sighs. And then there were the hands. Somehow, though manacled, they found her breasts, fondling them, teasing her already raw, red nipples until she wanted to scream around the rod in her mouth.

Jane felt her own juices, and she felt as if her labia were about to burst free, she was so swollen. One man found the most sensitive part of her nipples and stroked her, faster and harder—just as she stroked up and down on him—until she felt the shock of an orgasm shoot through her in soft, pulsing waves. She couldn't hold back a groan of her own, sighing around his thick cock as her body shook and shivered.

He came at that moment, bursting into the back of her throat with a hot, hard wad. She took him all, swallowing and licking the tip of his cock with a little thank-you for the bit of pleasure he'd given her.

Then she rose to her feet and stumbled to the next man. It was Captain Holt, and it was all Jane could do to keep from biting down on the massive hard-on that waited for her.

"Guess I should have taken you when I had the chance," he muttered as she dutifully closed her mouth around him. "But this will do…" His words ended in a soft grunt and he shuddered gently against her as she slid down to the root.

Jane's body was on fire, only half satisfied from the soft, superficial orgasm. She wanted more. She *needed* more. She sucked on his cock, licking and stroking with fervor, hoping he'd find a way to touch her…to bring her along with him. Her lips were so swollen and her jaw so tight she could hardly move, and she was becoming dizzy from lack of food and drink as well as the up-and-down motion…over and over and over….

She sighed and sucked and licked, her eyes closed, focusing on her own pleasure—as if she could *will* herself to orgasm. She gripped his taut buttocks, working her mouth around the head of his rod, playing, teasing, allowing herself to enjoy—

"Enough!"

All at once, Jane felt herself flying through the air. She landed on the ground a few feet from the two columns of men—half of whom had already been serviced by her.

Zenovia stood where Jane had been only a moment before. "You!" she said, leaning in toward Holt. "She is my slave. How dare you touch my property! How *dare* you presume!"

She turned in a whirlwind of barely controlled fury. "Out. Everyone out of here. *All of you.*"

VII

A S JANE LAY THERE ON THE GROUND, panting, throbbing, confused, and more than a little frightened, the entire chamber was vacated more rapidly than she could have imagined.

When they were alone, Zenovia turned upon her, yanking Jane to her feet with a painful grip. She braced herself for a blow, to be shaken or thrown...*something*...

But to her surprise, Zenovia began to unlock the chains around her waist, and those that threaded through the metal cup covering her quim. She tore them away, and the next thing Jane knew, she was dragged up onto the top of the dais and shoved onto the floor. Her legs trailed awkwardly down the steps, her thighs splayed wide and her red, ready quim fully exposed.

Zenovia followed, her body pressing Jane into the ground as her mouth covered hers. Tongue thrusting deep, she devoured Jane roughly, sending even more lust and arousal spiking through her sensitive body.

A powerful thigh slid between Jane's, and she felt the hot wetness of the other woman's quim sliding against her thigh as Zenovia straddled her, moving her toga out of the way. Panting and confused, Jane could hardly breathe as her mistress kissed her passionately, pressing her steaming self down against Jane's leg, then pulled her mouth away.

"You," Zenovia muttered into her ear as she covered one of Jane's breasts with her palm, "may *not* find pleasure with *anyone* except me. Especially a *man.* You are my *slave.*"

She shifted against Jane, her pussy slipping tightly against the top of her leg as she pushed her thigh up into Jane's swollen quim. The sudden pressure there had Jane crying out with surprise and delight. Zenovia began to move, thrusting herself against Jane while Jane's quim pressed against her, mimicking the same motion as fucking.

"Oh," Jane sighed, moving in tandem with her. The scent of female juices filled the air, and the curves and muscles of their bodies eased along each other, hot and smooth.

Zenovia was panting now as she moved faster, riding Jane's thigh with her slick quim while Jane writhed beneath her, thrusting her hips up and against her mistress's leg, trying to find an ending. They moved faster and faster, slick and urgent, grunting and moaning, hair tangling, breasts bouncing, fabric bunching…and when Zenovia's fingers moved between them to touch Jane's engorged clit, she immediately tipped into an orgasm.

She cried out as the powerful release shuttled through her, hard and hot and strong. Zenovia grabbed her hand and brought it to her own wet, swollen clit. Jane pressed the engorged kernel, still undulating from her own satiation, and felt Zenovia explode against her with a loud cry.

They lay there, the chieftain shuddering over Jane, their thighs wet and slick, panting and gasping. Jane's cheeks were hot, and her back hurt from where the edge of the dais step pressed into her…but she was sated. Satisfied.

Zenovia pulled away after a moment, still wearing her toga—which fell into place as she stood. She looked down at Jane, who was too weak to move.

"I tell you this now, Jane. You are my slave. You belong to me. You will not seek or receive pleasure from anyone but me. *Especially* a man." She pulled Jane to her feet, then bent her face to kiss her almost tenderly on Jane's puffy lips.

Zenovia released her and turned away. Moments later, she returned to the trembling, confused, and terrified Jane, holding the metal contraption that had been cupping her quim.

Jane shuddered as her mistress spread her legs and licked the juices from her pussy. She nearly collapsed as that tongue swiped and slathered over her, both soothing and teasing.

And then Zenovia shackled her up once more, fitting the golden cup back over her, tightening the chains, and then re-attaching the leash to her collar.

"Now," said the chieftain, "we shall continue with our day. Perhaps I shall even allow you a bit of nourishment. For we shall have a long evening ahead of us, my dear pet."

Jane's thoughts swam, and she was distantly aware of courtiers returning to the chamber, Zenovia giving orders, and, at last, a small plate of food and drink brought to her.

But instead of allowing Jane to eat, Zenovia insisted upon feeding her like a trick dog. She offered only one morsel at a time, though Jane was starving and hadn't eaten since the fateful dinner last evening.

She'd nearly finished the small plate of food, and Zenovia allowed her to drink some watered-down wine, when one of the guards approached. She appeared somewhat distressed.

"Your Highness," said the woman. "Lord Akenov has arrived."

Zenovia frowned. "Damn him. It's not time for his quarterly visit." She looked down at Jane, who, understandably, showed curiosity at this development. The chieftain smiled tightly. "You need not be jealous, darling slave. Akenov is my official concubine—for breeding purposes only. You need not fear he will take my attentions from you. No one could do that."

Jane had no idea how to respond to this, and so she merely nodded.

"Bring him in. Let us see what he gives for this unexpected visit." Zenovia was clearly irritated and put out by the situation, and it surprised Jane that she was so compliant.

Moments later, Lord Akenov strode in. He was accompanied by several men—presumably his personal guard.

Jane looked at him with curiosity. He was very tall—taller than Zenovia—and extremely handsome. Well built. Muscular. His hair was short and curly, cut straight across his forehead in the manner of the ancient Romans.

If one had to have a man for a concubine, she reflected, it seemed one could do much worse than Lord Akenov. Even his teeth were straight and white, and they gleamed when he gave Zenovia a sardonic smile.

"What brings you here, Akenov? I was not expecting you for another month."

"I cannot imagine a less hospitable welcome for your lover, my darling Zenovia," he said, bowing at the dais.

The chieftain made a disgusted sound, but remained silent.

"Very well, then, I shall get to the point. But first," he added, shifting closer so as to speak for her ears only, "I must say I have even less desire for our conjugal visits than you, my dear elephant." Then his eyes widened, for he had seen Jane, who knelt upright next to the throne. "By the gods," he murmured, his attention lingering heavy and hot. "She is lovely. No wonder you are displeased with my arrival."

"You were getting to the point, Akenov."

"Yes, of course." Akenov stepped back, but his gaze slipped down over Jane's breasts and tumbled hair. "I have with me a diplomatic retinue lately come from London." He turned and gestured.

Jane watched as three men near the back of the contingent separated themselves from the rest and walked forward. As they moved closer, her heart nearly stopped beating, and her body began to shake.

"May I present Lord Hampstead and his companions," said Akenov, but Jane heard nothing more.

Zaren.

Zaren was here.

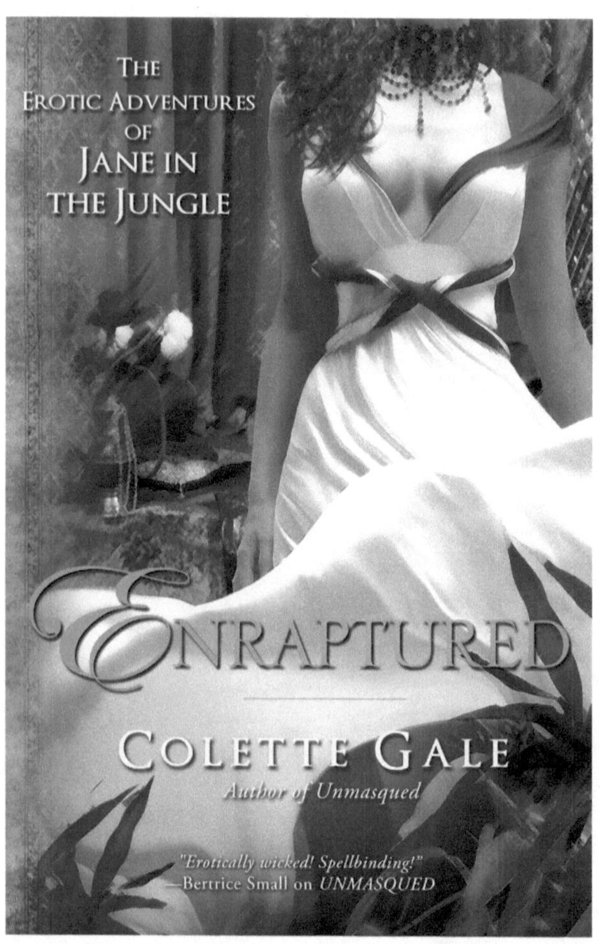

Jane finds herself the object of obsession of the Queen of Amazonia, enslaved by her with no opportunity for escape. When her mistress's concubine Akenov makes an unscheduled appearance, Jane is caught up in a whirlwind of eroticism.

Watch for a new series coming in late 2016 from Colette Gale!

Colette Gale is the pen name of a *New York Times* and *USA Today* bestselling and award-winning author who has written for three major publishers in a variety of genres.

She has also written several "seduced classics," including the popular *Unmasqued: An Erotic Novel of The Phantom of the Opera*.

Colette can be found on Facebook
(**facebook.com/colette.gale**)
or her website (**colettegale.com**)

For information about Colette's upcoming releases, please sign up for her newsletter at:
bit.ly/ColetteGaleBooks

www.ingramcontent.com/pod-product-compliance
Lightning Source LLC
Chambersburg PA
CBHW050559190726
48283CB00007B/2200